Dukes and Diamonds

Victorian Jewels
Book 1

Lauren Smith

ISBN: 978-1-962760-37-9 (e-book edition)

ISBN: 978-1-962760-38-6 (print edition)

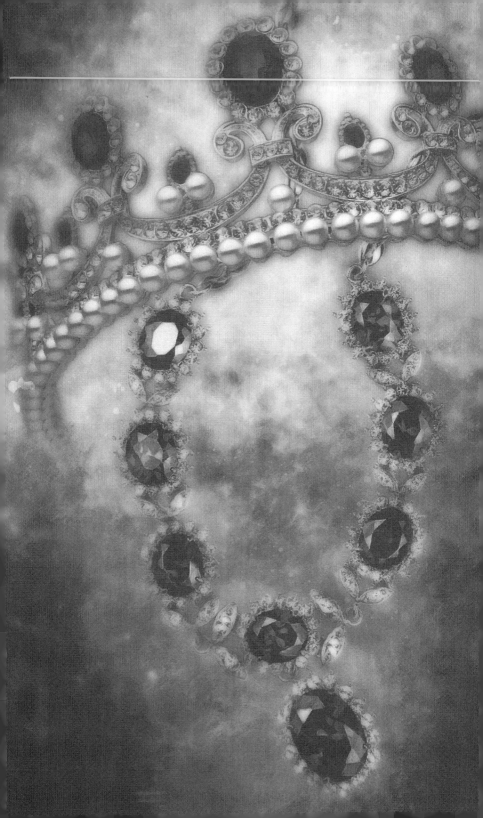

Prologue

London, England – 1876

Rain soaked the cobblestones, chasing away most of the usual market crowds that would have filled the streets and provided Tabitha Sherborne with prey. She lingered in the alley, clutching the lapels of her masculine coat about her neck, and pulled her flat cap down over her eyes. Drops of water drizzled from the brim of her cap, making it even harder to see through the downpour. Though she wore a dress underneath, her hat and coat gave her the appearance of a young man, which helped deter attention from her on days like today when she needed to be ignored.

A clap of thunder deafened her ears, and she watched the street entertainers scramble for cover beneath the narrow doorways of nearby shops. A few

1

peddlers braved the weather, calling out for the rare passersby to have their kitchen knives sharpened or pots and pans mended. On days like these, everyone in the marketplace lost a chance to feed their families. Rain like this chased away all but the most determined customers.

A handful of young children clutched baskets of drenched lavender and violets, their sad little figures tugging at Tabitha's heart. Only the vegetable sellers and fishmongers seemed to survive in this weather.

As Tabitha continued her vigilance on the street through the falling rain, she spied a tall gentleman with a cane. He strolled down the street, his hat tipped to shield his face from the wind and rain. The fine quality of his coat and boots caught her attention. He paused, reaching into the pocket of his waistcoat to check the time. The glint of a silver pocket watch was what she'd been hoping to see. She slipped out of the alley and trailed him. It would be harder in this weather to accomplish her mission, but she had to eat, and this was the only way.

She moved from one shop doorway to another and was careful not to stare at the man. Instead, she kept him in her peripheral view while she examined a set of gentlemen's trilby hats on display in the windows in front of her. When the man stopped to speak to a young lad selling newspapers, Tabitha joined him. She pretended to wait in line for a newspaper as well.

With practiced ease, she leaned past him to take a paper from the boy. In the same swift move, she lifted her palm up and slid it into his pocket, plucking the watch out and tucking it into her own pocket. The man had only recently checked the time, so he wasn't likely to check again for perhaps another half hour. She would be long gone when he discovered the theft.

With the watch secure in her pocket, she winked at the boy selling playbills and walked away. One *never* ran. She stopped by one of the little girls selling violets. Tabitha dropped a coin into the girl's palm, then removed her cap and placed it on the child's head to keep the girl a little drier. The child rubbed her red nose with a little fist and murmured a shy, "Thank you." She couldn't have been more than six. Something tugged at Tabitha's chest, but she could do no more for her than that single coin and the hat. She herself had nothing to survive on. What could she do for a child who was even worse off?

The rain relented by the time Tabitha turned the corner and passed by a bountiful stand of flowers on a wheeled cart. A beautiful blonde woman in a bright sapphire-blue walking dress stood by the flower stand admiring the freshly cut blooms. Her dress trimmed with a delicate rose fringe that lined the trailing bustle and the billowing bows that cascaded down the full back of the skirt, and those skirts were carefully lifted by a strap wrapped around her wrist that kept the lovely train from dragging on the wet ground. She wore red-tipped walking boots that peeped out from the front of her skirts.

The elegant picture she painted in front of the cart of blooming flowers was stunning. Tabitha didn't often see women like her out on the streets in this kind of weather and certainly never alone.

She spoke with the woman selling the fresh bouquets of flowers. The woman in the blue gown was a fine lady, born into a life with no struggle or suffering. Her skin was pale with a hint of a blush, and her hair was coiffed beneath the jauntily perched little hat. Tabitha searched for any signs of jewelry on the woman, but she wore no rings, necklaces, or any other finery that could be pinched.

Blast!

When the lady turned toward Tabitha, her basket tumbled from her arms and the flowers spilled to the ground in a colorful, beautiful mess.

"Oh no!" the woman cried in dismay. Responding instinctively to the stricken look on her face, Tabitha dove for the flowers and tried to retrieve them. She'd felt strangely compelled to help her, but pretty ladies were always like that, weren't they? They looked so helpless and kitten-like, and it was no wonder men were always bowing and scraping to please them and take care of them. Tabitha couldn't imagine a man ever doing that for her. A sudden pang of longing struck her so hard that she blinked away burning tears in her eyes. What would it be like to live that kind of life?

Something in the lady's eyes had said these flowers mattered to her beyond a pretty centerpiece. The woman blushed. "Thank you."

Tabitha finished placing the flowers in the other woman's basket.

"Truly, *thank you*. I was planning to take these to my ailing mother," she confessed. "Flowers are the only thing that makes her smile these days."

"It's no trouble," Tabitha replied. She was still in awe of the fine lady. They were of a similar age, although she guessed this woman might be a year or two older than Tabitha's twenty years. Tabitha had none of her polish or elegant glamour, yet the kindness in the woman's face drew Tabitha's sympathy rather than her jealousy.

She straightened and politely nodded at the woman before Tabitha rushed away. She couldn't stay in this part of town for long. She was so quick to escape that she bumped into a pair of roughly dressed men near a newsstand, and they cursed at her.

By the time she reached the area near Covent Garden, she felt secure enough to check on her prize. She dug her hand into her pocket, expecting to feel the cool touch of silver, but her fingers found only empty air. Tabitha searched deeper but still found nothing. She checked the lining for holes, then finally searched her other pocket, where her fingers closed around a scrap of paper. When she pulled it out, she noticed the emblem of a little bird. A robin, by the looks of it. She turned the paper over and found a handwritten note on the back:

Nicely done. We are impressed. To retrieve your item, visit us at two o'clock in the afternoon.

An address was printed neatly below.

"What the devil?" Tabitha scowled and glanced around. Someone had stolen her purloined watch. Or rather, more than one person, as the note had said "we." She hadn't felt a thing. Was she getting slow? It did happen to pickpockets occasionally as they got older. As she replayed the moments after taking the watch, she realized it must have been those two men she'd bumped into after helping that young woman with her flowers. Her empty stomach rumbled at the thought. If she didn't go to the meeting these people had arranged, it was possible she wouldn't have any luck pinching an item to sell before it grew dark. That meant she wouldn't be able to eat a real meal today.

It was a little over an hour before the meeting time specified on the card. She removed her coin purse and counted her money as she considered what to do. She could afford a penny loaf and a cup of coffee at a stall, but nothing more until she could get that watch back and fence it. She continued to debate her choices as she bought her bread and coffee. Then she settled on a portico to eat. Her belly was grateful, but she would be hungry again in a few hours.

She studied the address again and scoffed. It was a home near Grosvenor Square. That was where the rich toffs lived. Lord, what was she going to do? It was common enough for men of all classes to lure women into traps for forced prostitution—or worse. Thinking it over, Tabitha decided to go early and observe the house discreetly. See what she thought of it before meeting up with these "robin" fellows.

When she reached Upper Grosvenor Street and spotted the fancy townhouse from address on the card, she kept her distance. She lingered in the park square, pretending to take in the air now that much of the storm clouds had moved on. She couldn't see anyone coming or going out of the house.

I can leave now, or I can risk it for the watch . . .

7

Her stomach's needs eventually won out over her sense of self-preservation, and she finally crossed the street and rapped the silver knocker. She was a quarter of an hour early, but perhaps that would give her an advantage.

A butler answered. He was a tall man in his fifties with a distinguished look and a fine beard. Exactly the sort of man she expected to greet her.

"Yes?" It sounded like a challenge to prove she belonged on his doorstep. He stared down his nose at her pompously. It took her a moment to not let his tone or demeanor rankle her.

Tabitha held up the card she'd found in her pocket. "I have an appointment."

His eyes narrowed. "I was told to expect a young *lady*." His gaze roved over her drab gray woolen dress and tattered coat, soaked hair, and fingerless gloves.

"A lady, eh?" She snorted at his joke, but he didn't crack a smile. "Sorry to disappoint you, sir." She bobbed a sarcastic curtsy.

"This way, Miss . . ." He paused when he failed to have a name to address her with.

She laughed. "Oh, you're a clever one, you are. I won't be giving you my name, not so you can track me down and throw me in Newgate."

"I was not told to do any such thing, miss." He sounded as if she'd deeply offended him.

She followed the butler inside, and her eyes widened. Just beyond the door, a large hallstand with a mirror stood ready to hold coats and umbrellas. Tabitha caught a glimpse of her own appearance in that mirror and frowned at the drowned rat staring back at her. She carefully walked around the center table full of blooming flowers and glanced up at the glittering chandelier over her head.

This was a beautiful home. More beautiful than any she'd ever seen in her life. She'd never imagined people could actually *live* in houses like this. Tabitha shared a cramped attic space with half a dozen other girls in an old warehouse by the docks.

"The parlor is this way." The butler opened a door down the hall for her and ushered her inside. The parlor was a high-ceilinged room with bright blue-and-orange flower-patterned wallpaper that lent the room the feeling of an endless summer. It drew a smile to her lips before she could stop herself. If she lived in a place that had a room like this, she'd never want to leave. Sumptuous carpets covered the floor, and Tabitha was glad she'd wiped her boots before coming inside. Several portraits of distinguished lords and ladies hung over a writing desk full of papers and letters.

The fireplace was surrounded by towering book-shelves, each filled to the brim with books. She'd learned to read long ago and had vowed to never let that skill lapse. Her father had told her that a woman who could read had the world at her fingertips. Old memories, ones she kept close to her heart to relive whenever a deep pain threatened to surface.

She turned her attention to a display case in one corner of the room, which was filled with silvery objects that would be worth a fortune if she could sell them. She deliberately turned her focus away from temptation and studied the rest of the room.

There were two settees and a tea table arranged artfully near the fireplace. Despite the room's size, it felt cozy, like the set of rooms she and her father had lived before he'd died. The wallpaper had been peeling at the edges and the furniture worn and dusty, but it had been cozy like this. Again, her heart stuttered in a painful off beat.

"Please wait here." The butler's words broke her free of the past. He stepped into the corridor and closed the door, leaving her alone. Tabitha examined the room again before approaching the display case. Decorative trinkets, silver bowls, sculptures, and other things that looked heavy and expensive called to the thief within her. Her hands itched to touch, but she didn't dare. She did remove a letter opener from the nearby desk and slipped it into her pocket, in case she needed to defend herself. If the men who had summoned her here had any ideas about grabbing her, they'd get a nice little poke in the gut.

When the door to the parlor opened again, Tabitha gasped as a woman stepped inside. It wasn't just any woman. It was the one who had dropped all those lovely flowers at the market. The woman turned and closed the door behind her, her beautiful bustled blue skirts whispering over the carpets as she moved. Despite the voluminous fabric of the gown trailing behind her, she moved easily. Tabitha envied her careless grace that such ladies seemed to be born with. Tabitha might have the nimble moves of a thief, but she had no grace.

The woman smiled at her warmly. "Thank you for coming. I'm Hannah Winslow." She held out her hand to shake as though they were gentlemen at a club meeting for the first time.

Strangely, Tabitha liked the woman's frank, forward nature, but she couldn't afford to forget the potential danger. This woman had distracted her once, and she couldn't let that happen again.

"Where are they?" Tabitha demanded as she ignored the woman's offered hand.

"Who?" Hannah asked, her hazel eyes wide with confusion.

"The men who pinched my watch."

"You mean the watch *you* pinched first?" Hannah asked politely.

"Yes." Tabitha kept her eye on the parlor door. Any moment those men would come in here and . . . do whatever they planned to do.

"There were no men. Only me . . . and Julia, of course." The door opened and another woman entered as if she'd heard her name called.

"Sorry I'm late, Hannah—oh, she's here!" This new woman, Julia, paused in the act of unpinning her hat from her russet hair, and her warm brown eyes swept curiously over Tabitha.

"She's early," Julia observed as she set her hat down on a side table and smoothed her hands over her burgundy velvet walking dress. It was rich with embroidered patterns of robins, just like the emblem on the card.

"Yes, it seems she is," Hannah said with an amused chuckle. "This is my friend, Julia Starling."

Tabitha stared at the two women, utterly confused. Where were the pickpockets who'd taken her watch?

Julia slipped a hand into a hidden gown pocket at her hip and pulled out the silver pocket watch. It dangled in the air beneath her hand, spinning slowly in circles, the light glinting off its etched surface.

"How did you get that?" Tabitha demanded.

"The same way you did. I stole it." Julia's brown eyes lit with mischief.

"But—" Tabitha couldn't believe it. A fine lady had pinched the watch from her? She tensed when the parlor door opened again, but it was only a maid carrying a tea tray.

"Please sit, Miss . . . Oh dear, we still don't know your name." Hannah gestured toward one of the two couches by the fireplace.

Tabitha hesitated. She didn't trust these women, but this wasn't the danger she had expected to face.

"Please, we don't mean you any harm. We won't be calling the authorities. We invited you here to ask you something."

"Then go on and ask," Tabitha said.

"Would you sit and have some tea first?" Hannah offered.

Tabitha reluctantly lowered herself onto one of the two couches. Her empty stomach gnawed at her, but she wasn't going to let them know just how desperate she was. The two odd ladies sat opposite her, and Hannah poured tea for the three of them. Tabitha took the offered cup hesitantly, but when she caught a whiff of its aroma, she sighed with pleasure. *Real tea.* How long had it been since she'd tasted that?

"We saw you lift that pocket watch," Julia began as she handed the timepiece over to Tabitha. Tabitha snatched it and tucked it away in her pocket. "We were quite impressed."

"We were," Hannah agreed. "That brings us to why we invited you here."

Tabitha held her cup and waited for whatever bad news was to be delivered.

"We are on a mission to help those less fortunate. We want to do more, but even as well off as we are, we need a way to supplement our causes."

"That's where you come in." Julia grinned.

"I don't understand," Tabitha said. "How can I possibly fit in?" She took a hasty sip of her tea, anything to get something in her stomach. "Surely you fine ladies don't need a resident thief."

The two women exchanged glances, and then Hannah leaned forward. "That's exactly what we need."

Tabitha choked on her next sip of tea. "You're joking."

"We certainly aren't," Julia said. "We want you to continue to ply your trade."

"You want me to steal for you?" Tabitha asked,

slowly voicing the question to make sure she'd heard them correctly.

"More like *with* us. We stole your watch, after all. We aren't without skills," Julia reminded her with a grin. "But we need a third person to do this properly. We need someone who understands the city and its streets in ways that we do not if we're going to pull off bigger heists than mere pocket watches."

Tabitha's head was spinning. "Heists?"

"Oh yes," said Hannah. "We have a target in mind, and it is my opinion that we need two people to distract the target and a third person to retrieve the jewels."

These women were mad, surely, Tabitha thought.

"You plan on stealing from a jeweler or—?"

"No, that's the best part. We only intend to steal from those who are . . . well . . . *undeserving* of them," Hannah said.

"What she means is someone bad, or otherwise quite terrible."

"Right . . . ," Tabitha drawled. "You want to steal from the rich—"

"*Only* the terrible ones, yes, and give to the poor." Julia passed over a card, one similar to the kind that they had put in her pocket.

"We call ourselves the Merry Robins. You see, our

emblem is a robin." She pointed to the bird that was drawn on the card.

Tabitha inwardly groaned. *The Merry Robins? Like Robin Hood?* These women thought they were like the old English legend of the man who'd robbed from the rich to give to the poor. They couldn't be that naïve, could they? Surely they realized how silly that was.

"And where does the money go from the items you sell?" she asked. "You said the less fortunate, but I expect you don't intend to drop a bag of coins on people's doorsteps, do you?"

"Of course not." Hannah got up and went to her desk to retrieve a written list. "These are the orphanages, workhouses, soup kitchens, and other places that desperately need help. Even those in debtors' prison need assistance for the sake of their families. The charities we have on our list are run by good people. They do not embezzle money they receive or do anything that we consider immoral. But they also do not receive enough support from society to be as effective as they could be."

Tabitha still couldn't understand why these two women, who seemed to have everything, would care for those who had nothing. It made no sense.

"Why?" Tabitha asked. "Why care? You have your pretty palaces and your pretty gowns, and all that's ever expected of you is to attend teas and balls. You don't have to care about any of this."

For the first time, Tabitha saw a crack form in the politeness of the two women. Hannah's kind eyes turned hard as steel.

"Because we *can* help. Women and children are the ones who suffer the most when there is inequity in the world. I am tired of letting men make our gender victims, and I'm tired of seeing children starve on the streets. Have you ever seen the tide at the waterfront?"

Tabitha shook her head. The docks were a dangerous place to be, especially for a woman, no matter the time of day.

"When boats are stuck in the mud during a low tide, they can't do what they are meant to . . . which is sail upon the water. When a tide comes in," Julia explained, "it rises everywhere along the shore. As it does, it lifts every single boat floating nearby. That tide lifts *every-thing*. What if *we* became the tide? What if *we* lifted up our fellow humans? More food in their bellies, less moth-eaten clothing, more chances to find a home with shelter for the winter months. The more hope someone receives, the more they are lifted, you see. And when lifted by hope . . . they can find their way to sailing again."

The fine hairs on Tabitha's arms rose. These two

women actually *believed*. And what was more, Tabitha started to as well. She began to imagine what good they could actually do. No more children selling wilted violets and lavender on the street. No more boys chasing carriages in the dark, begging gentlemen to buy newspapers. No more bodies frozen on the pavement, no more crying babies who had no milk, no more pain and suffering.

"Is a world like that even possible?" she asked aloud, even though she hadn't meant to.

"Our world will never be perfect, and it will be a fight every day. But wouldn't you rather put your head on your pillow at night and sleep better knowing that *you* were a part of that fight?"

Tabitha was quiet a long moment as she considered what joining these women could mean, not just for herself but for others.

"Let's say that I agree. Who would we steal from first? And what would we be stealing?"

Hannah beamed at her. "Well, I believe we should practice a bit first before we hit our primary targets, but the man that we eventually plan to steal from is a particularly rude and arrogant duke who has *far* too many diamonds . . ."

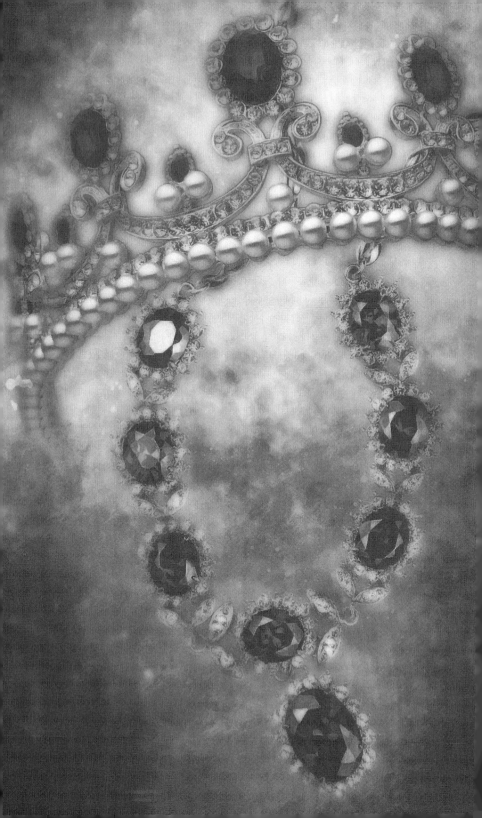

Chapter One

T HE STRING OF BURGLARIES IN GROSVENOR
SQUARE AND MAYFAIR HAVE LEFT AUTHORI-
TIES BAFFLED. NO SUSPECTS HAVE BEEN
IDENTIFIED. THE LATEST VICTIM IS LADY ASHBURG,
WHO HAD AN EMERALD NECKLACE STOLEN DURING A
GARDEN PARTY AT HER HOME LAST SUNDAY. SCOTLAND
YARD HAS INTERVIEWED EVERY GUEST AND SERVANT
PRESENT AT THE TIME OF THE THEFT. YET NO ARRESTS
HAVE BEEN MADE. REWARDS ARE BEING OFFERED FOR
ANY INFORMATION AS TO THE IDENTITY OF THE THIEF
AND THE LOCATION OF THE JEWELS.

—ILLUSTRATED POLICE NEWS, SEPTEMBER 1876

FITZWILLIAM SEAGRAVE, THE DUKE OF HELSTON, or Fitz, as his friends and family insisted upon calling him, folded up the illustrated newspaper that sat on his lap and frowned. The paper contained sensational, garish reports on crime and punishment in England. He set it on the reading table in front of him and sipped his brandy thoughtfully as he examined the frontpage illustration. It depicted a man in black clothing wearing a mask and gloves as he crept behind a beautiful young woman whose neck was bedecked with a large, jeweled necklace.

"Jewel thieves . . . Honestly, don't the poor wretches have anything better to do with their time than take things they have no right to?" he muttered to himself. For the last several months, the *Police News* and other papers had been carrying the story of the jewelry thefts as though it was a matter of national concern. As if a veritable wave of crime was crashing upon England's shores.

He stared around vacant chairs in Berkley's, his gentlemen's club. The reading room was usually empty this time of night. He was alone except for an elderly man asleep by the fireplace halfway between Fitz and the door. Most of the men were in the cardroom or the dining room at this time of night.

Normally, he would have been in the midst of that

crowd, throwing himself into games of risk, but they had begun to bore him of late. The usual amusements he relied on had lost their appeal. He was too good at choosing the right horses at the derby, it was too easy to take a woman to his bed, and he had exhausted the pockets of most of the men in the cardroom one floor below.

Fitz studied the portraits of past members on the wall. Nearly sixty years ago, life in England had been vastly different. There had been no industry, fewer mills to turn the northern cities white with cotton from the factories, or coal turning the industrial cities black with soot. The men on these walls had never known the hum of gaslights, the rattle of trains, or the feeling of a steam engine in a ship that could power across the water faster than any sail.

Yet Fitz had the sense that the men who graced these canvases had seen and done much in their lives, whereas he had not. It was strange to think that in a world of invention and industry, his life was far less adventurous than the men who'd lived in the past.

A door crashed open at the far end of the quiet reading room, and a tall man slipped inside. His entry disturbed the older member asleep by the fireplace, who awoke with a muffled grunt and cursed at the interloper.

"What in the blazes? Watch the bloody door!" the

man growled, his graying mustache twitching as his eyes searched the face of the newcomer. The man who had caused the ruckus was a familiar and welcome sight to Fitz.

"Evan, over here," he called out. The man spotted him and strode over, thunder brewing in his eyes. He slapped his own copy of the *Police News* down on the table in front of Fitz.

"Have you seen this?" Evan planted a finger on the article that Fitz had just been reading.

"Yes, quite unfortunate business, that."

Evan Haddon, the Earl of Brightstone, was one of his dearest friends. Evan's jet-black hair was slightly mussed, as if he was always dragging his hands through it. Given their long history of friendship, Fitz could tell when his friend was furious, though he was doing his best to hide it.

"*Unfortunate* business? Fitz, these thieves are a menace. My cousin, Lady Alice, had her diamond earbobs pinched in the middle of a bloody ball."

"You're sure she didn't leave them at home in a jewel safe, or perhaps misplaced them?" Fitz inquired. It wouldn't be the first time Lady Alice had had a complaint to make. Despite her beauty, she was not the most pleasant woman.

"No. Good God, man. They came right off her ears

during a dance somehow. Everyone searched the floor after she realized they were missing, but no one found them."

Fitz pictured Evan's pretty cousin dancing, and in the midst of a twirl, he imagined seeing a pair of black-gloved hands plucking her earrings clear off. Fitz suddenly laughed.

"It isn't amusing, Fitz. This is *serious* business. These thieves left a calling card like street magicians. Alice found this tucked down the back of her evening gown." Evan threw himself down in a chair beside Fitz and tossed a card on the table.

"A calling card?" Fitz was roused from his state of ennui. "Color me intrigued. The papers made no mention of such a detail."

"They wouldn't. It would encourage other gangs of thieves to do the same. Cards would start showing up all over London," Evan predicted, his fury turning to glum resignation. "What's next? We'll see a calling card sitting where the crown jewels used to in the tower of London?"

"Let me see that." Fitz leaned forward and took the card from where it lay next to Evan's hand.

"The card says, 'The Merry Robins,' and there's a little stamp of a bird. A card is left at the scene of each theft. That's what the detective from Scotland Yard told Alice when she filed her police report."

Fitz turned the card over, brushing his thumb over the emblem of the little robin. "Interesting." He was more than a little curious now about these thieves, given that they had robbed Evan's cousin of her jewelry. Wouldn't it be fun if he solved the mystery and caught these men? The thought spurred a fire in him that hadn't been there in a long time.

"More like *infuriating*. Someone needs to catch these bastards."

"The Merry Robins . . . You know who that reminds me of?" Fitz said softly, fighting off a smile. His and Evan's eyes met, and his friend's eyes widened with shock.

"You don't think . . ." Evan sat up, his face darkening. "Surely not. Beck retired from this sort of thing ages ago."

"I thought he had too, but he might know who these Merry Robins are." Fitz had a feeling Beck would know these men, or know how to find them, and the thrilling prospect of catching these thieves put him in the mood to act at once.

"Perhaps we ought to pay a call on our old friend," Evan agreed. "I swear, if he has Alice's earbobs . . ."

"Then I'm sure he will politely return them to you," Fitz said with confidence.

Evan checked his pocket watch. "It's nine thirty. Where do you suppose he would be?"

"Likely at the card tables." Fitz stood and Evan followed him out of the reading room. They descended a square-shaped staircase the cardroom one floor below. Cigar smoke formed a thick cloud above their heads, and the sounds of men wagering and cards fluttering filled the room as games were played. Fortunes had been won and lost in this room over the years.

It took a moment to find their boyhood friend, Walter Beckley, or Beck, as they called him. He was at a whist table with three other gentlemen. He and his partner had just finished a hand when he glanced up to see Fitz and Evan watching him. He calmly collected his half of the winnings, shook his partner's hand, and stood. Like Evan and Fitz, Beck stood over six feet tall and was handsome as the devil himself, which had always brought trouble in their younger days. His charming smile disarmed everyone he met.

Beck skirted around the table and gave his friends an inquiring look. Fitz returned the look with a tilt of his head toward an empty gaming table. The three of them crossed the room and seated themselves at the table where they could speak more freely without fear of being overheard or disturbed.

"Haven't seen either of you in a while," Beck mused. He placed his winnings into a leather trifold wallet and then tucked the wallet deep into his breast pocket.

Fitz felt the dig of his friend's words a little too deeply. It was true he had not spent much time with Beck in the last year. They'd nodded at each other in passing when in the club or out at social gatherings, but the long nights of talking over glasses of brandy and playing billiards or cards had fallen by the wayside for them all recently. Fitz realized he'd missed both of his friends more than he wanted to admit.

"I had affairs in Edinburgh most of this year. Business." Fitz had been seeing to his newly acquired book publishing company to make sure everything was running smoothly. It had demanded much of his time to get the offices and the employees up to scratch.

Evan shrugged. "Sorry, Beck. I was busy with an affair of a different sort, one who has since moved on to greener pastures."

Fitz frowned. "Lord Fairton's widow?"

A nod. "She left me for Lord Woolsey when I refused to buy her a bigger townhouse."

Beck snorted and pulled a cigar out of his pocket

and lit it. "I see not much has changed after all. So, what is the reason for this call between old friends?"

Evan gave Fitz a nudge with his elbow. "You ask him."

"Oh dear, Evan is too embarrassed to ask it himself? Whatever it is must be dire. Just *ask* me," Beck replied, clearly amused by Evan's discomfort.

"You heard of the recent jewel thefts?" Fitz asked.

Beck nodded, his gray eyes dimming a little, his amusement fading. "I have. What of them?"

"It has nothing to do with you, has it?" Evan asked. "These Merry Robin fellows?"

Beck puffed out a breath of cigar smoke and then calmly snubbed the tip in an ashtray. He glared at Evan as if his smoking had been completely ruined.

"I meant no offense, Beck." Evan's tone was sincere. "You're the only thief we know."

"*Former* thief," Beck emphasized.

"Yes," Evan echoed. "Former."

Beck raised a brow. "You assume it has something to do with me simply because I used to steal shiny, pretty things?"

"We made no such assumption," Fitz hedged carefully. "We merely thought you might have an idea as to who these fellows are, seeing as how they might run in your old circles."

"And if I did, what does it matter?" Beck asked. "Neither of you are listed as victims, at least according to the papers."

"Well, poor Evan's cousin would like her diamond earrings back. And me? I'd like to catch these thieves. I have been so *bored* of late, and these Merry Robins have been running circles around the Yard. Wouldn't it be fun to hand them over to Scotland Yard and see the faces on those clueless detectives?" The more Fitz thought about it, the more he wanted to do exactly that. He wanted to catch a thief.

Beck gazed at Fitz a long moment and then slowly leaned forward. He smiled that charming smile that had distracted many a woman, and more than a few men, as he parted them from their jewels or money without them being any the wiser.

"It's no use hoping to track them down the way a *proper* detective would," he confided. "You're simply not equipped for it. No offense, you are both bright men, but it's not something one does on a lark. Have you read *Criminal Man?* Have you studied criminal anthropology?" He saw the dejection on their faces and then added, "For you, a different approach is required. If you want to catch a thief, you'll need to set a trap. Something big, something *irresistible.*"

"Such as?" Evan asked.

Beck was still staring at Fitz, and Fitz realized suddenly what his friend was thinking.

"You can't mean . . . ," Fitz began.

Beck met his gaze. "Oh yes."

"But my grandmother hardly lets that diamond out of her sight. It's not even *my* diamond yet," Fitz protested.

The jewel in question was the Helston Diamond, a massive gem that could be inserted into a tiara by affixing it to a cleverly placed silver setting in the center. The tiara was a beautiful piece made of a graduated line of cushion-shaped and old-cut diamond clusters alternating with diamond-set scroll motifs. It had been in the family for more than a century, and it was meant to be a wedding gift from Fitz's grandmother for Fitz to give his bride whenever he married.

"We can't use that, Beck," Fitz argued.

"Nothing ventured, nothing gained, old friend," Beck replied. "If you want these thieves, hold that diamond out as bait and make the task of taking it appear deceptively easy."

"Does this mean you'll help us?" Evan asked.

"Do you *want* me to help you catch this thief?" Beck asked in return, a hint of bitterness in his tone.

"Yes," Fitz said honestly. "It will be like old times. The three of us up to our old nonsense."

"Very well." Beck smiled somewhat sadly, as though the mention of their past brought a bittersweet fondness to his heart. "Come closer. Now, here is what we must do . . ."

JULIA WAVED THREE INVITATIONS IN HER HAND. "We have our way in!"

Tabitha looked up from the newspaper she'd been reading. Hannah paused in her letter writing at the nearby desk. They had been resting in Hannah's parlor after dinner while Julia had been at her parents' home for dinner. Julia didn't live at Hannah's residence but she spent nearly half her time there rather than at her own home. She was one of the few ladies of her status who traipsed about London without a chaperone and yet her parents didn't seem to mind. They were a loving, indulgent couple that Tabitha had taken a liking to instantly when she'd first met them.

Hannah chuckled. "Dare I ask what you've gotten us into?"

"It is a legitimate invite, I assure you. My aunt is a friend of the Dowager Duchess of Helston. The three of us are attending a musicale this evening at the duke's home." Julia flashed the invitations in the air with a cheeky grin.

Tabitha almost smiled. Today, like most days, seemed like a wonderful sort of dream. She had moved into Hannah's townhouse shortly after that fateful encounter in the marketplace.

She had placed her trust in Hannah and Julia, and so far, she'd not come to regret that decision. Over the past six months, they had transformed her life from a street pickpocket to a gentle lady.

But what mattered more was that they had held true to their promise. She had helped them steal more than twenty pieces of jewelry, and every piece had been sold, with all of the proceeds given to those in need. Orphans, war veterans, single mothers, and widows fallen on hard times. She'd gone with them to deliver the funds to the very relieved and grateful people who ran the charities.

The children selling flowers now had new coats, pants, and dresses. They also had hats, mittens and gloves. She knew those children would continue to sell things on the street to support their families, but if she could keep them warm, keep them fed . . . that was enough for now. In the meantime, she was working on a better solution to keep those children from being on the streets in the first place.

Their secret work was on everyone's lips, it seemed, and the whisper of the Merry Robins brought a smile to Tabitha each time she heard it ripple through the markets. It had become a beacon of hope for those who had so few things in life. If her father could have seen her sitting like a fine lady wearing a lovely gown while in a fancy parlor, drinking tea and knowing that *she* was the one to help these less fortunate people, he would have been proud of her. He would have loved to have seen her feeding the poor and helping teach children to read and write, just as he'd taught her. She spent most of her days visiting the charities they helped with the profits from the stolen jewels; a quiet afternoon like this was rare.

"What time is the musicale?" Tabitha asked Julia as the other woman draped herself gracefully onto a chair by the fire.

"Eight o'clock."

"Eight! I must change at once!" Hannah leapt from her chair in a panic. Tabitha had only a moment to dive forward from her seat to catch the bottle of ink Hannah knocked over before it spilled all over Hannah's letters. Tabitha's quick reflexes often came in handy in such moments.

"You need not change your dress. You're perfectly fine," Julia argued and winked at Tabitha.

Since becoming a part of Hannah and Julia's lives,

she'd learned that Hannah, a young widow of only twenty-three, was always polite and perfectly dressed for every occasion. Julia, who was the same age, was almost Hannah's opposite in every way. Julia was a headstrong, wild, risk taker compared to Hannah's compassionate, gentle soul. They had been friends since they were young girls, and Tabitha envied their closeness. Their friendship had been built over years of trust. But luckily for Tabitha, they had been openhearted enough to let her into their circle of friendship and become a fellow Merry Robin.

"Tabby, do you wish to change too?" Hannah asked, using the nickname that they'd given her. Julia had said it was because Tabitha reminded her of a very brave and clever cat she'd once rescued from the streets. That cat was now an ancient, chubby, spoiled feline who rested in sunbeams and chased the occasional mouse. Once Tabitha had met the cat, she'd found it strangely endearing rather than annoying to be named after the old cat.

"I think I'll be fine with this." She waved at the blue-and-cream satin gown that she wore. They had only had dinner an hour ago, and she was dressed suitably for a musicale. More than once, she'd marveled at the change not only of her circumstances but of herself. The dirty-skinned, starving, thin-limbed young woman was gone.

Now she was a woman with softer curves from a healthy diet, and her once dull brown hair was lustrous. Her blue eyes seemed far brighter than they ever had been before. She wore clothing in the height of fashion, spoke like a fine lady, and walked as though she were on a bed of clouds.

But deep down, the fierce street urchin was still inside Tabitha. She felt she was fully of two worlds instead of one. It was not easy to feel like that, but she far preferred it to being trapped in the world she had been born into. She frequently had to face that she was becoming too complacent and accustomed to luxury. She often reminded herself that things could change at a moment's notice if something happened to Hannah or Julia, and she could be back on the streets again.

"Come keep me company while I change," Hannah said with a grin, and Tabitha agreed.

"I'll collect a notebook. We'll need to sketch Helston's house to remember where everything is," Julia called out to them while she searched Hannah's desk.

Tabitha followed Hannah upstairs. Her friend paused as she always did in front of the portrait of her deceased husband, Mr. Jeremy Winslow. He had been a handsome young man, and his face held a deep kindness that always made Tabitha's heart ache at the thought of him being gone. She would have liked to have met him.

Hannah kissed the tips of her fingers and touched the frame, then continued up the rest of the stairs. Hannah had only been married to Jeremy a few months before he perished in a railway accident. Julia said that Hannah and Jeremy had known each other for years and their marriage had been a true love match. It had been two years since he'd died, and Hannah, while still mourning him, had reemerged in society in the last year.

Over the past few months, Tabitha had grown protective of Hannah, just as Julia was. Hannah was too kind, too good to suffer such grief and loneliness. Tabitha had heard her weeping at night sometimes. The helpless feeling had left Tabitha guilt ridden, but how could she offer comfort to Hannah? What could she possibly give her friend to ease her pain? She'd seen her father mourn quietly at night the very same way after Tabitha's mother had died. She had been too young to know what to do then, and now she felt too beaten by life herself.

As Hannah entered her bedchamber and her trusted maid Liza helped her change, Tabitha pressed her with questions about their intended target. She leaned against the bedpost as she listened to Hannah from behind the changing screen.

"This Lord Helston, what is he like?" They'd spoken of the infamous Helston Diamond as one of their most important gems to steal when they'd first met, but it seemed so far away then. Now they were finally ready to take on a true challenge. Stealing little earbobs, rings, and necklaces from women had proved easy enough, but the Duke of Helston would be a far different matter. The diamond they sought technically still belonged to his grandmother, the one hosting this evening's musicale, but it would be his one day, as his grandmother intended it to be a gift for his future bride, and that had been enough for Julia and Hannah to put it on the list.

"Infuriating. Arrogant. He believes he knows everything better than anyone else. He wrecks the lives of others because he must always be right," Hannah said, her tone icy. Liza huffed in agreement as she began to lace Hannah's dress up in the back. Liza was loyal to a fault when it came to Hannah and helped the Merry Robins keep their secret. She's grown up in a poor house as a child and knowing that her mistress was finding a way to help children who lived in such conditions like she did had further solidified her loyalty and silence as to the identifies of the Robins.

"I get the sense he must have done something specific, or are we pursuing him for being generally unpleasant?" Most of their targets had done terrible, cruel things, while others were simply horrible people who dismissed the suffering of others as the price one paid for a civilized society.

"Helston is a tad more personal than the others," Hannah admitted as she came around the other side of the curtain.

She'd chosen her favorite silk reception dress made up of a dark-blue bodice and overskirt with a cream satin flower-embroidered pleated underskirt. Her deep square neckline was reminiscent of the fashion a century ago, with lace at the edges concealing her breasts enough to make the gown appropriate for a musicale, while still reminding any man present that she was young and beautiful, even though she was widowed. Not that Hannah ever seemed to think about gentlemen or marriage or her own beauty. She was far too modest for all of that.

"How is it personal?" Tabitha asked curiously.

"When we were in finishing school, Julia and I had a friend, Anne Girard. She was the sweetest girl, and quite brilliant in her studies. She was very lovely, though not vain at all. She was nouveau riche, her father earning his money through business rather than birth. Some of the girls were quick to judge her, but Julia and I adored her. The year after our debuts, Anne met a gentleman named Louis Atherton and they became engaged. She was quite happy, and we were happy for

her. Julia and I knew Louis. He was a good man."
Hannah frowned. "Then Helston whispered in Louis's
ear and poisoned him against her."

"What did he say?" Tabitha asked, intrigued.

"He said that Anne was beneath him. Unsuitable
for marriage. When Louis broke the engagement,
Anne's life was ruined by the scandal."

Tabitha's face must have shown her confusion.

"It isn't done, you see. A gentleman doesn't break off
an engagement. When a lady breaks it off, there is no
social cost, but for a man to throw a lady over . . ."
Hannah winced. "It raises questions as to why, and
people *always* think the worst. Anne was no longer
eligible in the eyes of society, and so not only did the
man she loved toss her aside, but now no other man
would court her."

"What happened to her?" Tabitha's heart tightened
for this woman she'd never met. How could someone do
that to her?

"Her family became desperate enough to send her
to America to find a husband. She sailed for New York.
She lost the man she loved, her reputation, and is now
cut off from her family, an ocean away—all on the word
of that bastard Helston."

"How horrible!"

"I suppose he's a wretched-looking old man?" She

couldn't help but picture a villainous man with a leer who used a cane to beat small children he passed on the street.

Hannah sighed as she collected her reticule and gloves. "Tragically, Helston is handsome, *far* too handsome."

Tabitha rarely thought of male beauty, or *any* type of beauty, really. She had been focused on survival for so long that beauty in any form escaped her notice. At least until she'd been pulled into Hannah and Julia's glittering world. Now she was starting to see the beauty in so many things . . . the rain that she'd once cursed, the petals of the flowers that the little girls sold and the smell of freshly baked bread. When given the chance to live, not simply survive, one could finally start to see the beauty in a great many things. It was why she was so determined to help anyone she could by stealing from the rich to give to the poor.

"That won't bother me," Tabitha said as she and Hannah went downstairs to meet Julia and wait for the carriage.

"You say that now, Tabby, but there are quite a few handsome men in this world. One day your head will be turned by one of them, and you will be lost in love."

"Tabby's lost in love, is she?" Julia asked with a grin.

"No, I'm not."

"Not *yet*. I was warning her about Helston, Julia."

"Oh yes." Julia's smile vanished. "He's a bastard, but a beautiful one."

Hannah gasped in shock at Julia's colorful language.

"Well, he is." Julia lifted her chin, offering no apologies.

Tabitha rolled her eyes. No man was attractive enough to rob her of her good sense, no matter how beautiful a bastard he might be.

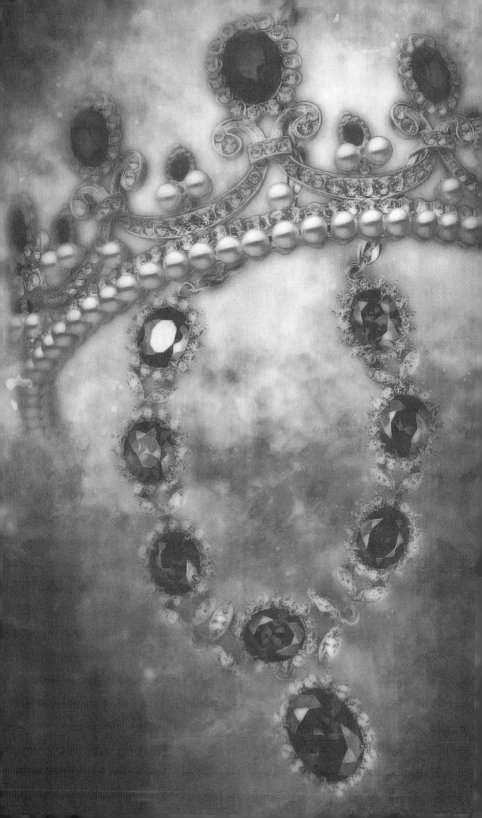

Chapter Two

Tabitha had attended a number of social gatherings since she had joined the Merry Robins, but tonight felt different. Perhaps it was simply nerves at knowing she and her friends would be scouting a real prize, or maybe it was something else. Whatever it was left her on edge as she descended from Hannah's private coach and followed the other guests. Everyone queued on the steps leading up to the entrance of the Duke of Helston's residence.

As Hannah had explained, the dowager duchess had a dower house for her own use on the family's country estate, but since her grandson the duke was as yet unmarried, she lived most of the year with him in the Helston townhouse and acted as his hostess for formal events. She was a well-respected, powerful but fair and kind woman. According to Hannah, Helston's relationship with his grandmother was the only good thing about him.

"It's unlikely Helston himself will be here this evening. He adores his grandmother but rarely attends such functions. You needn't worry about running into him," Hannah explained.

"She should be relieved," Julia replied. "The pompous, arrogant—"

"*Julia,*" Hannah warned, but Tabitha saw Hannah hide a smile as she hushed her friend. Tabitha quite liked Julia's intensity. She refused to be a lady if it meant letting anyone walk over her or those she cared about.

But despite their reassurances, Tabitha was inexplicably afraid that the duke would be there, that he would instantly see through her façade and she and her friends would be tossed out—or worse, arrested. It was nonsense, of course, yet her mind would not let go of the idea.

The three of them provided their invitations at the door as the butler gave them entry. It was a grand townhouse, grander than Hannah's home. They followed the guests ahead of them into a small ballroom that had been transformed into a concert hall with about thirty chairs lined up in front of a Byzantine piano. A string quartet accompanied a woman seated behind a harp, forming the rest of the musicale display. A table with refreshments sat off to one side with a fleet of footmen in attendance.

"Don't forget to smile," Hannah whispered to Tabitha. "And breathe."

Breathe. She inhaled deeply as she reminded herself to do just that. This was no different than any other day. They weren't here to steal the diamond tonight. They only wanted to see it and get a sense of the house. Just simple reconnaissance. She lifted her chin and smiled at several women as they reached the refreshment tables and took glasses of punch from a footman. She could do this.

Then everyone turned as a beautiful, proud-looking woman in her twilight years stood by the piano and addressed the crowd. The dowager duchess had arrived.

"I'm delighted to present Mademoiselle Lynette from Paris to sing for us tonight. These fine musicians will accompany her." The dowager's austere beauty softened as she looked at the musicians. "Thank you for entertaining us tonight with your talents. My grandson will be sorry to miss this performance as he is such a lover of music."

Tabitha relaxed. The beautiful bastard would *not* be here this evening after all. Not that she was afraid to meet him. Of course she wasn't.

"Enjoy tonight, and thank you for coming," the dowager said before she began walking through the crowd and greeting the guests. She paused when she reached Tabitha, Hannah, and Julia. Her two friends dropped immediately into gentle curtsies and bowed their heads. Tabitha rushed to do the same, but it did not escape the old duchess's notice that she hesitated for an instant. *Blast.*

"Mrs. Winslow, who is your companion? I've not had the pleasure of meeting her."

"This is Tabitha Sherborne, a distant cousin of mine from Yorkshire," Hannah supplied smoothly.

"Welcome, Miss Sherborne. I hope you enjoy the music." The dowager continued to study her, but it was not the look Hannah expected. She saw no derision, no judgment, only curiosity. The tiara the duchess wore had a large egg-shaped diamond in the center. The diamond that she'd often boasted she was gifting to her grandson for the moment he took a bride. The diamond they planned to steal.

Admittedly, the duchess was not someone Julia or Hannah would have ordinarily considered a target. She was a proud woman, but never cruel. Her grandson was another matter, Tabitha knew, and it was only through his grandmother's tiara that they could teach him a lesson.

"Thank you, Your Grace," Tabitha replied, her throat strangely tight as the old woman fought off a smile.

"It's a pity Fitz misses these engagements. Such *interesting* ladies he could meet," she said, half to herself, before she walked away.

"Interesting?" Tabitha echoed to Hannah and Julia. "What on earth does she mean by *that*?"

"Well, you are rather interesting, Tabitha. You are so pretty with such delicate features, yet those same features seem to be full of fierceness."

"What she means is you look like a lioness, not a kitten," Julia added. "Men expect kittens. But you have faced the hardships of life like no one else here. That strength shows in your face."

Tabitha reached up to cover her face with her hand, wondering how awful she must look. She didn't have Hannah's graceful looks or Julia's sharply intense beauty. What did strength look like? A collection of sharp angles and gaunt shadows upon her face? A hardness to her features that made her look as though she'd been cast in stone?

"You must stop seeing yourself in such a harsh light," Hannah said, catching Tabitha's hand and pulling it away from her face. "You're *stunning* to look at."

Tabitha glanced at Julia, needing the more honest of her two friends to give her the unvarnished truth.

"She's right. Courage and strength are beautiful and interesting."

Hannah got the other two back on track. "We should take our seats. Tabitha, once the first song is over, slip outside and tell the servants you need to visit the ladies' retiring room. Take your time and examine as much as you can of the house. Note any promising points of access we can use at a later date," Hannah said.

Tabitha gave a nod to indicate she'd heard the instructions as the three of them sat in the back row.

A pretty Frenchwoman in a pale-rose bustle gown festooned with flowers around her neck took a position by the pianist, and the concert began.

The first song was a pretty tune, one full of teasing, amusing lyrics with a quick tempo. After the first song ended, Tabitha stood and excused herself from the ballroom. A helpful footman gave her directions to go to the floor above to reach the ladies' retiring room.

She purposely missed the correct door and began to slip in and out of each room in the corridor. She opened each door, assessed what was inside, and moved on. When she came back to the landing at the top of the stairs, she heard a slow, mournful melody as the concert continued below. One of the servants must have left the door open because the music now carried through the entire house. She placed her palms on the railing and listened. The notes and words burrowed deep into her soul.

My lord was a handsome man,
With laughing eyes and a warm smile,
He was mine, he was mine,
The wind and rain would not keep him away,
No storm could hold him at bay,
He was mine he was mine,
But my lord fell ill with fevered dreams,
And his laughter died, his smiles faded,
But he was still mine, he was still mine.
His last breath was carried by a bitter wind,
And on his cold grave my heart did rend,
But he was still mine, still mine.

Tabitha closed her eyes, feeling the woman's loss, sensing her heartbreak on such a deep level it was as though she'd lost a lover herself. Tears escaped her eyes and she sniffed, wiping her face.

"Lovely, isn't it?" a deep voice asked from behind. She stiffened and fought to compose herself. She must have disturbed one of the footmen. She turned to see who, and her heart stopped.

The tall man standing close to her was handsome. *Too* handsome. Everything in his features conveyed strength, and for once she understood what Hannah had said when she'd mentioned strength showing in one's face, but she felt in that moment that it was far more attractive on this man than it would be on her.

His jaw was square, and his eyes were a dark blue and full of turbulent storms. His mouth was full, and the hint of a cleft in his chin was softened by the gold blond hair that fell boyishly into his eyes. He sported no beard or mustache despite society's dictates with the current trends. His shoulders were broad, and his waist narrowed to muscled but slender hips. The evening suit he wore was perfectly cut to his muscled physique.

It took Tabitha a moment to remember he had spoken to her. He reached into his waistcoat pocket and handed her a handkerchief, his gaze still fixed on her face.

"I shouldn't say a woman is pretty when she cries, but damned if you aren't a beautiful creature." For some reason that made Tabitha laugh, even though the sound came out watery.

"It is such lovely music," she agreed, answering his earlier question.

He joined her on the landing at the top of the stairs and braced himself on the railing with his forearms. The song continued to float up from the floor below, dancing in the air around them. Each swell of the strings and the descending patter of piano notes filled her mind with memories of her childhood.

She saw her mother lying in a sickbed. It was an old memory, one that had begun to fade more each year like a photograph left out in the sun. Memories of her father, grieving the woman he loved while raising a child on his own. Her father had never let her feel unloved, despite his own broken heart. Fresh tears sprang to Tabitha's eyes, and her throat tightened as she thought of him.

"What does this song make you think of that you feel so much it brings you to tears?" the gentleman asked. His voice was quiet, an emotion she couldn't quite name layered in his words.

"My father," she answered. "He would cry sometimes at night when he thought I was asleep. He never remarried after my mother died. A love lost like that destroys you. This music makes me feel it, but somehow I can see it through his eyes now, not the child I was. I can't explain it." She used his handkerchief to wipe her eyes again. "Does it make you think of anything?"

"Strangely, it makes me think of my father as well. But his story is a little different than yours." The man stared down at the open door to the ballroom. "My father was in the Crimean War. I was but a child when he fought in the Battle of Balaclava."

The name of the battle was familiar to Tabitha. She'd heard it somewhere before, but she couldn't remember where or when she'd learned it.

"What happened?" she asked.

"The British, French, and Ottoman forces were besieging the naval base at Sevastopol. The Russians tried to break through on horseback, but a Highland regiment of foot soldiers were ordered to hold them off. My father was among them. They had no horses. All they could do was form two lines to face down three thousand Russians on horseback. They called it the battle of the Thin Red Line, because of the uniforms they wore. The phrase now means a military unit spread thin but holding the line against attacks. It's a badge of courage, but to my father, it was the worst day of his life, watching his friends and countrymen die. But they held the line." The gentleman was quiet a long moment.

Tabitha moved closer, her arm touching his as they stood side by side. She had the strange urge to touch his face and comfort him. She had never wanted to do that with anyone before.

"Tennyson wrote a poem about that battle. I remember my father weeping once when he heard it spoken after a dinner. Some man deep in his cups recited it to the men while they had their brandy and cigars. My father came home, tears still in his eyes, and wouldn't speak to anyone for hours."

"Do you remember the poem?" she asked.

He flashed her a rueful smile. "I couldn't recite it all from memory, but I do remember one part."

> *When our own good redcoats sank from sight,*
> *Like drops of blood in a dark-gray sea,*
> *And we turn'd to each other, whispering, all dismay'd,*
> *"Lost are the gallant three hundred of Scarlett's*
> *Brigade!"*

"Heroes and fools on the field that day," the man sighed. "That's what my father used to say. But it's been years since I thought of that." His sensual mouth still held a hint of a smile.

"Is your father . . . still alive?"

"No, he died about ten years ago. My mother passed a year later." The gentleman turned her way. "What of your father?"

"He died when I was thirteen."

"So young." She saw grief and empathy in his face. "You had kind relatives who took you in?" His gaze swept over her fine evening gown. Of course he would assume that she was well-off. He never would have guessed that six months ago she was little more than a pickpocket.

It was on the tip of her tongue to tell him about growing up on the streets, about learning early how to steal, but that was a secret she could not share, even if she wanted to. That sudden impulse to unburden herself was so strong it shocked her. She never liked to tell anyone anything about herself or her life. The only two people she could trust with her past and the truth about her life were Hannah and Julia.

"Yes, my aunt Cecile took me in," she lied. "I'm visiting my distant cousin. She's been kind enough to let me experience the excitement of the city."

Applause followed the end of the haunting melody downstairs, and the sound drew Tabitha's focus back to her mission. She had wasted too much time talking to this man. She needed to get back to her friends, lest anyone wonder why she had been gone so long.

She stepped back to escape him. "I should go. I mustn't let my cousin worry."

He caught her hand briefly as it trailed past him on the banister.

"Thank you for this evening," he said, and for a moment she wondered if he would draw her close and dare to kiss her, such was the intensity of his gaze upon her.

"For what?" she whispered in the darkened corridor.

"For reminding me of the past. I so often keep it at bay, but the pain of it tonight wasn't as sharp because I shared it with you, just as you shared your tears with me."

His frankness stunned her. This man, this complete stranger, was making her feel things she wasn't used to feeling, things that threatened to destroy her very small and carefully controlled world. She blinked as her eyes burned.

"I really must go," she gasped and pulled away from him, their hands separating, and in that moment she saw the wall go back up on the man's face. Whatever vulnerability he'd revealed in the dark, it was hidden once more as he stepped back from her.

With only one foolish glance back at him, she hastened down the stairs and ducked back inside the ballroom to resume her place beside Julia and Hannah.

"How did it go?" Hannah asked.

She nodded in response, unable to trust her voice at this moment. She did not mention the gentleman, nor the foolish way she'd unburdened herself to him.

It was only long after the musicale ended, as she undressed in her room, that she discovered she still had his handkerchief in the pocket of her skirts. She removed the finely woven cloth and traced her fingers over the dark-blue initials upon it: F. S.

She had never even gotten his name. Was he a Frank? Perhaps Frederick? Ferdinand? Whoever he was, she knew his voice and his stunning eyes would haunt her as much as the melody of the song would. It was the first time she had felt *seen*, somehow, in a way she could not explain. The gentleman had gazed into her soul and hadn't looked away at whatever he'd seen there.

She climbed into bed and pressed the handkerchief to her nose, taking in the faint scent of the man's cologne that still lingered upon it. As she felt sleep creeping in that a new question presented itself in the darkness.

What had the man been doing there? She hadn't seen him among the other guests earlier that evening. And where had he come from? Because she'd checked every room before returning to the stairs and all the rooms had been empty.

If she hadn't still held the handkerchief in her hand as proof of his existence, she could easily believe it had been a dream she'd manifested into reality. Who was he, and how had he come to be there? The mystery tangled itself in her thoughts long into the night.

Fitz watched the beautiful mystery woman flee, her discomfort at the intimacy of what they'd just shared apparent. The moment had been more powerful than a kiss. He hadn't expected to find anyone upstairs during his grandmother's musicale. No one ever missed a song when she hired a talented singer to perform. Yet there *she'd* been, a vision in an evening gown of blue-and-cream plaid. Her bustle created a waterfall of silk from her lower back down to the floor, and was accented with two-tiered pale-blue silk revers that framed the plaid fabric. She looked like a colorful sweet from the confectioner's shop, and he'd always loved a pretty gown on a woman.

There was nothing more enticing than watching the bustle on a woman's backside sway with her hips as she moved. It reminded him how much fun it would be to take his time to slowly remove her elaborate outfit. He thought of a dozen ways to seduce her, but then he'd heard her make a soft, distressed sound and he'd realized she was hurting. As he'd come home earlier that evening, he'd heard the music whilst in the kitchens stealing a bit of food from the cook since he was famished. It had drawn him up the servants' stairs to a better spot to hear it. The music had also moved this woman. He'd wanted to pull her into his arms and kiss away her tears even before he had glimpsed her face.

It had been a long time since he'd been affected by someone else's emotions. Perhaps it was the music. His grandmother always chose the most wonderful singers and musicians. Fitz, like her, also had a soft spot for music. It could reach him despite every barrier he'd built to hide his heart from the world. He didn't like to feel pain because so much of his childhood had been full of it. His father had once said that all of life was simply moving from one moment of pain to the next.

Despite his wealth and station, Fitz had always felt the truth of his father's words. One could have everything that mattered and yet find that none of it *truly* mattered.

His father had swallowed the end of a pistol after nightmares of the war had left him too long without peace, and his mother had died of a broken heart soon after. Fitz wanted none of that in his carefully controlled world. Yes, he now lived a damned hollow existence, but it was without pain, at least most of the time. He would take feeling nothing every day over feeling too much.

But the moment he'd spoken to that woman, it was as if his fortress was nothing more than mist. Her pretty tears had slipped straight through that misty barrier, and she'd beat her fists against his heart, making it come alive, if only for a moment.

Why her? He could have any woman he wanted. He'd had mistresses who knew every way to please a man, but this woman . . . Christ, he did not even know her name, and yet she was like no one he had ever met before. They'd had said little, and yet what they'd shared had been of such *deep* things. She had unearthed his heartache in mere seconds, all because she'd shed tears at a mournful tune.

He closed his eyes, burning the image of her face in his mind. *Cornflower-blue eyes that held an unquenchable fire, a mouth that trembled as though she dreamt of his kiss, and a faint rose-colored hue in her cheeks that reminded him of paintings of Persephone—a fragile spring goddess stepping into the underworld, the taste of pomegranate upon her lips.* He wanted to pull her into his darkness, to kiss her as though he were Hades, claiming this woman's soul for all eternity.

Puzzled by his own reaction, Fitz remained on the landing above the stairs observing the guests' departure, hoping to spy the mystery woman once more. He caught a glimpse of that blue-and-cream plaid gown as a flock of lovely ladies moved toward the front door. He waited until the butler, Mr. Tracy, gave a heavy sigh of relief as he closed the door for the last time that evening. Fitz's grandmother stood beside the butler, cleaning her spectacles.

"Well, that was quite an evening," the dowager duchess said to Mr. Tracy.

"Indeed, my lady. Indeed," the butler agreed before he went down the kitchens to see to the downstairs staff.

Fitz descended the stairs, and his grandmother spotted him. Her eyes first brimmed with joy, then darkened with disapproval.

"Fitz, dear. I thought you were out this evening, yet here you are. You came back early and refused to meet our guests?"

He kissed his grandmother's cheek and chuckled. For as long as his parents had been gone, his beloved grandmother continued to teach him the art of being a duke.

"I had a meeting at my club. I'm sorry to have missed the musicale."

"You should be," his grandmother huffed. "There were some lovely young ladies here this evening."

"Indeed. I saw a few pretty ladies as they left. Tell me, who was the woman in the blue-and-cream plaid silk gown?" His grandmother would have to know who the mystery beauty was. She kept detailed guest lists, but she often extended extra invitations to her friends to bring others to events like these because she so loved sharing her love of music. Still, she would have made sure to introduce herself to any guest she didn't previously know.

"Blue-and-cream plaid . . . ah yes. Mrs. Winslow's cousin, if I remember correctly. Tabitha Sherborne. Beautiful creature. Tell me you're finally taking an interest in marriage, dear boy. Your father was already married and had you at this age. You are positively ancient now."

Fitz couldn't help but laugh. "I'm not even thirty. Men marry and father children well into their dotage. Age is of little concern to a man."

Her gaze narrowed, preparing for the coming battle. "That may be true, unfortunately, but think of the ladies, Fitz. No young woman should have to marry a man three times her age. Be fair. You are young and handsome now. Marry while you can attract the best woman as a wife. A happy wife leads to—"

"A happy life," he finished. "Yes, I know. But I do not feel the call to marry."

"That is your *first* problem. Marriage isn't simply a calling. It's a *duty*."

Fitz was enjoying this verbal sparring. "But Grandmother, you always said marriage is about love, like you and Grandfather."

"It *is* about love. You have a duty to find the right woman to fall in love with and marry."

Blast, she had him there.

"Then perhaps I need to host a country house party to revive my spirits in regards to love. Will you act as my hostess? Invite everyone on this list to a house party at Helston Heath, including Miss Sherborne and her cousin." He removed a list of guests from his pocket and gave it to his grandmother. She studied the list, still clearly suspicious.

"You must have some scheme in mind, Fitz. What are you up to?"

"No scheme, Grandmama," he assured her with a smooth smile. But she knew him too well. She had helped raise him, after all.

"You are up to something. That charming smile you're giving me has only ever brought trouble down on your far too handsome head, my boy. I will not invite anyone unless you tell me *why*."

"Very well, it's about your diamond tiara," he said as he nodded at the circlet that rested in her silvery hair.

She reached up and touched it self-consciously. "Yes?"

"I'm worried someone might try to steal it."

"Steal it? Whyever would they do that?" she demanded.

"Haven't you read the papers, Grandmama? There is a gang of jewel thieves robbing the rich of their best pieces. You're wearing one of the most famous diamonds in England as part of that tiara. The center stone alone is worth a fortune, let alone all the other smaller diamonds surrounding it."

"Oh, I'm not worried about that," his grandmother said loftily. "The Merry Robins wouldn't steal from me."

Fitz narrowed his gaze on his grandmother. Did she know something he did not? "And why is that?"

"Because it's clear those thieves only target the *worst* sort of people."

"Rich people," he clarified.

His grandmother sighed dramatically.

"No, dear. They steal from *cruel* people. Have you not examined the list of victims? I have. I can't think of a single person on that list whom I actually like."

Fitz stared at his grandmother. "You mean all the victims have something in common aside from money and influence?"

"Yes, of course, haven't you realized that?" She appeared stunned that he hadn't made the connection. "And to think I thought you were clever," she teased him.

"Wait a moment." He left her waiting in the corridor while he retrieved a newspaper from the day before that listed the victims. He pointed out the name of a gentleman to her once he rejoined her in the corridor. "What has Lord Blotten done?"

She adjusted her spectacles for a better look. "He bankrupted a decent family by convincing them to invest poorly. He knew they would lose everything. He then bought their property for next to nothing."

"And her?" He gestured to a woman's name that was next on the list.

"She had a Crimean War veteran tossed into Newgate for begging near her townhouse. The man was missing a leg and had no other way to earn a living."

He gestured to the third name on the list. "Him?"

"He took advantage of an upstairs maid. The girl died in labor with his child."

"This one?" He pointed to yet another name.

"She spread wretched rumors about another young lady that were entirely unfounded. It cost the young woman an advantageous match."

"Are all of these things public knowledge?" he asked his grandmother.

"Not all of them. Many are things that occurred behind closed doors. In some cases, not even the servants know. I only happen to know about this because I've made inquiries on my own."

"You have?" He couldn't imagine his grandmother

skulking about seeking information like some silly Scotland Yard detective.

"Of course. Someone is targeting my level of society, and I wished to understand why. Now that I do, I commend the thieves. They are striking out in revenge for those who can't defend themselves. I think it's rather noble."

"Nobility aside, someone must get to the bottom of this. Perhaps it's a servant."

"Impossible. Many of the thefts occurred when no servants were present," his grandmother supplied.

"Or so we are led to believe," Fitz countered. "But assuming you are right, who would have access to all these victims?"

His grandmother laughed. "I should think that was quite clear. It's one of *us*, dear boy. It's a good thing you do not own any jewels or you might well be next."

"What?"

She shrugged. "You broke up that friend of yours last year, Louis Atherton, with that darling young woman he was in love with, simply because you didn't like the girl's father. You said he was an old blustering fool who'd schemed his way up the social ladder. It wasn't as if he was to become *your* father-in-law. I told you not to interfere, but like always, your pride was too much to leave things alone. Now they've sent that poor young woman to America. Her family has been publicly embarrassed because of you, and her father won't show himself in society. It's rumored that he's trying to drink himself to death."

This part was news to Fitz, and his eyes grew wide.

"I adore you, my boy, but your pride will be the end of you. You are nearly thirty. You cannot keep making the sort of mistakes that far younger men would make. Louis put his faith in you and believed you when you convinced him that his marriage to that girl would reflect poorly on his social standing, to the detriment of his business interests. You never once asked what marrying a woman he loved would provide him that business successes would not."

Fitz's collar was suddenly too tight. He slipped a finger under the stick collar and tugged a little. Even at his age, being chastised by his grandmother was an unpleasant experience.

"If I were a jewel thief with a social vendetta, I might come after you for that. I love you, Fitz, dear, but damned if you aren't a prideful fool sometimes. Thank heavens all the jewels of note in this house are still mine. At least for now." His grandmother pressed a kiss to his cheek and went upstairs to retire for the evening.

Fitz stood in the hallway, mulling over his grandmother's words. She had spoken the truth, but Christ, he couldn't imagine Louis and that woman's father getting along. The man was a nuisance. Always saying the wrong thing, embarrassing everyone. He'd done Louis a favor, hadn't he? He'd have only dragged poor Louis down with him and . . .

Fitz leaned against the wall, his arms crossed as he glared at the portrait of an ancient Duke of Helston. It had been months since he'd spoken to Louis, let alone seen him. Fitz had been as close to Louis as he was to Evan and Beck. Was Louis avoiding him? Surely not. Louis had *thanked* him for his help. Told him he had saved him a lifetime of regret. And yet . . . Fitz shook off the feeling of guilt and directed his focus back onto his mission.

If his grandmother was right, the thieves wouldn't target the diamond because it technically still belonged to her. But they *might* target him because of what he had done. So he had to make it clear that the diamond was to be his legacy, make a public display of its importance to him, perhaps. That might entice the thieves to pursue the gemstone. It might work.

He would host a country party at Helston Heath and create a whisper in society that he was taking his grandmother's tiara with him to the country. He would invite all the people who had been present at the thefts. He, Evan, and Beck had narrowed the potential suspects down to a list of twenty people. And those were the names on the list of guests he had handed to his grandmother. One of them had to be one of those damnable Merry Robins. And he, like the Sheriff of Nottingham, would set a trap to catch the fellow.

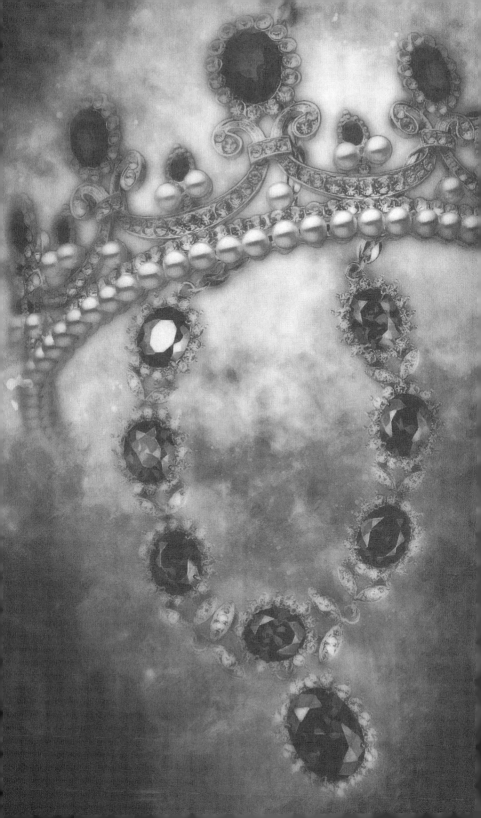

Chapter Three

Three weeks later

"Are you certain this will work?" Fitz's grandmother pressed as she handed him the black velvet box that contained the jeweled tiara with the large, lustrous diamond at its center.

"Quite certain," he assured the dowager duchess. "The guests will be arriving soon. Why don't you go and greet everyone? I will join you once I've seen this stored securely."

His grandmother's blue eyes sharpened. "You are trying to dismiss me, Fitz. I am leaving now because I agreed to act as your hostess and I mean to do it properly, but we *will* talk more about my diamond later." She swept from the room, her dark-blue skirts and train whispering behind her as she left his study.

Fitz grinned as he opened the box and carefully removed the large diamond from the center of the tiara. He put the priceless stone in a brown leather pouch and then crouched by the corner of his desk. He pulled back part of the rug to reveal a loosened floorboard. Taking a letter opener, he pried the plank up. In the opening he'd created, there was a small iron chest. He opened the lid and placed the diamond inside before he locked the box and returned the plank and rug to their original positions. Then he stood and removed a small object from his trouser pocket. He held up the object to better see it in the daylight.

It was simple glass, hand cut to resemble the shape and color of the diamond from his grandmother's tiara. Beck had referred him to one of London's best paste jewel makers. Any expert would be able to tell the difference between this paste imitation and the real diamond, but in the heat of the moment a thief wouldn't have time to check for such things as air bubbles in the glass, nor would they have time to notice the warmth of the paste stone versus the coolness of a real diamond.

He hadn't told his grandmother that the true diamond would be safe. To her knowledge, the real diamond would be stored with the tiara. She had made it clear to him that she respected the Merry Robins and only reluctantly agreed to let him use her diamond as a lure to catch the thieves, so a part of him feared she would let something slip in the wrong company and his clever ruse would be for naught. It was better that she be kept in the dark on this matter.

He inserted the paste stone into the center of the front of the tiara and nestled the tiara back into its velvet box. Then he opened a locked cupboard in the wall with a small key and placed the velvet box inside before locking it up again. Fitz needed to catch the man, or men, red-handed, which meant he couldn't make it too hard for them to steal the jewel. An iron chest might provide too much of a challenge, but picking the simple lock on this cabinet would be easy enough for any thief.

During the day, a footman would be stationed outside the room, making it impossible to enter without his say. At night, he, Evan, and Beck would take turns guarding it in secret. Night would be the only time the thieves would come because he would not let the jewel be taken out and worn during the house party. The usual modus operandi of the thieves was to steal during public events or gatherings, but he wasn't going to make it easy for them. If they wanted the diamond, they would have to steal it under his terms. And when they did, he and his friends would be ready for them.

Once he was satisfied with the tiara's safety, he left his study and nodded at the footman waiting outside.

"Stay on guard, Oscar. I'll have Lee ready to relieve you in a few hours."

"Yes, Your Grace." The footman stood by the closed door of the study. Fitz had brought two of his most trusted footmen in on the scheme to catch the thief, as well as his valet, Stewart. They'd agreed to take turns watching for anyone who might try to steal the jewel.

When Fitz reached the grand entryway of Helston Heath, he found his grandmother greeting the steady flow of incoming guests. Fitz leaned against the wall of the corridor as he watched the men and women parade through his home from a safe distance. No one noticed him, as his grandmother had their full attention, which gave Fitz the chance to scrutinize each man carefully. Which were the thieves? Fitz would find out soon enough.

"We have tea on the back terrace for everyone," his grandmother announced. "Please feel free to freshen up, or you may go ahead and join the others outside."

Most of the men headed for the terrace, following the butler. Mr. Tracy, their longtime family butler, had preceded Fitz and the dowager from the London townhouse to open the country house and prepare for the party. Half of the ladies chose to be shown to their rooms, and footmen stood ready to lead them upstairs. More than one woman noticed Fitz lounging in the doorway as they passed, and each one blushed and glanced away. Most were young things, though a few were more matronly, but even they blushed when he nodded and smiled at them. He knew he could be charming when he wished to be.

"Welcome," he murmured as they passed him by like a colorful flock of birds.

A new trio of women came up the steps out front and entered his home. The first two he recognized as Hannah Winslow and Julia Starling. The two barely spared him a glance as they whispered, their heads bent toward each other. His lips twitched. Neither of them liked him, but Julia's aunt and Fitz's grandmother were old friends.

He had known Hannah's husband, Jeremy, when they'd been lads at Eton, and it had been a great blow to England to lose him at such a young age in that train accident. Fitz had spoken to these two women socially, even danced with them upon occasion, but they certainly weren't considered friends. The woman who followed Hannah and Julia, the one whose cornflower-blue eyes widened as she swung her gaze over the grand marble entryway of his home, was the woman he had been both dreading and hoping to see ever since he'd asked his grandmother to invite her.

Had he imagined what he'd felt for her the night he

had met her? He'd convinced himself he had dreamt it, but now that she was here, he couldn't deny his fascination was as strong as ever. This woman held him spellbound. Her long dark hair was pulled up in loose waves with a red silk ribbon. She wore a red silk damask walking gown with a cream-colored bustle that tumbled into a short train behind her. The bold colors were regal on her, and she moved so carefully, so *gracefully* into his home, that he briefly felt as though she were some lost princess who had found her way to his door. It was a foolish, romantic notion, but it seemed she had a way of bringing sentimentality out of him.

When her eyes finally swept his way, his heart stuttered for a moment and he held his breath. Her luminous, expressive eyes revealed surprise, then delight, then apprehension. It was as if she was a damned mirror of his own soul.

Hannah and Julia slowed their steps to wait for her, and she blinked, breaking the spell between them before she rushed to join her cousin and her friend.

Tabitha Sherborne. At least he now had a name for his mysterious beauty.

Fitz smiled as he watched her flee a second time. She could run, but he loved to chase. Perhaps this was what he needed. A romantic diversion. Something to keep his mind at ease during his pursuit of these thieves.

He hadn't had a mistress in more than a year, and only a few brief nights in Scotland with a few ladies who had expected nothing of him come morning.

Fitz's smile widened as he realized there was one very big problem with what he wanted. Tabitha was *not* the kind of woman a gentleman had a brief affair with. She was clearly a gentle-born lady from a good family who had not yet married. He couldn't, or rather shouldn't, seduce her. She also had an uncanny effect on him. She made him lose control of his emotions, made him forget to breathe and forget where he was.

Looking at Tabitha was like falling into a dream full of moonlit palaces and the heavy aroma of blooming flowers. He'd heard of the hazy dream worlds that opium addicts lived in, and it reminded him of how Tabitha made him feel now. Drunk with desire and out of control.

More guests trickled through the front doors, and he finally joined his grandmother to perform his duties as host.

"There you are, my boy," she murmured between greeting the next few guests.

"Here I am," he chuckled.

"Your Miss Sherborne was just here."

"She isn't mine," he reminded her.

"Yet." His grandmother smiled, the sheer determination of a woman of her age and status warning him she meant to see it happen.

The word "yet" should have been a threat to his carefully controlled world, but instead it felt strangely like a promise.

THE HOUSE WAS LARGE. *TOO* LARGE. TABITHA FELT exposed by the open spaces of this palatial country home. She'd spent the last several months in London with Julia and Hannah in Hannah's townhouse, not the country. This was an entirely new experience for her. Every marble surface glowed. The staircase was wide and the rugs were new. The portraits and tapestries that covered the walls were stunning. There was so much to take in, she didn't know where to start. Her gaze darted around at everything, trying to soak it all in.

And that was when she saw *him.* The mysterious stranger she'd met the night of the musicale. She froze in place as his gaze locked with hers. He was leaning against the wall and the corridor stretched behind him. He wore a fine three-piece suit of dark blue, absent a frock coat or morning coat, which somehow wonderfully yet subtly indecent to her eyes. He wore a crisply folded ascot of a bright white that offset his dark suit. He looked like a bemused Roman god watching over the mortals entering his realm.

"Tabby, come on," Julia whispered.

She pulled away from the man's gaze. Her friends were much farther ahead of her on the way to the terrace, where tea was being served. She rushed to catch up with them, trying to put the mysterious man out of her mind for now.

They had a diamond to steal. The mission that had brought her into the world of the Merry Robins was even more important than before. Only last week, Hannah had received a letter from Anne, her friend in America who'd been ostracized in London because of Lord Helston's actions.

Anne had written to say that she couldn't make a match in New York either. The unanswered questions surrounding the breaking of Anne's engagement had doomed her prospects in England. But those questions had followed her across the ocean and manifested themselves as wild and unsubstantiated rumors of gross misdeeds and inappropriate behavior. It had taken on a life of its own to the point where she dared not show herself in public anymore. Julia and Hannah had decided that they couldn't wait any longer to punish Helston for his misdeeds. They had hoped to wait until he'd chosen a bride and given her the diamond, but

Hannah had been adamant about her need for revenge, even though the diamond still belonged to his grand-mother. The man simply had no other weaknesses they could exploit.

Tabitha joined Hannah and Julia as they crossed the threshold onto a large stone terrace decorated for a fine afternoon tea. She recognized many of the guests here from previous engagements where the Merry Robins had struck, which would make things tricky. But this house was far more intimidating. Not only were there the other guests to avoid, but here there were triple the number of servants present.

"We will have eyes on us everywhere," Tabitha said as she accepted the teacup Hannah offered her. The trio walked to the edge of the terrace to drink their tea where they could avoid being overheard.

"I suppose night will make it easier, won't it?" Hannah suggested. "There will be fewer servants about. If we go after the diamond sometime between midnight and four o'clock in the morning, everyone should be in bed."

"That brings us to our next obstacle. Where would the jewel be hidden? This house has a thousand rooms. We can't rely on any of our plans from when we were intending to steal it back in London." Tabitha nodded at the back of the vast manor house. All she saw was an endless row of windows stretching into the distance.

"Hannah," Julia began. "You know Helston better than I do. Perhaps we could get him to give you a tour? He will treat you better than either of us. You could investigate the house while he shows you around. I think he would tell you quite a bit if you asked him *nicely,*" Julia said, batting her eyelashes for effect.

"I doubt he would," Hannah said with a soft laugh. "The last time he and I spoke, I slapped him."

Julia gasped. "You didn't, did you? When was this?"

"The week after Anne sailed for New York. I ran into Helston at a ball and he asked me to dance. I lost my head—or rather, lost my hand." Hannah bashfully sipped her tea. "I don't regret it. The look on his face when he reached up to touch his cheek—he clearly hadn't expected me, of all people, to strike him."

Tabitha bit her lip to hide a grin at the thought of sweet, gentle Hannah slapping the beautiful bastard's face. It would have shocked her to witness that as well.

"Oh Christ, there he is," Julia hissed and nodded at a man who had just stepped out onto the terrace.

Tabitha studied the people around her but noticed only one gentleman who had joined the guests in the last minute. The mysterious stranger from the musicale.

She was about to ask who they were referring to, only it was clear on their faces it was indeed him.

"No . . ." She hadn't breathed a word of her encounter that night to her friends. It had been too personal, too special to tell anyone.

No, no, no . . . He couldn't be the duke. A duke would have introduced himself to a lady if they'd met under such circumstances. A duke would not have hidden at the top of the stairs with her, would he?

"Julia, is *that* Lord Helston?" She flicked her gaze toward the gorgeous man in the three-piece suit who was slowly making his way toward them.

"Yes, that's him," Julia scoffed softly. "I told you he was a beautiful bastard."

"Steady yourselves. Here he comes," Hannah said a moment before Lord Helston stopped directly in front of them. His stormy blue eyes took the three of them in, and his lips twitched as he bowed.

"I missed my chance to welcome you to my home. Miss Starling, Mrs. Winslow." He addressed the other two first. "It's good to see you again."

"Thank you for the kind invitation, Lord Helston," Hannah replied smoothly, though a little icily.

"Given our last encounter, I'm surprised you accepted."

"Yes, well, between you and your lovely grandmother, only one of you needed their behavior corrected," Hannah said crisply. "I would never refuse Lady Helston's invitation."

The duke laughed, flashing straight white teeth like a wolf. The rich sound of his laughter did something strange to Tabitha's belly, turning it into a warm mess of chaos. She placed her hand on her stomach, fighting to remain calm, but her small movement didn't escape his notice.

"Forgive me, I must request an introduction to your companion, Mrs. Winslow."

"Ah yes. This is my cousin, Miss Tabitha Sherborne," Hannah said. "Tabitha, this is His Grace, the Duke of Helston."

Julia nudged Tabitha, who instinctively flung her hand out toward the duke. He bent over and pressed a kiss to the back of her hand. Heat flared from the point where his lips touched her skin and rippled through the rest of her like a stone cast into a deep lake.

"Welcome, Miss Sherborne."

"Th-thank you."

"We were just speaking about how beautiful your home is, Lord Helston," said Julia. "Tabitha doesn't often see houses of such grandeur. Could we trouble you to give her a tour of the house and grounds?"

Tabitha stiffened and shot her friend a questioning

look. Julia nodded her head ever so slightly to encourage her.

"Would you like that, Miss Sherborne? To tour a home of such grandeur?" A devilish mischief lit up Helston's eyes.

"Y-yes," she replied. Lord, she was mad to think this was a good idea.

He offered his arm to her. "I'd be happy to show you around."

"Wonderful." Julia gave Tabitha a little shove, and she almost stumbled into Helston forcing her to clutch his arm. She shot a glance back at her friends, who gave her nods of encouragement that she should go with Helston. This wasn't to be just a simple tour. She was to examine the house for any place where he might hide the diamond. So be it.

"This way, Miss Sherborne." Helston covered her hand on his arm with his own. She noticed that he wore no gloves, and neither did she. That skin-to-skin contact was warm and as electric as theater lights. She was far too aware of him.

"Helston Heath was built in 1549. After a fire in 1703 they rebuilt the wooden Tudor manor house with the stone one you see before you." He led her along the garden path that traversed the length of the back of the house. When they were far enough away from any of the other guests, he met her gaze.

"So, we meet again, properly this time," he said with a chuckle. "I've been most curious to find you since you fled like some cinder princess, only you left no shoe behind on the stairs for me to clutch to my chest."

She blushed and reached into her skirt pocket, producing the handkerchief of his that she'd kept with her since that night.

"This is yours. I didn't mean to keep it, but I didn't know who you were to return it to you." She was reluctant to part with it, however. Even now that she knew this man was a bastard, she didn't want to let go of something that held such a wonderful memory for her. In that moment, she'd been no thief and he'd been no duke. They'd simply been two people in the dark, sharing a personal moment from the depths of their souls.

"Please keep it if you wish. There is always a chance you will be moved to tears by my house and wish to cry again," he teased.

Unable to resist, she laughed. "It is an *absurdly* large house," she observed and clamped her mouth closed in embarrassment.

"It is, isn't it? It will be nice to have all those rooms filled for the house party," he admitted. "The emptiness can be lonely."

She thought of her old living quarters in the warehouse by the docks and how, even surrounded by other young girls, she'd felt entirely alone.

"It's possible to also be lonely in a crowded room," she observed.

He sighed, the sound so weary that it tugged at her heart. "How right you are."

"Let me show you the inside." He escorted her to a back entrance past the gardens and a large hothouse, where he held open a door for her.

"Do you enjoy reading, Miss Sherborne?" he asked as she stepped inside with him.

"Yes."

He joined her, closing the door behind her as they faced a long corridor of rooms.

Helston flashed her a charming yet arrogant grin as he began to quote from a book:

"The White Rabbit put on his spectacles. 'Where shall I begin, please your Majesty?' he asked. 'Begin at the beginning,' the King said gravely, 'and go on till you come to the end: then stop.'"

"*Alice's Adventures in Wonderland*," Tabitha said with a delighted smile. She'd read the book a month ago, and it had struck a chord with her.

"Exactly. So, let us begin at the beginning." He waved around at the portraits as they passed. "These are

Helston ancestors. Stuffy-looking fellows, aren't they?" His tone was still teasing, and Tabitha leaned a little closer to him, her arm still tucked in his as they walked. He showed her a series of grand rooms, ending in one that was a blend of white walls, gilded surfaces, red damask curtains, and impressive furniture. The ceiling depicted a vast fresco of Greek gods at play on Mount Olympus.

There was also a large family portrait at the far end of the room, which they now headed toward. It depicted a lovely couple and a young boy of six or seven relaxing by a lake in a pastoral scene, while a hunting dog sat beside the boy as he petted it affectionately.

"Is this you?" Tabitha asked.

Helston's gaze softened. "Yes. That is me with my parents." He looked away quickly, and she saw a flash of old pain in his eyes. He was quick to pull her away from the painting. "Right, shall we continue?"

"Your Grace." Tabitha pulled on his arm, forcing him to stop. "I never had the chance to say thank you for sharing about your father the other night."

A tic worked in his jaw as he struggled for words. Was he angry with her?

"I . . . I usually don't speak about my father," she added softly. "But it was nice to talk with you about mine, and about yours."

His features grew harsh in their beauty as his lips parted, but he hesitated a moment before speaking.

"Miss Sherborne, we should continue the tour."

She did not bring up the subject of fathers again as he led her from the room. He had shut himself away in some inner tower where she could not reach him.

As they passed by a series of rooms, she saw a footman standing guard quite obviously in front of one of the doors. It seemed strangely out of character for a servant to be so visible, given how invisible servants were supposed to be.

"What's in that room, Your Grace?" she asked, pointing to it.

"What? Oh, that's my study. I decided a little extra security was necessary. With those Merry Robin thieves running about London, I decided to bring my grand-mother's tiara to the country, where it would be safe. Those thieves are less likely to come out here when they have plenty of jewels to steal in London."

Tabitha was well practiced in hiding her reactions to things that might otherwise catch someone off guard. "Surely you don't think those thieves would steal from your grandmother?"

"The principal diamond in that tiara is second only to those found in the Crown Jewels, and it is meant to be a wedding gift for my bride, when I decide to marry. All of London knows that gem is all but mine. It's my duty to protect that diamond."

Tabitha saw the flash of arrogant entitlement in Helston that her friends had spoken of, but she also saw something they hadn't. Yes, he seemed quite arrogant, but she was good at reading people, and she saw that Helston's mannerisms were a carefully constructed façade. Just like hers. She was no highborn lady, yet here she was, strolling along with a handsome duke, enjoying a respectable tour—

Helston suddenly pulled her into an empty drawing room and pressed her against the wall, one hand covering her mouth as he pinned her with his body. The flare of panic at being so close to a man she didn't know faded beneath the strange sense of rightness to it, to him. He smelled of woods and wildness as her skirts tangled about their legs when he slipped one of his feet between her own, moving them even closer together.

"Hush," he whispered, his lips caressing her ear. She started to struggle, afraid of what he intended to do. No matter how much she liked him this close, she couldn't let him do anything so dangerous as kiss her because she'd give in to her own desires and let him. She had to keep herself from treading down a dangerous path that would complicate her mission to steal his diamond.

"Do you trust me, Tabitha?" he asked in a rough whisper that sent shivers through her.

She shouldn't. She ought to shake her head and push at his broad shoulders and escape him . . . but she didn't, so she nodded because she trusted him. After a moment, she realized that his focus wasn't on her, but on something outside in the corridor. Someone was coming.

"Good. Now, be very quiet or they'll hear us," he warned and lowered his head toward hers.

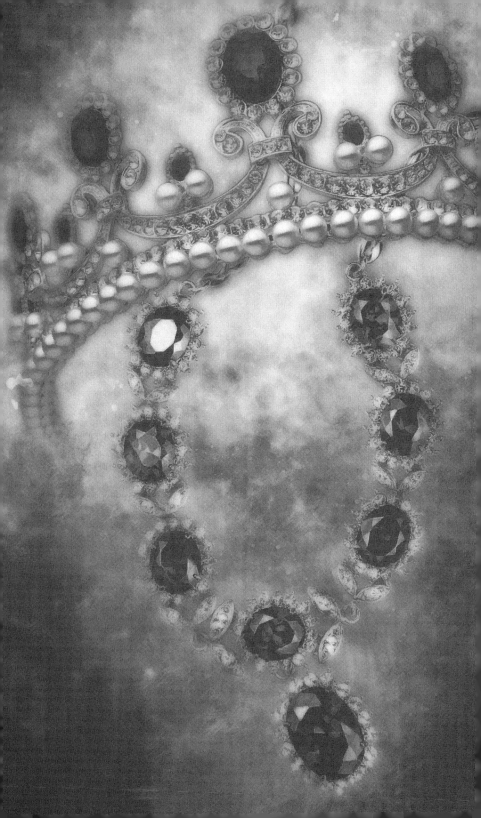

Chapter Four

Tabitha's throat was dry and her skin burned as she gazed up at Helston and his sultry, arrogant mouth that at that moment seemed just ripe for kissing.

Was he going to kiss her?

He lowered his head toward hers but didn't uncover her mouth with his hand, nor did he try to kiss her. He held very still, his head tilted, his cheek ever so slightly touching her arm as the faint sound of voices carried down the hall. He held perfectly still, and it gave her mind just enough space to remember that someone was coming down the corridor toward them. She recognized one of the voices as the dowager duchess, but her words were broken up a bit as she whispered to someone.

"Mr. Tracy, you must keep a close watch on Fitz . . .

acting so strangely . . . I can't figure out why . . . I do have my hopes set on—" Her words halted abruptly.

"Set on what, Your Grace?" she heard the butler ask.

"Oh, it feels silly, but I want to see him married. I'm not getting any younger, and after losing his father, I need to know he's settled down and happy."

"He seems content," Mr. Tracy said.

"Content and happy are not the same thing. I fear I've failed him, Mr. Tracy. If his father hadn't ended his life, if he hadn't gone to that damned war, I wonder if Fitz might have seen the world through different eyes. My grandson has known more pain than joy. Finding a woman, the *right* one, could save him."

"You believe he has found someone?"

"He asked me to invite the Sherborne girl. I think he's taken with her. It's the first real interest he's shown in a woman. I'll be damned if I don't press that advantage."

Tabitha held her breath and Helston stiffened against her as the voices grew louder and they feared being discovered.

If his grandmother found them like this, it would cause a scandal. He might even be forced to offer his hand in marriage. That couldn't happen. It didn't matter that she liked him, that his very nearness and spell-binding touch did wonderful things that made her feel wildly alive. Even if she wasn't here with the intent of punishing him for his misdeeds, marrying someone like her could only end in disgrace.

"I assume you have a plan to bring them together?" Mr. Tracy said, his voice starting to grow softer again as they passed by.

"Yes, I want them seated together at every meal and . . ." The rest of the dowager's words trailed off as she and the butler moved farther down the hall and turned a corner, carrying them out of earshot.

For a long moment, neither Tabitha nor Helston moved. He remained tense against her as he slowly let out a breath. He dropped his hand from her mouth, and they stared at each other a long moment, their faces still close.

The dowager's words tumbled in her head like a spinning kaleidoscope. *"I think he's taken with her."* Was he? It baffled Tabitha to think that a duke would have any kind of interest in her.

Helston raised his hand to her cheek, brushing the backs of his fingers over her skin. The caress felt wonderful.

"Your Grace . . ." Her words were faint, as she was still overcome by their heated closeness.

"Tell me to let you go, Tabitha. Tell me now . . ." He used her given name even though she hadn't told him he

Lauren Smith

could. Something about the way he simply claimed her name flushed her body with a wild and primal heat.

"If you don't, I'm going to kiss you," he warned. "Christ, I'm liable to do much more than that. My grandmother is right, you know. I am taken with you." His voice grew deep, a hint of gravel to his words. "*Taken* doesn't seem to be quite strong enough of a word, though. I feel *possessed* by you."

"Possessed?" she echoed as she found her own hands had moved up to grip his waistcoat. Until that moment, she hadn't even realized she'd been reaching for him.

"This is your last chance . . . Push me away. Tell me to stop."

But her lips couldn't form the words. They felt wrong. She craved a connection like this with him, even knowing it would be brief.

She tilted her face up to his, her lashes lowering as she gazed at Helston's beautiful mouth, and she was lost.

With a soft growl, he captured her wrists in one of his hands and raised them over her head, pinning them in place against the wall. The sensual assault of his lips upon hers was like nothing she'd experienced before. She fell into a euphoria as her lips opened to his and his tongue thrust into her mouth, flicking against hers. He kissed her ruthlessly, devouring her whole. She understood the feeling. She wanted the same—all of him, every fiber of his being to join with hers in every way possible. A fierce ache started between her thighs and she whimpered, pressing close to him, searching for the ease to her ache.

He tore his lips from her mouth to trail kisses up to her ear, and she protested the loss of his mouth upon hers with a whimper.

"Do you ache for me, darling? Do you *need* me?" he demanded in a rough pant.

"*Yes.*"

He pulled her right leg up, holding it against his hip. This allowed her to rub herself against his thigh, which only heightened that wild need inside her, a desire for things she'd long thought she'd never have.

"That's it, darling," he murmured, and then he was kissing her again. His deft fingers slid under the vast layers of her skirts to find the bare, vulnerable skin of her inner thighs and the aching center of her body that throbbed with need.

That first caress of his fingers upon the place so hungry for his touch made her cry out in shock. He swallowed the sound with his mouth, and she bucked into him, urging him to continue. After a long, torturous moment, he gave her what she needed. He slid a finger into her, pushing it deep. She moaned as a thousand sensations rioted within her.

"Yes," he encouraged in a gruff whisper. "There's my good girl. Take what you want." He continued to thrust his finger, and she pressed herself into him, trying to rock that finger in and out. They developed a rhythm, him moving his hand against her mound and her jerking as the tension built inside her.

They made a soft *thump—thump—thump* against the wall, such was the rough urgency of their movements. The way he murmured for her to take what she wanted, how he called her his good girl, it all lit some deep fire inside of her and she cried out again. He didn't cover her mouth this time, he didn't kiss her, he simply gazed at her as she dissolved into a creature of pure bliss.

Their eyes locked, and she knew in that moment he *owned* every part of her. His gaze consumed her, and she could do nothing but surrender to the moment. Her body spasmed as little aftershocks quaked inside her. Helston absorbed every one of her little tremors, his gaze still intense as he kept her wrists above her head and her body pinned against the wall.

"Was that your first time?" he asked when her shaking eased.

"My first?"

"The pleasure. It's called climax. Have you ever felt it before?"

She slowly shook her head, and he let out a breath and leaned in, pressing his forehead to hers.

"It's never felt...like that before...when I dared to..." she didn't finish.

"When you dared to touch yourself?" he asked and she nodded. "You are innocent," he mused, his eyes closed. She briefly closed her eyes as well, reliving the feeling of what they'd shared. It felt so deep, so *real* compared to anything else she'd ever experienced.

"You have such a beautiful response to pleasure. My God . . ." Helston smiled as he opened his eyes. "If I wasn't that mad to have you before I'm certainly mad for you now."

He slowly withdrew his hand from beneath her skirts, making her twitch and her legs tremble.

"Don't move." He used a handkerchief to clean his fingers and then used it to wipe between her legs. She covered her face with her hands in mortification but then peeped through parted fingers at him.

"Don't be shy now, not after what we've been through," he said with a chuckle. Then he lifted her into his arms and carried her over to a couch. He sat down with her on his lap. She tried to slide off to sit beside

him, but he tsked at her as though she were a misbe-
having child.

"You need a minute to get your legs back. Just rest,"
he said. "No one shall see us."

She was silent a long while as she regained her
breath. "Did . . . er . . . have you done that with a lot of
women?" she finally asked. She had been changed irrev-
ocably, but she feared it meant nothing to him. What
she knew of men, the men she'd been around on the
streets, they spoke callously of women and often treated
them even worse. She had been lucky to be taken in by
the warehouse girls for so many years. They had kept
her safe from the dangerous realities of the streets.

"I have done it before," he answered. "But never so
quickly. By that, I mean we've only seen each other
twice and I just jumped you like a wild animal." She
heard the puzzlement in his tone. "I should apologize,
should admit it was wrong, but—"

"Don't," she said. "It was wonderful, even if it was a
little frightening."

He lowered his head to nuzzle her cheek. "You are
quite a mystery to me, Tabitha. Most women would
have slapped me and run away for what I did."

She reached up to place her palm on his cheek.
"Why would I hurt you when it felt so wonderful?" she
asked.

"Because I'm supposed to be a gentleman, though I am not acting like one with you." He sighed. "Who knew that a house tour could be so scandalous?"

Tabitha smiled a little at his joke, feeling strangely laid bare after what they had done.

"My friends . . . I mean, my cousin and my friend would be furious with me."

"You mean Mrs. Winslow and Miss Starling." He spoke their names with a dark chuckle. "Yes, I'm quite aware they don't like me."

"They call you a bastard." Tabitha stiffened as she realized what she'd just said. Her old pickpocket self would've had no problem with speaking in such a way on the streets, but this was not how a proper lady spoke.

He looked a little startled. "A bastard?"

"A beautiful one," she added. "I'm sorry, I shouldn't have said anything."

"They are your friends. I understand. Believe me. I suppose I have been a bastard at times, but it's because I know I'm right about a great many things. You would be surprised to learn that very few people want to be told when they are wrong. I am often the one telling them that they are wrong, which I suppose incurs their dislike."

He said this so matter-of-factly that she simply stared at him. Did he really not understand that he couldn't simply dictate to others what their life choices should be?

"But how can you be so certain you are right *all* the time?" Tabitha asked, more than a little curious that he could believe such a thing.

He flashed her a cocky grin. "Because I am. I was a duke at an earlier age than most men. It is the same for shouldering responsibilities. I've been in a lot of situations and seen much of the world. I would challenge you to find something I know little about."

Tabitha almost asked him what he knew of the conditions of the poor in London, but she didn't want to ruin this moment. No one had ever told her how good it would feel to be held in a man's arms like this. She felt safe, secure, and cherished.

"How are you feeling now?" he asked.

"Better, but . . ." She hesitated, feeling shy.

"But?"

"But I don't want to move just yet. This feels nice." It was likely a terrible idea to be so open and honest with him, but it was so easy to feel like herself when he was there. Yes, she had lived on the streets, she had faced down danger and fought off cold and hunger. Despair had been her constant companion, but it hadn't hardened her as it had most of those who lived on the streets. She was still a person seeking warmth, safety, security. And most of all, love. Helston could, for the moment, offer some of that to her, and she let it comfort her for as long as she could.

"We can stay here a little longer unless we hear my grandmother again."

Tabitha giggled and pressed her forehead against his shoulder.

"I can't believe they didn't hear us," she whispered.

Helston chuckled. "I'm damned good at being quiet when it counts. How long will you be in London with your cousin?"

"I'm not sure." She honestly hadn't thought about that far-off day when the Merry Robins would retire from stealing. What would be her future then? Hannah would never cast her back out onto the streets, but she couldn't live forever on her friend's generosity. They had discussed that someday they might help her find a man to marry, if she so wished, or that she might find work at a reputable shop or even that she could take a part of the proceeds of the sale of the jewels. She'd refused the last option, of course. There was no way she could sleep at night knowing that she had a warm bed and food and was also keeping some of the money of the thefts. In the past, she'd only ever stolen things to survive. Now she didn't need to. She stole for others and therefore couldn't keep any of the money for herself.

"I can't stay with Hannah forever. I will need to marry or find some other means of supporting myself."

"You will *need* to?" He seemed surprised.

"I suppose you believe I come from money like Hannah, but I assure you I do not." She guessed it was safe enough to admit some things about her life without giving away the larger truth.

He waited for her to continue, so she did. "I lived in a small set of rooms my entire life until my father died. He worked as a clerk for a private banker and made very little money. But as poor as our lives were, our home was rich in love." She smiled as she remembered her father reading to her late into the night, never worrying about wasting precious candles.

"When he died, things were not easy. There were nights with empty bellies and cold days." It was as close as she could get to telling him that she had lived on the streets.

He rubbed her back with one hand, trying to soothe her, and it was only then that she realized she'd started to tremble from the memories of those hard, lean years.

"I wish I had known you then. I would've helped you," he said, his tone a little rough with emotion.

"Would you?" she asked, her tone hardening a little. "Do you know how many *fine* gentlemen and ladies pass by someone in need and do nothing? You think, *What a poor, pitiful wretch. They should be able to take care of themselves by finding work, and since they haven't they must be lazy.* Their fates must be their own with no help from you." She said the words harshly and pulled herself off his lap to stand. He let her go and sat there watching her with those stormy eyes.

"But the truth is, there isn't *enough* work, there isn't *enough* food. There isn't enough of *anything* for a good majority of the people in this country," she said.

Helston's posture now grew defensive. "If you're suggesting I part with my coin to allow a few gin-soaked men to drink more so they might go home and beat their wives and children even worse than they already do—"

She spun away from him, her anger flaring hot out of nowhere as she interrupted him. "Of course you think of the men. But what of the women, the children? The starving flower girls, the boys selling matchsticks. The frail elderly women with hands too old to sew and eyes too weak to see by candlelight to work, the old men who can no longer work in the factories, and the veterans from the wars. *They* are the ones you fail each day."

"Now hold on." He got to his feet and caught her arm, turning her back to face him. "You're throwing accusations at me. Have you seen me deny a child or an old woman anything?" he challenged.

"I've seen enough men of station turn a blind eye to

believe the worst." The words left her mouth too quickly, before she realized they were a mistake.

The flash of fire in his eyes frightened her. But rather than strike out at her the way the men she had just spoken of would, he released her and stepped back.

"I'm very sorry you think so poorly of me, Miss Sherborne," he said. "I believe it's time I returned to my guests. Please excuse me." He gave a slight bow and left her alone in the drawing room.

She stood there a long moment, her heart pounding as she fought off the urge to burst into tears. Why had she said such things to him? Why did he wield such power to break down her walls and make her speak with such painful honesty? How she felt and acted around him was a jumbled mess of contradictions she didn't understand. If she wasn't careful, she might reveal too much and give away her true motives for being here.

When she finally collected herself, she found her way back to the terrace. Almost at once, her friends descended upon her.

"Where have you been? Helston came back alone a short while ago and . . . Good Lord, Tabby, are you all right?" Hannah took one of Tabitha's hands in her own and gave it a squeeze.

"Er . . . yes. Of course." But Tabitha was the farthest thing from all right. She snuck a glance at the duke, who stood at the far end of the terrace. He watched her with a quiet, challenging look as he studied her in return. She felt as though they were on the opposite sides of a giant chessboard, the pieces moving between her and Helston, with no way of knowing what his next move or hers. She could only pray that he didn't know what the stakes of this game between them truly were. For him, it was a game of seduction, but for her? It was a game for a diamond. A diamond that could help so many people— or cost her her freedom if she was caught.

"Helston wasn't a brute to you, was he? He can be so rude. What did he say to you?" Julia asked. She looked ready to march across the terrace toward the duke and do battle.

"No, he wasn't. I'm afraid I might have been too honest when speaking to him, and he, in turn, was far too blunt with me. I fear I may have hurt our chances for gathering more information from him."

That was true enough. She didn't want to tell her friends about what had happened. It was too intimate, too personal.

"Why don't we go upstairs and rest a bit before dinner," Hannah suggested. "You can tell us everything once we're alone."

"Yes, let's," Tabitha agreed. "It will give us a chance to talk. I believe I know where we must direct our *atten-*

tion." She emphasized the word with a raising of her eyebrows.

Julia's eyes glowed with excitement. "Oh?"

"Yes. It's here, as we thought. We will have to go at night, and I believe we'll need to access the room through a window. He has a footman stationed at the door."

"I see." Hannah tapped her chin. "Once we have it, he will know it's been taken. We will have to be careful. We need a place to store it safely, though, as he will search the guests."

"I wish we'd been able to get a replica made in paste," Tabitha said. "But we would need to get our hands on the real one in order for the closest match to be made."

"Yes, it is a pity. It would have been far easier, but we shall simply have to do this as we've done the others," Hannah replied.

"In that case, we have much to plan," Julia said as the three of them left the group of guests gathered outside.

Tabitha cast one last glance at Helston, who stood at the far end of the terrace with two other men. He was still watching her and doing nothing to hide the scowl on his face.

She feared their quarrel had destroyed his interest in

her and he would leave her be, which would be for the best. But perhaps not, if the intensity of his focus was anything to judge by. She turned her face away, a flush of mortification heating her skin. It would be wise to avoid him as much as possible for the duration of their mission.

"WELL, *THAT* CERTAINLY LOOKS LIKE TROUBLE, FITZ. What the devil did you do?" Beck gave a subtle nod to the three retreating women, who all darted harsh glances in their direction. The women looked furtive as they whispered to each other in the way women did when they wanted to discuss their secrets.

"I suppose I acted a little rashly," he admitted. *And harshly,* he silently added.

"Rash? *You?* Bloody hell, man, the world must be ending," Evan teased, but his grin faded as he saw the black look on Fitz's face.

"What did you do, Fitz?" Evan asked more quietly.

"I conducted myself in an ungentlemanly manner with Miss Tabitha Sherborne."

"Who is she?" Beck asked as he watched the three women vanish inside the house.

"Hannah Winslow's cousin from the country." A

flash of Tabitha in his arms shot through his body like lightning. The feel of her mouth, the taste of her, the erotic way she'd panted his name between kisses and how it seemed to remake everything he understood about the universe. That moment had been heat and light in their purest forms, and it had rocked him to his very core.

"She cannot be Hannah Winslow's cousin," Evan said.

Fitz felt a new tension vibrate within him, one that had nothing to do with his unfinished business with Tabitha. "What do you mean?"

"Hannah doesn't *have* any cousins in the country, at least none named Tabitha Sherborne," Evan declared confidently.

"You're sure?" Fitz asked.

"Quite."

Beck leaned in. "How do you know?"

"Because . . . because . . ." Evan rubbed the back of his neck, an uncharacteristic red hue coloring his face as he glanced away from Fitz and Beck. "Because once upon a time, I was madly in love with Hannah. I made it my mission to know everything I could about her."

Fitz stared in shock at his friend. "You were in *love* with Hannah the Harridan?" He'd had no idea that Evan had ever felt strongly about any woman. He'd had mistresses by the score over the years, but he'd never once mentioned having any affection for Hannah, let alone a mad love for her. This was something he would have to discuss with his friend later, after these jewel thieves were caught.

"Yes, I was, and she's no harridan, as you well know. She was never the same after losing him." Evan glanced away from them. "What I felt for her was a long time ago." He cleared his throat. "One thing I'm certain of is that she has no cousin named Tabitha Sherborne."

All three men turned to look in the direction the women had gone, and Fitz frowned.

"Then who the devil is the woman I just kissed?"

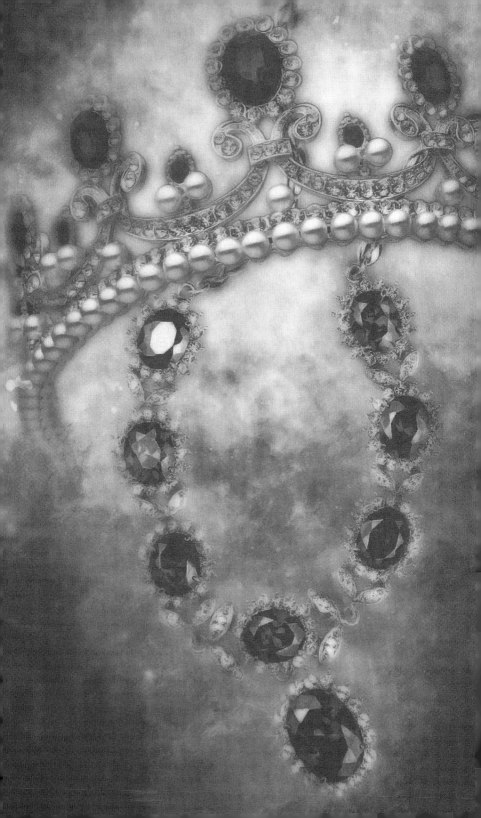

Chapter Five

Fitz let his valet, Stewart, finish dressing him for dinner. His mind was miles away as he struggled to understand what had happened that afternoon. From the moment Tabitha Sherborne set foot in his home, he had been on edge. She had disrupted *everything*.

It wasn't simply the passion that had ignited between them in the drawing room, although he could die a happy man with that memory alone. Lord, the way she'd pressed her body so eagerly against his own, the softness of her skin, the way she'd tasted . . . Those memories would fill his dreams for years to come. But what would haunt him forever was the way her corn-flower-blue eyes had filled with wonder as she'd experienced carnal pleasure for the first time. He had been enraptured by the expression on her face, the intensity, the shock, and then the delight he'd felt as she'd allowed herself to trust him in that moment.

They were practically strangers, and yet that thread of connection from the night of the musicale had proved stronger than he'd imagined.

Which was why the pain on her face when she'd spoken of her past—of cold days and empty stomachs—and her turning away from him, had struck through him, hot and angry. Though his anger was not directed at her. Far from it.

He needed her to trust in him, and he felt eager to prove himself worthy of it. Her inability to confide in him made him question himself more than he cared to. He stared unseeing at himself in the mirror as Stewart used a soft brush to remove dust from his coat. Stewart then gave Fitz's patent leather shoes a quick shine.

"Thank you, Stewart."

Fitz left his bedchamber, replaying his conversations with Tabitha as he walked. He was still confused about who she truly was. He knew three things for certain: she held a distrust of wealthy men and women, she had gone through a lengthy period of hardship, and she wasn't Hannah Winslow's cousin from the country.

He trusted Evan enough to know that if the man claimed to have researched the matter, it had been researched well. If he said there was no cousin from the country named Tabitha, then there wasn't.

So who the devil was she?

He could easily confront Tabitha and Hannah about their deception while they were here at his home, but there was no guarantee they would tell him the truth. They would most likely leave the house party in disgust, and he might never have the answers he so desperately wanted. Until he understood why he was obsessed with Tabitha, he didn't want to scare her or her friends away with bold accusations.

His mind caught upon a memory of her hands, the fading calluses on the pads of her fingers and palms. What had she done to earn them? His stomach knotted at the thought of her working in some match factory late into the night, desperate for coin to feed herself. But the calluses were faded, so something had changed in her circumstances for the better. How could one woman create a so many questions?

As he descended the stairs, the butler rang the gong for dinner. Blast, he was late. That hardly ever happened. He met the guests and his grandmother as they left the main salon. His grandmother waved him over and leaned in to whisper when he reached her.

"You will escort Miss Sherborne to dinner."

It was a command, one he had expected since he'd

overheard her plotting. Normally he would have battled her, but in this instance he was happy to comply. Although he'd been upset with Tabitha this afternoon after her accusations about his character, he still wanted to be near her. She was a puzzle begging to be solved.

He slid through the crowd and halted at the sight of Tabitha. Among all the other ladies, she stood out like the first spring flower to grow after a hard winter. Her evening gown was a blend of exquisite colors, with a cream underskirt embroidered with jonquils, dahlias, and peonies amid green leaves. The exquisite embroidery made it appear as though a garden grew on her underskirt. The bodice and overskirt were coral, and the front of the overskirt was pinned back to flare at her hips, displaying intricate folds with a sunny yellow satin backing. Fine layers of lace trimmed the hem of her underskirt and bodice. He could see the swell of her breasts through the wispy layers of lace along her décolletage.

She turned his way, and their eyes met across the room. His pulse quickened. The world beneath his feet shifted, and he braced his legs a little wider so as to stay steady. What was wrong with him? The mere sight of a woman shouldn't have affected him like this, but it did.

He moved toward Tabitha, aware of everyone's eyes upon him as he approached. He offered her his arm in silent invitation. For a moment, he feared she wouldn't accept. Then, with a rising blush in her cheeks, she slipped her hand through the crook of his arm. Together, they led the rest of the procession into the large dining room.

Neither of them spoke as he seated her next to him. He was seated at the end of the table as host, and she was placed directly to his right. Mrs. Higgs, a friend of his grandmother, sat down to his left. She was in deep discussion with her escort, who happened to be Beck. Beck flashed Fitz a subtle, questioning look, flicking his gaze quickly at Tabitha and then back to Fitz.

Fitz returned the look, silently assuring Beck that he would delve into the question of Tabitha's story further, just not at this moment.

"We have activities planned tomorrow. A picnic, riding, badminton, and croquet," Fitz found himself saying as Tabitha placed her napkin in her lap and sipped from the goblet of wine a footman had placed in front of her.

Tabitha glanced his way. "Oh?"

"Yes . . . and I thought perhaps we might play a game together, or . . ." He paused, trying to best assess how to broach the matter of their reacquaintance. He kept his voice low, even though Beck had thankfully captured Mrs. Higgs's full attention now. "We could try again."

"Try again?" Tabitha asked innocently, but her eyes held a fiery challenge, assuring him she knew *precisely* what he meant.

"Yes. This afternoon was . . ." He struggled for the right word.

"A mess?" she supplied, a hint of mischief in her eyes.

"Yes." He hoped she would admit they'd both been *a mess*, as she put it, but she didn't. She let him claim that blame fully on his own. Perhaps he deserved it, since he had been the one to kiss her, to take such liberties that opened up the discussion that followed and their subsequent quarrel. But he was committed to starting over with her, and if that meant accepting all of the responsibility for their last encounter, so be it.

"Right, well. My given name is Fitzwilliam, but I would like very much for you to call me Fitz, as my friends do."

"Do you wish to be friends with me, Fitz?" Tabitha inquired, her tone softening. Her gaze grew pensive as she studied him. He was finally having a victory of his own.

"Yes," he said without hesitation.

Her gaze shot down the length of the table, where

Hannah and Julia were engaged in lively discussion with their own dinner companions.

"Then I suppose it would be all right if you called me Tabitha."

By the flush in her cheeks, he knew she was remembering that moment when he'd spoken her name while he'd pleasured her. He wanted her to remember that when he called her Tabitha, the delicious pleasures that could be had.

"Excellent." He drank his wine as the footmen set out dishes to be passed around the table. His grandmother preferred a less formal dining style where most of the dinner dishes were cut up on the sideboard table, then handed around to the guests. It required fewer servants to handle the demands of the guests. His grandmother liked the intimacy of a gathering where people shared food between each other, rather than having servants do all the work for them.

As they dined, Fitz juggled his conversations with Mrs. Higgs and Tabitha with more ease than he expected, in part because Beck was purposely keeping Mrs. Higgs distracted to allow Fitz to focus on Tabitha.

"Tell me, did you and your cousin see much of each other as children?" he asked as the dessert course was brought around. He'd avoided any sensitive subjects the entire meal as he sought to gain more of Tabitha's trust, but now he was ready to test her.

She glanced away, her gaze focused on the brightly colored little cakes being laid out in front of her. "Oh, not often."

"Do you enjoy sweets?" he asked. The desserts weren't overly fancy, but rather something one might find in a confectioner's shop in the shopping district. His grandmother had a soft spot for pastries and asked for them rather than the fancy desserts one expected to eat in a grand house.

Her hands moved restlessly in her lap. "I used to, but I don't eat them anymore."

Hoping to tease her into a better mood, he lowered his voice a little so that only she could hear.

"Oh? Tell me you aren't a woman who worries about her figure. You are beautiful, and any half-decent man likes curves on a woman. It gives a man something to hold on to when—" He stopped, but only because he realized his scandalous comments were being completely ignored by her. He reached under the table and gently clasped one of her hands, which had fisted in her skirts. She jerked a little at the touch and turned her head his way. Her face had drained of all color.

"Tabitha, are you all right?" he asked. "You've gone very pale. What's the matter?" The poor creature looked ready to faint. He prayed it wasn't what he'd said to her. He'd only meant to tease her and win a blush, or perhaps a smile.

"I . . . I am almost too embarrassed to admit it." Her gaze turned down toward her plate, which was empty of sweets. He squeezed her hand gently, encouraging her silently to continue.

"When I was about thirteen, I went with a few girls I knew to buy sweet cakes from the confectioner's shop near where I lived." Her eyes darted briefly toward the cakes on the plate. "The girls became violently ill. Two of them died. They seized violently and seemed to have been poisoned. Someone finally realized they'd all eaten the same thing, those cakes. They were found to contain chromate of lead. The baker had used it as a substitute for eggs. It was a sort of yellow substance, as I understand, and he believed it would be fine to use to achieve the color he desired when creating an egg-based glaze."

"He adulterated the cakes." Fitz's tone was grim.

"Yes." She swallowed, her eyes darting back to the desserts. "I just keep seeing those girls shaking upon the floor, frothing at their lips as their faces turned blue . . ." She shuddered.

"Keep your eyes on me, darling," he whispered and squeezed her hand. It drew her focus back to him. "Food adulteration is all too common a practice among lower-end food sellers."

It wasn't unusual for people to add things to food to increase the weight or change the color. He had once heard that some poorer bakers in town added ground-up bones, plaster, lime, pipe clay, and alum to bread. Well-off families only purchased food from reputable shops who did not take part in such practices. But a good reputation carried a premium price. Until this moment, he hadn't thought about those who had no choice but to take their chances, nor had he considered the idea that one could die from such unethical behavior.

"Did you fall ill?" he asked in concern.

"No. I gave my cake to another girl who needed food more than I did. She was one of those who died." A sharp hitch in Tabitha's breath warned him she was deeply upset. "I *killed* her."

"No, you didn't," he whispered. "That irresponsible baker killed those girls. Not you. Do you understand?"

Her teary eyes met his, and she drew in a shaky breath. They both knew she couldn't cry at the table in front of everyone.

"Right, yes," she said slowly. "Of course."

Fitz's heart stilled in his chest as she recovered her composure. The grief that lay inside him reminded him she was a fellow sufferer. She truly had been through something terrible. If she had once lived as poorly as he now suspected, he couldn't begin to imagine what else she might have endured. This was no pretty young woman raised in the protective shelter of a rich family. Tabitha had endured things that he likely could not fathom. And simply knowing that created a deep chasm in his chest, making it hard to breathe.

"Forget dessert," he said. "Perhaps I can show you more of the house?" She nodded, and Fitz caught his grandmother's eye at the end of the table. He gave her a nod to indicate he wanted to break tradition and allow some people to leave the table early. She acknowledged his silent message with a returned nod.

He released Tabitha's hand and stood, catching the attention of his guests.

"If you are done, the gentlemen may gather in the billiard room. Ladies, you have the salon at your disposal. Otherwise, please stay at the table and enjoy dessert."

Beck said something to Mrs. Higgs, and she blushed and thanked him for the lovely dinner conversation. Then Beck stood up. A few of the ladies and gentlemen followed suit. His grandmother remained at the table with the guests who wished to stay seated and finish their desserts.

Fitz offered Tabitha his arm. "Miss Sherborne." She

stood and followed him out of the dining room, her arm tucked in his again. It was strange how the practice of escorting a lady had always been something he felt obliged to do per the requirements of his station, but with Tabitha it was different. Any excuse to touch her, to shield her, to have her close to him was fast becoming an addiction. One that he was too afraid to examine closely.

"This way," he whispered in her ear. They left the other guests behind and quickly snuck away. He led her down a dimly lit corridor and out of one of the side doors of the house onto a narrow gravel path. The night was clear and full of stars. They both took in the fresh air and let out a deep breath together. The tension in her expression receded almost immediately.

He tilted his head back to look up at the blanket of thousands of stars over their heads. "Feel better?"

"Much, thank you."

"Of course. It is what friends do, isn't it?"

She laughed. "How are you somehow both charming and infuriating at the same time?"

"It's part of being a duke," he joked. He had never considered himself an amusing man. Evan was usually the more jovial one of his set of friends, but he wanted to make Tabitha laugh.

"It is better out here," she admitted. "Just seeing

those cakes brought back all those terrible memories. In all my recent social engagements, I've somehow been lucky enough to avoid such desserts. Usually, I find other ways to occupy myself and manage to escape dessert altogether."

"These are quite atypical of a grand dinner party dessert. My grandmother likes more common desserts like these, and the cook knows she does."

Fitz made a mental note to instruct the cook to avoid all future sweet cakes.

He patted her hand as he led her to the hothouse. The windows were fogged with the warm air inside, and it would afford them some privacy.

"You had a difficult childhood after your father died, didn't you?" He gently pressed upon the subject he wanted her to discuss.

"Yes," she answered, but didn't elaborate more than that.

He buried his frustration. He wanted this woman to trust him, to realize that he would do anything for her if she but asked. She had that power over him, and he would not deny it. He also wasn't used to a woman who didn't readily accept his help, and it confused him more than he cared to admit.

"You can trust me, Tabitha. Nothing you say to me will be spoken of to anyone else."

"You wish for me to spill my secrets?" she teased.

"All of them." Even though he was rather serious about it, he flashed her a crooked grin that never failed to charm women.

She let out another soft laugh. "Well, I suppose all women do have secrets, don't we? 'Tis our nature. The moon has secrets, as does the sea, and women are connected to both. So why shouldn't we have secrets as well?"

"I quite agree with that logic, and you should have secrets—it's part of what makes you so charming and mysterious," he agreed.

Fitz opened the door to the hothouse, and she entered ahead of him. He wasn't a romantic sort, but the separation of their hands, even so briefly, sent a pang through his body, as though she might slip away from him forever.

He closed the door behind them and joined her on the gravel path, taking her hand again as they stood in the middle of the hothouse. He threaded his fingers through hers, and the moment she curled her fingers against his hand in return, a heady warmth that had nothing to do with the air around them blossomed inside him.

"Shall we test your knowledge of the language of flowers?" Tabitha asked.

With a grin, he plucked a nearby hyacinth and held it to his nose, taking in its scent. "Will I win a kiss if I do well?" She had no idea that this was a game he would win. His mother had long ago taught him the language of flowers, and he'd never forgotten a single lesson.

"I suppose that would be fair enough . . ." She touched the flower he held. "What does a hyacinth mean?"

"Your loveliness charms me," he said. His mother had brought him to this hothouse every Sunday in the spring and explained to him what each flower meant and how it could someday help him find the woman who would hold his heart. He'd thought it silly at the time, but now he cherished the memories of those hours with her.

Tabitha laughed in delight. "Correct."

Fitz slid an arm around her waist and pulled her into him. He claimed his prize and kissed her softly, sweetly upon the cheek.

Then he glanced about before he retrieved a red fuchsia bloom. He trailed it over her lips, and her lashes fluttered.

"And that one?" Her voice was breathless as her lashes flared up and their eyes met.

His voice dropped as he stared at her mouth. "I like your *taste* . . ."

"Correct again, although I feel you're imbuing the word *taste* with a different meaning." Her cheeks gave a blush that even the reddest rose would envy. "I'm beginning to believe you might know *too much* of flowers."

"I had a most excellent teacher. My mother was a woman who adored flowers. She would put them in the rooms of every guest, fresh blooms daily. She loved the possibilities that flowers and things that grow in the soil had to offer. 'New life is beautiful,' she used to say."

"She sounds like she was quite wonderful," Tabitha said.

"She was," Fitz agreed. Tabitha was still in his arms, and he leaned down and kissed the tip of her nose. She laughed again, the sweet sound filling him with delight. He chose a red carnation next and looked at her expectantly.

"Your turn."

She took the carnation, her eyes softening. "My heart aches for you," she finally said. "That's what a carnation means."

He placed the carnation in a nearby vase as she moved away from him to look at the other flowers. He plucked a wild red rose and came up behind her, gently taking her by the waist as he kissed the shell of her ear. Then he lifted the wild rose up to her face.

She reached up, her fingers careful to avoid the

thorns of the stem. "Pleasure and pain," she breathed, her breasts rising and falling as her breathing quickened.

"All of life is torn between those two," he said as he nuzzled her neck and pressed a kiss to her bare shoulder. "When I first saw you, it was your eyes that held me rooted in place. They are the color of cornflowers."

"Do you know what cornflowers mean?"

She pressed back against him, and he wished they were free of their clothing so he could enjoy the feel of her skin against his.

He turned her face so he could kiss her, but a moment before their lips met, he spoke the words that her eyes now begged of him. He wanted her to know that he understood what she was asking of him. "*Be gentle with me . . . that is what a cornflower means.*"

She nodded, as if silently asking him that now with eyes that spoke the language of flowers.

He wanted to sweep her up in his arms and carry her to bed right then and there. He wanted to show her how gentle he could be and that someday, when she trusted him, he could set her free, teach her to be a wild creature in his arms when she finally felt safe enough to let go.

"Who are you?" he whispered as he turned her in his arms to face him. "Tell me something about you, *anything*," he begged. He wanted to know everything.

Right now, he'd only glimpsed the surface of the sea that was this woman's soul.

The heavy blooms around them and the soft moonlight seemed to make him feel like there was no past and no future, only this present moment with her.

Her lips parted, but she betrayed no secrets, shared none of that glowing soul that burned so fiercely in her eyes. She clung to him, and if all he could have in this moment was her trust in him to hold her, he would take it.

"Anything, Tabitha, please," he whispered as he closed his eyes and covered the crown of her hair with soft kisses.

"Please, Fitz, *please* . . ."

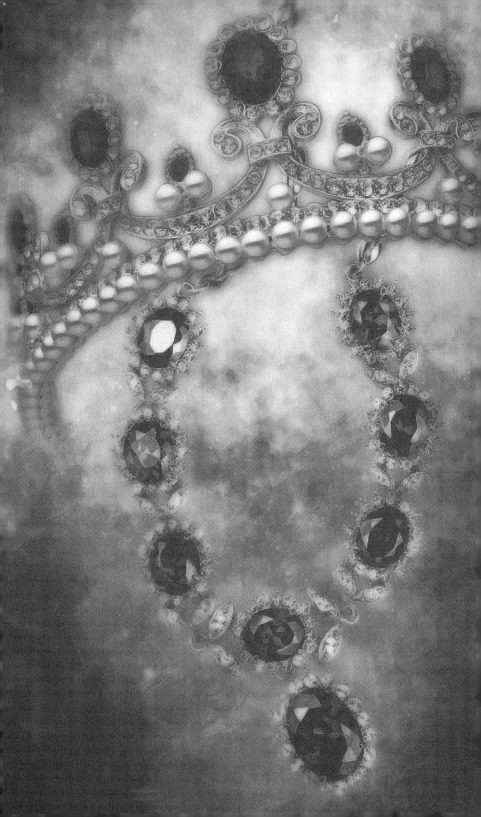

Chapter Six

"Christ," he breathed. "I want you, but this isn't the place for your first time."

"My first time for . . . oh!" she replied, her eyes widening with understanding. She stroked one hand down his body, lightly cupping his shaft as it pressed against the front of his trousers.

He groaned as she explored the feel of him. "Keep doing that and I'll have trouble controlling myself," he warned.

But she didn't stop teasing him—far from it. He turned her away from him, pressing himself against the bustle at the back of her gown.

"Do you know why women accent their bottoms with bustles?" he asked. He grasped her waist with one hand as his other gently moved up to her throat, touching it lightly with his fingertips.

"Why?" Tabitha asked, her voice breathless.

"Because it entices a man, reminds us of what we love. When I take a woman from behind, I pound into her, my hips slamming into the plushness of her backside. It feels glorious." He breathed into her neck, smelling the sweet scent of her, and she trembled beneath his touch. "This damn bustle makes me want to bend you over right here and take you in the dark with the flowers all around us. Here, we could be as primal as the beasts that dwell in the ancient forests."

Her responding shiver wasn't one of fear.

"I must confess something," she said, and he held his breath. "But I worry you will pass judgment on me when you hear it."

He tightened his hold on her waist, wanting to show her he wouldn't let go or cast her away no matter what she might say. Perhaps now she would explain her connection to Hannah Winslow.

"What if I confess something to you first?" he offered. "Then we shall be on even ground."

She nodded. "That would help." She pushed her back against his chest again, leaning into him, and he enjoyed that continued trust she gave him.

"I spoke of always being right," he began. "But I'm

discovering that perhaps I'm not always right about everything."

"Oh?" She tried to turn around, but he kept her facing away from him. He couldn't bear to see her face if he disappointed her.

"Yes. It seems that meddling in the lives of my friends has had unintended consequences. I was not ready to deal with that." He paused, considering his next words carefully. "I'm facing the hard truth that perhaps sometimes other people know their own lives better than I do and are therefore better suited to make decisions for themselves than I am. It is a newly discovered flaw in myself that I do not like admitting it, except to you."

He nuzzled her hair and breathed in the sweet scent that clung to her. It was as though she had bathed in flower petals that morning.

"That sounds like a terrible flaw indeed," she said. "But perhaps you will still wish to be free of me when I speak *my* truth, should it outweigh your own."

Fitz couldn't imagine what she could say that might drive him from her.

"When you touched me, and I experienced pleasure, it was for the first time, but it wasn't the first time that I have been with a man. There was someone a long time ago, when I was younger."

"Ah, I see." She wasn't a virgin, but this revelation did not disturb him. "You must have been very young." That was the part that worried him more. Men often took advantage of young women and it was wrong.

"I was sixteen . . . the young man I was with was seventeen," Tabitha admitted.

"Did he hurt you?" That was a thing that Fitz feared. Sixteen was terribly young, and it was possible the overeager boy could have hurt her.

"No. It was a little uncomfortable in the moment and there was a brief pain, but it soon eased. I was willing to be with him, and it seemed to give him comfort to be with me. I had no one to offer me advice, no one who explained that intimacy of the heart is not guaranteed. But he and I found comfort that night, where we'd both been cold and lonely before."

"I understand that more than you know. I have had mistresses in the past, and while I have held an affection for them, there was never anything more than a physical intimacy for me, despite my wish to feel more for someone. I never felt that way about anyone."

Until you, he added silently.

He finally allowed her to turn in his arms, and she clutched his coat in her hands.

"You truly don't judge me for having been with someone?" Those cornflower-blue eyes spoke the language of flowers for her, forever asking him to be gentle.

"I have my failings, but judging you won't be one of them. I'm glad to hear that you haven't been hurt and that if we . . . Well, I wouldn't want to cause you any pain."

Her hand slid up his chest to curl around his neck. In that moment, he knew he would wait forever if he had to, to have this woman.

"I've ruined our moment, haven't I?" Her blue eyes filled with tears, but she didn't cry. He was relieved. If she'd cried, he wasn't sure he could have survived it.

"No, darling, you haven't. I still want you desperately, but it's made me want to wait for the right time. When you're ready, I can make that moment all the things lovemaking should be." He didn't care that he sounded like a romantic fool. It felt right to speak what lay in his heart now that she'd exposed it to the world.

"When, not if?" she asked. "You promise me that? I've never been so stirred in my life as you have stirred me now, Your Grace."

"Fitz," he said.

Her lips curved in a smile that melted his soul. "Fitz. How are you wicked and sweet all at once? I've never met a man like you."

"You keep saying things like that. I can't be certain if I'm honored or insulted," he chuckled.

She pressed her face against his waistcoat and her hands curled into his sleeves as she clung to him.

"Just kiss me," she breathed. He gently tilted her face up to his and saw the ghost of tears clinging to her lashes.

His mouth came down on hers, hard, desperate, filled with a longing he knew he should hide, but he couldn't. Her lips parted beneath his questing tongue as he delved deeper, tasting her until she was imprinted on his very soul. He cradled the back of her head in one hand while his other grasped her lower back, holding her close to him. The flowers around them seemed to whisper soft, sweet words in their quiet language of wild beauty. Tabitha's lips were softer than the petals of any bloom, and the heat that kiss created lit a spark of desire once more inside him.

How had he been so cold and not known it? The chill that had encased his heart and kept him hard and frozen these last few years was now fading beneath the heated touch of her lips. He was not a man given to thoughts of divinity, but in that instant, he believed and finally understood what some people meant when they said that to love someone was to bask in the divine.

Did he love her? Could someone love another so

quickly? Surely it was madness, some trick his mind was playing upon him because he'd secretly longed for a deep connection to another soul.

Their mouths broke apart, and he struggled to regain his breath and his senses, as the experience of kissing Tabitha grew more intense each time.

Those cornflower-blue eyes held his gaze, and he forgot why he had demanded to know any of her secrets. A woman should always keep her mystery, wearing it like a fur-lined cloak or donning it like a glittering diadem upon her brow.

Finally, he found his voice. "Come, let me take you back to the house." He pressed one more lingering kiss to her lips and sighed. "Blast and damn, I hate being a gentleman sometimes." That drew a gentle laugh from her. "But rest assured, Tabitha, I *will* ravish you."

"And I shall let you," she replied with an adorable cheekiness that made him want to crush her in his arms again and never let her go. Where the devil had this perfect woman come from, and why couldn't he let the matter of her past simply remain a question that needed no answer?

TABITHA BID THE DUKE GOOD NIGHT AS HE WENT TO
join the other gentlemen in the billiard room, leaving
her alone at the foot of the grand staircase. Rather than
go to the salon where the ladies would be gathered, she
snuck up to her bedchamber to rest and prepare for the
coming mission.

She called for Liza to come up and help her undress
and bathe. Liza was technically Hannah's maid, but she
was sweet enough to help Tabitha in addition to her
duties to Hannah. She was one of the few people who
knew the truth about the Merry Robins, and she was
more than happy to keep their secret.

"Thank you, Liza. I'm planning to try for the
diamond later tonight, to see if I can take it or at least get
a better idea of where and how it's secured. The duke's
study appears to have a guard posted outside, so that's
where I'm going to start my search. I'm going to retire
early and try to get some rest first."

"What time are you going to go look for the
diamond? Would you like me to come back and wake
you?"

"Yes, please. Around three?"

"Of course, Miss Tabitha. Let's get you out of this
gown and into the bath."

As the maid helped her undress, Tabitha found her
thoughts drifting back to those stolen moments in the

hothouse with Helston. It had been years since she'd thought of the night she'd shared a bed with young Joseph.

He had been the one who had taught her the art of the light-fingered trade. He had walked her home to make sure she wasn't snatched. At sixteen, she was vulnerable to men, especially those looking for fresh girls to enslave in prostitution.

He'd offered to stay the night. It had been so very cold, the other girls were gone for the night, and she'd been lonely enough to accept. One thing had led to another, and she and Joseph had fumbled together in the candlelight, tugging at each other's clothes until they had stumbled into the nest of her little bed. It had been an awkward and sweet moment, the way he'd tried to make sure he hadn't hurt her. She hadn't even minded sharing her bed as they'd both fallen asleep.

Joseph died six months later from typhus, and while she had not loved him, she'd mourned his loss and had buried those memories deep until tonight. He was among the many reasons she'd been so afraid to let her guard down. But Hannah and Julia had torn down so many of those barriers that someone like Helston had been easily able to storm the battlements of her heart.

With Helston, she'd broken all of her rules. He made her want to trust her heart to someone, to lie beside him at night and be assured he would still be there in the morning.

He made her feel a hunger for wild, primal things that a man and woman could do together. She'd never let herself think about that before, but tonight she'd practically begged Helston to take her with a desperation she'd never thought possible.

She'd thought she had no interest in men, but the truth was she'd simply not met the *right* man yet. And Helston was indeed the right man . . . and it was damned unlucky that he was also the *wrong* man at the same time.

After her bath, the lady's maid left her to get some rest before her late-night mission to look for the diamond. As she drifted off to sleep, her thoughts kept returning to Helston.

When it was close to three o'clock in the morning, there was a light knock upon her door. Tabitha eased the door open and allowed Liza to slip inside the room with her.

"Thank you for waiting up, Liza," she said once the door was firmly closed.

"Here, Miss Tabitha." Liza helped her don her black trousers and black blouse. Each of the Merry Robins had their own outfit just like this that they could wear during their thefts if those thefts couldn't be done with practical lifts during balls or parties. Whenever a jewel couldn't be stolen during an afternoon tea or ball, they'd returned at night and used a servants' entrance to access the house, taking the jewel with relative ease.

Tabitha finished dressing quickly and pulled a black hood over her head that covered her entirely except for her mouth and eyes. This kept any of her skin from showing if she needed to hide in the shadows, and it also kept her identity as a woman concealed by not showing her hair. She'd cut eye slits in the mask and she used a bit of dark soot to conceal the skin that a person could see through the slits to disguise her even further.

"I drew a map of the grounds for you, Miss Tabitha. You are right about the duke's study being under guard. He has two footmen and his valet taking turns watching the door." Liza placed a sheet of paper down on the little table by the chair facing the fire, and Tabitha bent over to examine it closely. It was a detailed drawing of the house and its many passageways and staircases, which, along with her previous tours of the house and grounds with Fitz, gave Tabitha a quick understanding of where she needed to go.

"The guards are only on the outside of the room? Not the inside?"

"I believe so, but I cannot be certain. I have only

seen the footmen standing outside the door. I suppose they think that's enough." Liza shrugged.

"It might be for some, but I will get into the study using the window outside." Tabitha gave the lady's maid a quick hug. "Wish me luck." Tabitha then snuck out of the bedchamber and crept down the back servants' stairs.

Helston Heath was quiet as she moved soundlessly through the corridors. She made her way beneath the cover of night until she reached the back door that would take her to the gardens. She met no servants along the way, given the late hour. The scullery maids would not be up to light the fires for another two hours.

She exited the door that Helston had used earlier that night when he'd shown her the hothouse, because it also faced the duke's study. Once outside, she counted the windows of the house and made her way to the room that she was certain was the right one. When she reached it, she crouched down in the flower beds beneath the windowsill.

Her heart raced and she felt strangely sick at the thought of taking Helston's diamond. A flash of a memory from earlier tonight, when Helston had held up the cornflower in the hothouse and spoke of her eyes, made her lips tremble. She'd seen a gentleness in him, this man who could be so domineering and dictating to those around him. And he'd shown that gentleness to her. He'd even admitted to faults and spoken of confessions and desire that transcended mere physical need.

She closed her eyes, trying to strengthen her resolve, but it didn't come. Instead, she saw Helston again. She was back in the hothouse and could feel his arms around her as he dared to ask if she'd been hurt that first time a man had lain with her. How could he not have judged her? Gentlemen *prized* virgins, but that hadn't seemed to matter to him. He'd even sounded relieved to learn she had not suffered.

No. She couldn't do this. She couldn't take his diamond. She pushed away from the wall of the house and crept back inside. She found Liza waiting up for her in her bedchamber.

"Did you get it?" the maid asked, her voice hushed.

"No. The window was locked. I will try again tomorrow." The lie felt bitter upon her lips. Orphans, widows, and wounded war veterans were relying on her, and tonight she had let them down.

"Are you all right?" Liza asked as Tabitha flung herself back onto the bed with a heavy sigh. "You look a bit peaked."

"Yes . . . I am. Why don't you go on to bed, Liza" she urged. "It's late. We'll try again tomorrow. I can change back into my nightgown on my own."

"Very well then. Good night, miss."

Liza left her alone, and Tabitha stared up at the ceiling. It was only then that she saw the bouquet of flowers that sat on one of the tables by the window. The vase was overflowing with red tulips, and she knew the meaning of tulips.

Tabitha rose from the bed and went over to the table. Had the duke left these for her? The unique arrangement had to be from him. The flowers must have been delivered while she'd bathed after their time in the hothouse when she'd been in the adjoining room. Liza must have taken the flowers and put them over here and forgotten to tell her about them.

She buried her face against the velvety soft blooms and whispered the message the flowers carried. *"I declare my love."* She noticed that mixed in with the tulips were clovers. They too carried a message. *"Will you be mine?"*

What was she going to do? She nuzzled the flowers again and let out a breath.

Damn you, Helston, she thought. *Damn you for making me fall for you.*

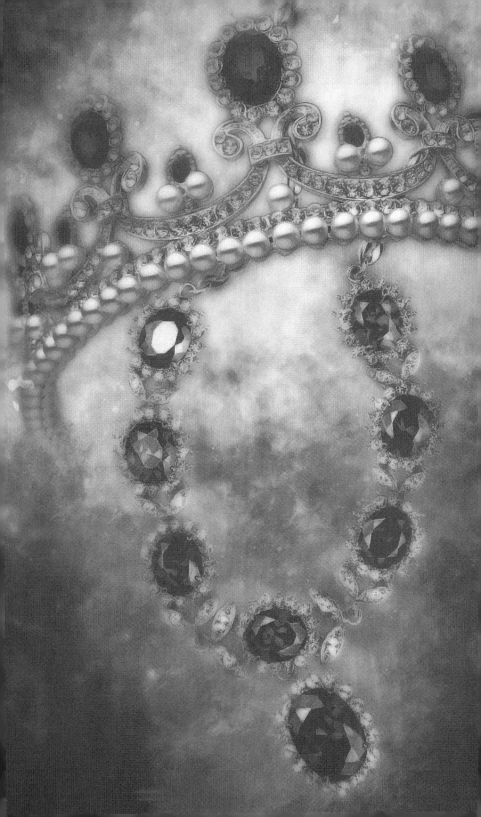

Chapter Seven

"Quiet night?" Beck asked at breakfast the following morning. Fitz had had the footmen who usually manned the dining room wait outside until more guests came down to breakfast. This allowed them to be alone in the dining room. Most of the gentlemen had stayed up late into the night drinking and smoking, but Fitz was used to rising early and couldn't break himself of the habit.

"Yes. I waited all night. No one even tried the hallway, according to my servants. I think we may have to send the footman away from the door during the night."

"I agree," Beck said. "It's not as though the real jewel is at stake."

They kept their conversation to a low murmur so as not to be overheard by anyone outside the dining room.

"I'll take tonight's watch," Beck offered.

"Actually, I believe I should go again this evening. Given that I'm meant to be the target, the thief likely won't open up to me. You and Evan will be less suspicious. I want you to work your way through the gentlemen guests and see what you can learn through conversation."

"So we interrogate them without letting them know they're being interrogated."

"Precisely."

Fitz finished his breakfast and gazed at the cornflowers on the table, which had been arranged in a lovely bouquet, along with other flowers from the hothouse. He smiled a little as he remembered delivering a bouquet much like it last night to Tabitha's bedchamber while she was having a hot bath. Her lady's maid had taken it from him and assured him she would see it in the morning.

He couldn't wait to see her, to ask if she liked them. He nearly laughed at his own childlike foolishness to be so excited over a woman's reaction to a bouquet.

Evan slipped into the dining room and joined them at the table. "Good Lord . . ."

"What?" Fitz glanced away from the bouquet to look at Evan.

"You've got a look about you," Evan replied.

"A *look?*" Fitz snapped. "What the devil is that supposed to mean?"

Beck and Evan exchanged a worried glance.

"He's right. You have got the *look,*" Beck agreed.

"You're both acting like I've come down with consumption," Fitz said with a glower. "What is this *look* you speak of?"

Evan relaxed. "And just like that, it's gone. For a moment there, I was worried. You looked as though you were thinking about something wonderfully pleasant . . . like a woman. And this isn't the time to dally with anyone. I thought you were here to catch a thief, not a bride. This entire plan was your idea, if you remember," Evan said.

Fitz arched a brow. "And if I *was* thinking of a woman?" he asked.

"You are by far the *least* romantic of us. If you fall into the pit of matrimony, then Beck and I are surely doomed," Evan huffed. "I don't want to fall in love again. Having my heart obliterated once was quite enough, thank you." He reached for a plate of scones on the table.

Beck hid a chuckle as he sipped his coffee. "I have

no qualms about love with the right woman, but that's rather a challenge, isn't it? Women are far too predictable these days. I require someone exciting who won't mind me being who I am and all the scandal that I bring."

For the first time in years, Fitz saw a hint of the old Beck from before his father had died and left his family penniless.

Beck had kept his dire straits a secret as long as he could, until creditors had swarmed their townhouse, taking everything of value. Then he had shown up at Fitz's door just after midnight, his mother and little sister in tow, and begged for a pair of rooms to sleep in for a few days while he tried to make other arrangements.

Fitz had eagerly provided three rooms and insisted they stay a few months rather than a few days. Beck had argued, but once his mother and sister had settled into their rooms, he'd reluctantly accepted the offer. Fitz had never told Beck that having his family under his roof had been wonderful. He'd felt like he had a family again for the first time in years.

Within a few months, Beck had become an infamous burglar, one the press had dubbed the Merry Rogue, and soon he had been able to afford lodging for his family again. He'd even been clever and began investing half of the money he stole, while gambling the other half to win more. No one but Fitz and Evan had ever known the truth of Beck's rapidly rising wealth.

Being with Tabitha in the hothouse the previous evening had reminded him of when Beck and his family had lived with him. He'd felt . . . complete somehow, having someone he cared about near him. The way she made him feel, that dizzy, delightful fullness in his chest made him excited and yet deeply serene all at once.

"Dare we ask what has you looking so dreamy this morning?" Evan asked.

Fitz snorted. "I'm not *dreamy*, nor will I ever be."

"But you are, old boy. That Sherborne girl has you all twisted up. Stealing kisses and courtly walks to the hothouse under cover of darkness . . ." Evan chuckled. "You'd best be careful. Such things would have had our ancestors married with babes on the way by now."

"She's fascinating, I admit that. I can't help but want to put together the pieces of her mystery." He toyed with his teacup and then leaned a little toward his friend. "I blame you, Evan."

"Me?"

"You are certain she isn't related to Hannah? Even by a distant marriage?"

Evan shook his head. "I learned everything about Hannah, including her family tree. I traced her lineage back to William the Conqueror and I know all her cousins and even second and third cousins. Not once did I see any Tabitha or any Sherbornes. Even the female relatives who married and took different names did not escape my search."

"You don't suppose that this mysterious Miss Sherborne is . . ." Beck began thoughtfully.

"The thief?" Evan completed Beck's thought, and then they both burst into laughter.

Fitz didn't laugh.

Women were more than capable of such activities, and to be fair, the possibility had occurred to him. After all, Tabitha had admitted the desperate life she'd once led. Was it not possible that these thefts were the reason she was able to afford her current lifestyle? Beck was proof that such things were possible.

However, he had his reasons for dismissing her as a suspect, namely because of her companions, Miss Starling and Mrs. Winslow. They were well-born daughters of aristocrats and were the farthest thing from thieves that could be imagined. They also clearly trusted Tabitha, so much so that they had concocted a story about her being Hannah's cousin. The three were clearly good friends, and as gentle-born ladies, Hannah and Julia would not be given to such petty actions as theft. What would be so important about

Tabitha that Hannah and Julia would lie to society for her?

Suddenly, the truth struck like lightning. He knew of one very important reason that two gentle-born ladies would lie about another woman's background and introduce her into society as they had.

"Miss Sherborne is not after any jewel. She's after a *husband*," he murmured to himself, catching the attention of his friends.

"Miss Sherborne wants a husband?" Beck asked.

"Of course! That must be why Mrs. Winslow and Miss Starling have concocted this cousin story. Miss Sherborne told me things in confidence that would give me reason to believe that her spending time on the marriage mart would be unsuccessful." He did not tell his friends all of the private things Tabitha had shared in confidence with him. Those were not his secrets to share. It did not bother him, but it would sour most men toward her. And assuming she managed to keep her situation a secret, most men would want proof on the wedding night that she was a virgin. It was a silly, medieval notion, but men were often medieval in their thinking when it came to a great many things, women included.

"So, she's after you," Evan said. "I wonder at her courage to come after a duke. Bravo for her, but I daresay she won't catch you. She'd have to win over your grandmother as well."

"She's already captured my grandmother's interest," Fitz admitted. "I overheard her ordering Mr. Tracy to push the two of us together whenever possible during this house party. She's set on me marrying, and she seems to like Miss Sherborne very well."

"Good God, man," Evan declared. "You'd best watch your back or you'll be married by Christmas."

Married by Christmas . . . Why did the thought strike both terror and excitement through him at the same time? The vast dining room suddenly felt small and stifling. He tugged at his collar, trying to escape the strangling feeling of his ascot.

"I think I need some air." Fitz pushed his chair back and stood. "I'll see you both later, shall I?"

"Indeed. I heard croquet is the game of the day." Evan grinned. "I always enjoy whacking the hell out of that ball."

Beck rolled his eyes. "And when you do, it takes half a dozen men to go find it in the underbrush. Meanwhile, you flirt with every pretty woman in attendance."

Evan lounged back in his chair with a gleeful look. "I never claimed to aim for the wickets. Besides, once the rest of the gents chase after the ball, I have the ladies all to myself."

Beck snorted. "You're a bounder, you know that, don't you?"

"I happily own up to it." Evan grinned.

Fitz left his companions to bicker in the dining room while he headed to the back terrace. Once outside, he sighed in relief as the chilly autumnal breeze tousled his hair and invigorated his senses.

His thoughts were a mad jumble as he left the terrace behind and cut through a garden path that led him to a dirt road. The road passed through the woods that bordered his lands and bisected the side of a steep meadowy hill that was covered with sheep in springtime. He moved fast, stretching his legs and watching the rain clouds gather on the horizon. The faint rumble of thunder was only a minor distraction as he focused on the problem of what to do about Tabitha.

Was she here for a husband? And did she want *him* in that regard? More importantly, if she was secretly looking to find a husband, was she putting on a performance or was she presenting herself truthfully? Women sometimes tailored their performances to men when attempting to win a husband or even a protector. Was Tabitha the kind of woman who would do that? Or was she being herself with him? And if she was being herself . . . what did he think of the idea of marriage to her? Because they were certainly moving in that direction if she was indeed husband hunting.

He had never liked being reminded of the fact that he would *have* to marry someday. He didn't like being told what to do, ever. Naturally, he avoided any matters that might lead him to a wedding . But when he thought of Tabitha walking toward the altar to meet another man, it created a strange buzzing in his ears and made his fists clench.

Tabitha's face, half-hidden beneath a wedding veil, flashed across his mind. She would look exquisite in a creamy satin gown, orange blossoms adorning her hair and . . .

He cursed as he lengthened his strides. Since when was he the sort of man to daydream about a bride? Since when was he the sort of man who fell in love with a woman in the dark while listening to music? Apparently, when a man met a woman like Tabitha, he became a romantic fool with a longing for kisses and speaking the language of flowers.

TABITHA QUICKENED HER PACE TO A BRISK TROT THE moment she heard the rumble of the storm behind her. She was dead tired, as she'd not been able to sleep much the night before. The flowers that Fitz had left for her had sent her mind spinning. She also harbored quite a bit of guilt at not telling Hannah and Julia about her growing feelings for Fitz. She'd just kissed a man they both despised, a man who'd ruined the engagement and life of their friend, which had resulted in the veritable exile of the poor woman to America.

And if that wasn't bad enough, she'd failed to steal the diamond last night. Technically, she hadn't even *tried*, and that was somehow infinitely worse.

With all of those thoughts pounding at the inside of her head, she hadn't been able to go back to sleep so she'd decided to go for a walk. The early morning exercise across the fields had the added benefit of helping her avoid Julia and Hannah, at least for a while. She couldn't afford to talk to them yet, not until she had worked out how she was going to excuse herself for not retrieving the diamond.

She heard the rain coming long before she felt it. The dull roar of heavy drops swept across the meadow and the path she was on. She broke into a desperate sprint as the deluge chased her. She didn't want to return to the house dripping like a drowned rat.

When the rain inevitably overtook her, she was stunned by the sheer force of it. She tried to keep to the path, but the mud soon made it impossible. Even the thickening foliage above her did little to stop the torrential downpour. She felt like she was running through an endless waterfall.

Blast! This was not what she needed. There was nothing more irritating than getting soaked through to the bone. At least now she could return to the house, change her clothes, and request a hot bath. Before she'd met Hannah and Julia, she would've been wet the rest of the day, with an empty belly and a chill that likely would have resulted in a cold, or worse. Thank heavens she no longer had to face such conditions. She resolved in that moment to hug Hannah and Julia when she returned. The other women had truly saved her from the miseries of her old life.

But even thinking about that raised the deep fear that she would only ever have one purpose in life: to steal. Was she nothing more than a petty thief in a pretty dress? For so many years, she'd been a pickpocket, nothing more. Was she worth being anything, or mattering to anyone beyond her special skill set? It was probably silly to even worry about any of that, but she did.

Tabitha took a path up a small wooded hill trying to steer clear of the thick mud forming on the path, only to slip on the slick meadow grasses. She cried out more from alarm than pain as her ankle gave beneath her and she tumbled to the ground and began to slide and roll down the steep hill, hissing out in pain each time she rolled.

With a thud, she collided with a boulder, stunning her for a moment. But this boulder had grunted and rolled with her.

When she finally stopped, she bumped up against the boulder again. Only it *wasn't* a boulder. It was a man. When she blinked away the rain from her eyes, she was staring into the face of Fitz, his eyes as stormy as the clouds above them. His wet golden hair was hanging in damp tendrils over his eyes like burnished gold. He was staring back at her while lying on his side. He blinked slowly, as if trying to decide whether he was seeing her or if she was a dream.

"Your Grace," she gasped.

He slowly sat up and winced. "Tabitha?" He had a gash across his forehead. It wasn't deep, but blood was trickling down his face.

"Oh God, you're bleeding." She dug into her drenched skirt pocket and pulled out the token handkerchief he'd let her keep that bore his initials. She lifted up the damp handkerchief to wipe his cut. He winced.

"Hold still," she said and held his chin firmly as she wiped it. "I think the cloth is too wet. We need to get somewhere dry before I can tend to it properly."

Fitz smiled softly. "Are you a nurse, then?"

"Well, no, but I've handled my fair share of scrapes. Any cut must be taken seriously, especially in the city. What on earth were you doing out here?" she asked as she gingerly touched her left ankle.

"I was walking." He squinted up at the rain that fell in soft sheets around them. "Then this storm came out of nowhere. What about you?"

"I was out walking as well until I saw the clouds. I thought I could make it back to the house, but I was wrong."

"I'd be amazed if you had managed. We're a mile from the house. How did you get so far?" Fitz asked.

She blushed and glanced away. "I like being active. I walk often. I even run when no one is around to see. It feels good to stretch my legs. I don't believe those silly doctors who say it wrecks female fertility. Women have been walking and working long before those stuffy old men came along. Fresh air and movement are better than standing still."

The duke chuckled. "On that we agree. I can't stand to sit still for too long." As he said this he tried to stand, but he wavered on his feet unsteadily.

"Lord . . . I . . ." He slumped back to the ground. "I feel quite dizzy."

"That must be my fault. I hit you when I fell. Do you think you could walk if you leaned against me?"

"I might," he said uncertainly. His eyes had grown rather glassy, and she feared he may be concussed. She had hit him quite hard.

"All right, I'll try to lift you up. Then you lean on me." She stood and held back a whimper as her ankle twinged sharply. She could walk though, and had survived far worse. She held out her hands, which he accepted, and he stood. He wavered again, but she was quick to put one of his arms around her shoulders.

"Hold on and let's move up the path. We have to be careful of the mud."

Their progress was slow, but in time they reached the path higher on the hill and started the long walk home. They had gone perhaps a hundred yards when a dark-bearded middled-aged man emerged from the woods with a shotgun resting loosely in the crook of one arm. He had two dead pheasants tied to a line that was slung over his shoulder. He tipped his floppy hat back at the sight of them.

"Your Grace?" the man asked. "Are you ill?"

Fitz sighed with open relief. "This is John Cress, a tenant of mine," he said to her in introduction, and then he spoke to the man. "John, thank God we've crossed paths. We need a place to warm up. Might we avail ourselves of your home until the rain stops?"

"Of course, Your Grace." John nodded and squared his shoulders with pride. "The missus will have some soup on the stove, I imagine." John came over and took stock of their bedraggled state and Tabitha's limping movements.

"Here, lass, hold this. We'll be faster if I take care of him. You shouldn't be putting weight on that foot of yours." John passed Tabitha his shotgun and then took Fitz's arm and put it around his shoulders, easing the burden from her.

"Follow me," John said. They turned down the path toward a deep wooded area that flattened out to reveal a small paddock with a tiny barn. Goats, a few pigs, a dozen chickens, and one cantankerous-looking milk cow were all feeding at a trough in the shelter of the barn. Beyond the enclosure was a cozy little stone house. It was a welcome sight, and Tabitha found herself smiling despite the pain she still felt. She turned to Fitz and found him watching her with soft eyes. Perhaps it was only the concussion, but the look made her blush, nonetheless.

"Oy! Maddie!" John shouted across the clearing. The cottage door flew open, and a middle-aged woman stared back at them.

"What is it, John? Oh heavens! Your Grace!" She bobbed a quick curtsy as they approached.

"I'm so sorry, Mrs. Cress. But Miss Sherborne and I had a little accident up on the hill."

"I can see that, Your Grace. Come on in." She stepped back and let the sodden trio into the house. John took Fitz to a chair by the fire and then gently pried the shotgun from Tabitha's frozen hands.

"Go on and sit by the fire, lass." John gave her a nudge toward the other chair beside Fitz, and she collapsed into it gratefully.

Mrs. Cress tutted fretfully as she came over to them. "Miss Sherborne, is it? Are you hurt?"

"My ankle was turned a little, but I can walk. I am more concerned for Lord Helston . . ." She nodded at Fitz's still bleeding forehead, but the blood seemed to have clotted enough to slow the bleeding. "He seems to still be a bit dazed."

"I'll fetch a poultice. We'll get him right as rain— well, maybe not rain." The woman chuckled nervously. "Lord, there's a duke in my house, John. Can you believe it?" She whispered this loudly to her husband, who winked at Tabitha as if amused at his wife's excitement. Mrs. Cress retrieved her medicinal supplies from a cabinet by the coal stove.

She tended to the cut on Fitz's forehead and then poured them both some tea.

"We'd better get you changed out of those clothes. You don't want to catch your death. You first, Miss Sherborne." She escorted Tabitha to a small bedroom at the back of the cottage.

"It's not much, but it'll keep you warm," Mrs. Cress said as she removed clean undergarments, underskirts, a walking jacket, and a blouse from the drawer of a cabinet. Tabitha shivered as the other woman helped her pry her soaked walking gown off and put on the borrowed garments.

When they returned to the main room, Fitz was nursing a cup of tea, staring at the fire. He glanced up when she approached, and she blushed at him seeing her in simple homespun clothes. They were far more comfortable than the fine gowns he'd seen her in, and she feared for a moment he might be able to tell that this was what she was more accustomed to wearing. He simply smiled at her, his face weary, but his expression soft and full of a heat that only deepened her blush. Had they been alone in this little cottage, just the fire in the hearth and the rain outside . . . she knew that her clothing would have been the farthest thing from her mind.

"All right, Your Grace, you're next." John helped him stand, and the two men went back to the bedroom.

While the men were gone, Tabitha assisted Mrs. Cress in spooning a hearty wild hare stew into bowls for everyone.

"It's a good thing my John found you before the rain worsened," Mrs. Cress said.

"It is indeed. Helston and I are deeply grateful." The thought of walking all the way to the manor house in the cold rain made her shiver.

Mrs. Cress handed her a bowl and a spoon for herself. "Are you and his lordship . . . er . . . courting?"

Tabitha would have been surprised by the woman's honest question had she been a gentle-born woman, but she'd grown up not much richer than this woman, and in that part of society, frankness was valued above other social graces.

"No . . . no, we aren't."

"Oh." The woman spoke the single syllable with such meaning that Tabitha stared down at her soup rather than meet the woman's gaze.

"He is . . . above me in station, Mrs. Cress. So much so that . . ." She didn't have the right words to finish, but the other woman nodded solemnly.

"Ah, don't fret, love. I understand. I was a mere rag

seller, if you can imagine. But John came into London one day and saw me on a street corner, trying to purchase any bit of old cloth from fine folk I could get. If I got decent cloth, I could resell it for a little bit above what I paid and fill my belly every other night. John saw me and offered to sell the shirt off his back. He was so charming, so sweet, you see, but honest. I told him I had nothing to my name, and he didn't care. He just wanted me."

Tabitha smiled at the other woman. "You're very lucky to have found him."

Mrs. Cress shrugged. "Funny thing is, he says he is the lucky one to have found me. I think sometimes we women forget that titles and fancy dresses aren't what truly matters, not to good men. It's our hearts they cherish, not our riches." She nudged Tabitha. "Eat up before the men come back."

She'd no sooner cleaned her bowl than the men returned.

"Feel better in some dry clothes, Your Grace?" Mrs. Cress planted Fitz in the chair by the fire once again, and once more Fitz sought Tabitha's gaze. Something electric and powerful shot between them in that simple shared look. It was a look that dared to give her foolish heart hope for a future she couldn't have.

"Yes, thank you, Mrs. Cress. We appreciate your generosity," he said.

Tabitha took in the short trousers and the short shirt and the boots Fitz now wore. He looked like a giant in John's simple clothing. Despite him looking terribly silly, or perhaps because of it, Tabitha found herself smiling at him. Fitz smiled back, toying with the too-short sleeves of the borrowed shirt as if he could somehow make them longer.

"Once the rain stops, I'll take you both back in my wagon. I don't want to risk the roads until it has a chance to dry up a bit," John explained.

"Until then, you can warm up here, and if you want to rest, the bed is clean with fresh washed sheets."

"Oh, we couldn't," Fitz protested.

"Nonsense, Your Grace," Tabitha argued. "You've had quite a day, and you took hard a hit today when I knocked into you. You need to rest your head."

Fitz said nothing as he ate his soup, and he finally nodded after a few moments. "It is true, I do feel a bit dizzy still," he admitted with a frown.

"I'll help him to bed," Mrs. Cress said.

"Please, Mrs. Cress. I'll see to him. You've done so much for us already." Surely Mrs. Cress had much to do, and Tabitha didn't want her or Fitz to be the source of any additional strain.

"Come along, Your Grace." She helped Fitz up and escorted him to the bedroom, easing him down onto the small bed, the mattress sagging beneath his weight, and he let out a weary sigh.

"I feel quite wretched," he confessed. "We're putting out one of my tenants, and I can't even go home because of the rain. Nor can I properly take care of you. You are injured." He nodded at her ankle.

"Your Grace, really I'm fine now—"

"Fitz," he corrected with a boyish smile.

"*Fitz.* This is all my fault. I was the one who slipped on the hill and struck you."

Still grimly looking at her, he held out a hand. "A gentleman always takes responsibility, but I could have my injuries alleviated with a kiss or two."

The irresistible charmer, she thought. Tabitha put her hand in his, and he pulled her toward him. This was likely going to be a mistake, but she owed him a kiss, and more importantly, she *wanted* to kiss him. She reached up with her hands and threaded her fingers through the wet strands of his hair. His eyes half closed in pleasure.

"Come here," he said and pulled her closer. She fell onto his lap and his mouth slanted over hers in a hot, languid kiss.

Tabitha was lost. All that existed was the feel of his body, the heat of his mouth, and the dizziness that she felt. She struggled to get closer to him and pulled on his hair, needing to grasp him harder as she let him consume her very soul with that kiss. Their warm breaths mingled in the dim little room while thunder rumbled outside. The sound was low and deep, vibrating the air and the very earth around them.

If only we never had to leave this room, she thought with an aching longing. *Let us stay here forever, just like this.*

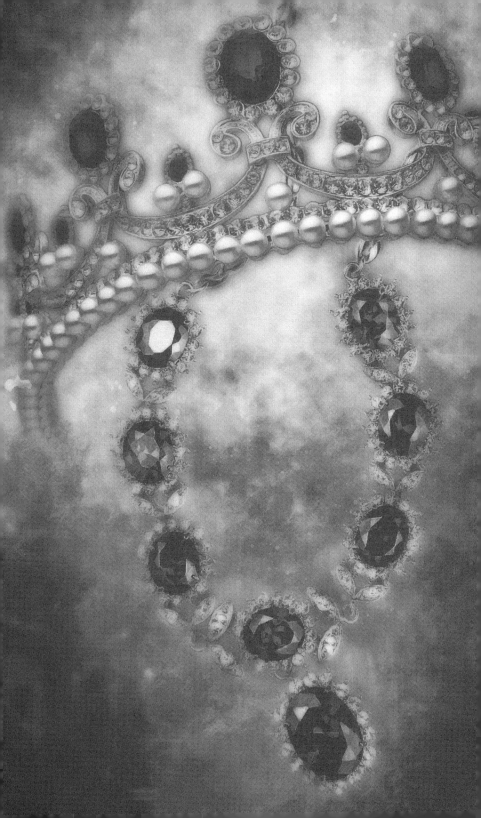

Chapter Eight

F itz ignored the throbbing in his skull and gave himself over to the moment. He had his little mystery creature bundled up in his arms again, right where he wanted her, and she was kissing him back with a passion that matched his own.

She tasted so bloody good and felt *perfect* in his arms. Wet tendrils of her hair had come loose, and he fisted his hands in the silky strands near the base of her neck. Tabitha moaned against his mouth and wiggled on his lap. He smiled against her lips, pleased that she seemed to enjoy his rather vigorous handling of her. He could be gentle, and he would be with her, but it was a relief to be himself in this moment and find that she felt the same way. Her hands tugged on his hair and her teeth nipped at his bottom lip in a way that made his body turn hard as stone. She moved her bottom again, and he nearly died at the torturous pleasure he felt as she rubbed against his cock through his trousers.

Somewhere in the back of his mind, he was aware that if his guests were to discover what he and Tabitha had shared in the last few days, it could force him to offer marriage to her. The thought did not create any of the expected rebellion within him that had always come before at the thought of marriage. If it came down to honor, he would agree and take this bewitching creature as his wife, his friends and their protestations be damned. But something kept him from choosing that fate willingly. Because each moment he thought of how happy he would be with her at his side . . . the inevitable thought of losing her brought him low and made it hard to breathe. Unwilling to let his thoughts ruin this kiss, he held on to her as if the world might tear her from his grasp at any moment and he would fight to keep her.

Their mouths parted, and she rested her forehead against his. A sudden deep connection to her snapped into place.

"You feel like *home*," she whispered. She stroked her fingertips at the base of his skull, the touch soothing. "How is that possible?"

"You feel like home to me as well. I can't remember the last time I felt like this . . . There have been times when I've smelled a certain brand of tobacco and I cannot help but think of my father in his study, or how my mother would be there in a chair reading while he answered his letters." Fitz looked into her eyes as the memories took over, and his heart constricted. "I remember standing in the doorway as a boy once, watching them in that cozy little scene. I didn't know then that such familial joys didn't last, and that one day I would see them like that for the last time. Perhaps it's foolish to dwell on those halcyon days. But kissing you . . . it brings me *home*."

Tabitha feathered her lips over his in the ghost of a kiss. "It isn't foolish. I've been so long without a home that my memories of them seem so dim. But when I'm with you, it makes those memories real once more."

"Do you think of your past like that?" he asked. He wanted to believe she had some sunny memories like he did.

She nibbled her bottom lip as if debating whether to speak. But after a steadying breath, she seemed to make a decision.

"Until recently, I felt trapped between my past and no future. I want to be honest with you, Fitz."

He stroked her back gently. "Be honest, then." What kind of admission could make this strong woman hesitate?

"I told you before that my life was not an easy one. The truth is, I was barely surviving," she confessed. "After my father died, I lived with some girls who took me in. They kept me from living on the streets. It was harder than you can possibly imagine."

Fitz had begun to wonder how much she must have suffered. Now he was getting more of the truth and it was breaking him apart to hear it. He didn't dare let her see his pain, not when she needed his strength and his compassion.

He gently took one of her hands in his to examine it. "I had wondered what caused these calluses." When she tried to pull her hand away, he pressed kisses to the pads of her fingertips.

"I keep thinking about how it would shame you to be with me," she whispered. "I am no one, nothing. I know that you are a man who cares about one's social standing."

He let out a weary sigh. "I do, likely too much," he admitted. "I enjoy the comfort of knowing that there is an order to the world, and that I know my place in it. Still, I know it has caused some to despise me, like your cousin. Not long ago, I had a friend who wanted to marry a girl. She was a good woman, I found no fault in her, but her family was so atrocious that marriage would have ruined my friend's life."

She turned away with a scowl. "You know how terrible that is, don't you?"

"Unfair, perhaps, but I did not think it was terrible to be concerned about my friend's future at the time. When you marry someone, you marry their family, and that affects everything you do, not just your social standing. Gentlemen would refuse to do business with my friend because of his father-in-law, and the mother would have brought him shame at balls and parties with her crass behavior. With his business prospects shattered and his social connections severed, he would be bankrupt within a decade. I saved my friend from a slow death."

"Perhaps . . . but all you did for certain was save him from true happiness," Tabitha countered.

"What happiness would he find if he and his wife became destitute? I have seen men marry for the deepest love in the world and be broken apart when life took its toll upon them. When a man loses his fortune and his home, his happy marriage often is the next thing he loses. Better to never marry than to lose one's wife like that."

"You have no way of knowing it would come to that, yet you are so certain of it. What if you were to stand by his side when others turned away? Would that not send a message? Or do you fear that you would be shunned along with him?"

That honestly hadn't occurred to him, and the fact that he hadn't even considered that as an option left him feeling at a definite loss.

His pride demanded that he challenge Tabitha's presumptions, and yet he found himself without the strength to do so. He had been so sure he had done the right thing. Louis had even thanked him for looking after his interests, yet each time he'd reached out to Louis, his messages hadn't been returned. He'd been busy with his affairs in Edinburgh that he'd simply lost track of the last time he'd shared a drink with his friend. But as he did the count of days in his head now . . . he realized with dawning horror that he hadn't shared company with his friend since that night Louis had agreed to break off his engagement to Anne Girard. Had his interference truly cost him his friendship?

"I haven't had a true chance to speak to him since that night he agreed to take my advice and cry off the wedding," Fitz said, resigned. "It's as if the last fifteen years of our friendship have vanished. Now that I'm thinking about it, I believe he gave me the cut direct in the card room the other night and I was simply too . . . bloody arrogant to have noticed his actions for what they were."

Louis had indeed ignored him that night, but the room had been boisterous. Louis had been engaged in discussion with a few other gentlemen Fitz was not acquainted with. Fitz had assumed that Louis was simply busy and would catch up with him later, but it never happened.

Fitz's throat tightened as he spoke of the incident. He'd done his best to dismiss it as his friend merely not seeing him, but now that he was telling Tabitha about it, all the guilt he felt and the hollowness of losing his friend came crashing back. He found it hard to breathe.

Tabitha stiffened in his arms. "Then I certainly would not be good enough for you." Her tone no longer held any bite, nor any accusation, but he heard the sorrow in her voice. She slid off his lap, and the loss of her warmth left him as cold as the deep of winter.

"Fitz, we must stop this before we go too far." The resolve in her expression turned that coldness creeping through him into a dark, empty void.

"Yes," he agreed, but the word tasted bitter upon his lips.

Just then, John knocked upon the closed door. "Your Grace? My wagon is ready. The roads are drying up. I can take you to the house now."

"Thank you, John." Fitz stood and waved for

Tabitha to go ahead of him as they exited the bedroom. Mrs. Cress was there waiting to see them off.

"You poor dear," she said to Tabitha. "John will get you home, don't you worry. Do you need any food for the road? I will have your clothing dried before I send it back down to the house."

"No, thank you, Mrs. Cress. You have been wonderfully kind." Tabitha embraced the woman and followed John outside. Fitz lingered a brief moment longer in the house.

"Thank you, Mrs. Cress. I won't forget your kindness. It will be rewarded."

Mrs. Cress smiled, her face soft with a motherly look. "Nonsense. The reward is knowing we were here at the right time to help. We need nothing else, Your Grace. You give us so much by letting John hunt on your land."

"Nonetheless, I won't forget," he promised her. A few deer and pheasants didn't feel like much compared to this woman's kindness.

The Cresses were *his* tenants, and it was his duty to look after them. Instead, they had looked after him and Tabitha. He would see them repaid for their generosity.

By the time he joined John and Tabitha by the wagon, the farmer had pulled out a large oilcloth and wrapped it around Tabitha's shoulders to shield her from any rain that might come during the drive to Helston Heath.

"The hay is dry, and this will keep you warm," John assured Tabitha, then offered a second oilcloth to Fitz.

"You keep it, John. We're not too far from the house. You will need it if the rain returns."

When the farmer hesitated, Tabitha scooted over in the hay and lifted part of her cloth blanket.

"Yes, please take it, Mr. Cress. His Grace and I can share this one."

"As you wish." The farmer climbed onto his perch on the buckboard wagon, and Fitz crawled through the hay to Tabitha. She held up the cloth on one side, and he wrapped it around his shoulders and pulled her close against him, letting her absorb his warmth as he curled his other arm around her shoulders.

"Are you warm enough?" he asked, his voice huskier than he'd intended.

"Y-yes, thank you."

Use me, take my heat, my darling, he silently urged her. *And I shall cherish this moment of you beside me for however long I have.*

For the first time in his life, he wanted something— or rather, someone—that he couldn't have. Tabitha was not a woman a man could simply walk away from. She was the sort of woman who changed a man forever once he held her in his arms. A smart man would take her to the altar and never look back.

But as she'd reminded him, he couldn't do that. He was a duke, and society had expectations as to who he could marry. Fitz could tell them all to be damned, might even enjoy that, but those same people could make his wife's life a bitter thing if he failed to choose wisely.

These grim thoughts only made him hold Tabitha tighter. It felt like those months long ago when he'd lost his father, how he'd dreamed of seeing him, touching him, only to wake and discover it was naught but a dream. The person who had felt so real that he could touch him, hear his voice, had been only in his mind . . . and his breaking heart.

He held on to Tabitha now, but when would he wake up and feel her fade away like every other dream?

As the wagon rolled forward, Tabitha tucked her head under his and he settled his chin on the crown of her hair. Neither of them spoke during the ride to the house. He feared that even uttering her name might shatter the dream. The storm had moved off into the distance, leaving behind a light mist that chilled the air. Tabitha shivered in his embrace and he rubbed her arm, trying to give her more of his heat.

As the wagon took the final bend to the front drive

of Helston Heath, one of Fitz's grooms rushed down the gravel path toward them.

"Thank God! They're here!" a footman shouted back to someone at the house. He waited for the wagon to stop in front of the door before he offered assistance to Fitz and Tabitha. They both broke apart and made for the edge of the wagon.

Fitz got out first and told the footman to have John brought inside and warmed up by the fire in the kitchens and that he was to be given a warm meal as well as a basket of food to take back with him.

"Don't let him give you any excuse. Tell him I insist on it." Then Fitz turned and grasped Tabitha by the waist and helped her down. "Let's get you inside."

"You still need to have your head looked at," she reminded him.

He touched his forehead and winced. She was right. It wasn't a deep cut, but he'd felt damned dizzy for a while after the accident. He wasn't sure if it was due to a concussion or the blood loss, but it would be good to have the doctor take a look, nonetheless.

Mr. Tracy and Fitz's grandmother hovered in the doorway, waiting for them.

"Good heavens, Fitz, what happened? And what on earth are you wearing?" As his grandmother took in the sight of him, it reminded him that he and Tabitha had left their own clothes at the Cresses' cottage. He would need to have the clothes he wore cleaned and pressed before returning them to the farmer and getting his own back in return.

His grandmother's face was pale. His disappearance had no doubt frightened her. She had lost her husband, her son, and her daughter-in-law. Fitz was all she had left of her family. He couldn't put her through something like that again. He resolved to be more careful with himself in the future.

"I was walking in the hills when I ran into Miss Sherborne, or rather she ran into me. She slipped in the mud and fell down the hill, and I'm afraid she took me along with her. My tenant, John Cress, found us. Could you have a doctor brought round to see to Miss Sherborne's ankle? It took a bit of a turn."

Tabitha spoke up. "And he needs his head examined. I struck him quite hard when I fell."

His grandmother put an arm around Tabitha's shoulders. "Good gracious! Come in and let me call your cousin to you. She's been worried sick wondering where you went. The footmen and grooms have been searching the gardens and the road for the last hour. You're soaked to the bone. We must put you to bed at once." His grandmother's anxiety was clearly showing in her panicked speech.

"Oh, please, I'm fine. Quite fi—"

"Nonsense, I insist. A warm fire and a bed with a foot warmer. That's what you need."

Tabitha shot Fitz a pleading look, but he found he liked the idea of Tabitha cuddled up and warm in bed even if he could not join her.

"My grandmother is always right. You must do as she says," he replied in his most serious tone. "Tracy, please fetch Mrs. Winslow. Then send for the doctor."

Fitz's butler left and returned shortly with Hannah and Julia. Fitz watched the other two women fuss over Tabitha, who blushed and tried to insist she was fine. It was clear that they deeply cared about Tabitha, no matter how she'd found her way into their lives. That was his only consolation for knowing he could not be the one to care for her. She had friends. *Good* friends.

"Come now. Let's get you upstairs, Miss Sherborne," his grandmother said.

Tabitha took one step, but he noticed her limp had worsened as she'd climbed the steps into his home a few minutes ago. Not wanting her to injure herself further, he stepped forward and scooped Tabitha up in his arms before she could prevent him from doing so.

Her face turned a bright red. "What are you doing?"

"Yes, Your Grace, what *are* you doing?" Julia demanded beside them.

"Miss Sherborne injured her ankle. I insist upon taking her upstairs myself so that no further injury occurs." No one could dare argue against him carrying her under such circumstances.

Julia glared suspiciously at him, and he held back a laugh of triumph at finally catching Miss Starling off guard for once.

Thankfully, Tabitha ceased her protests and allowed him to carry her. If he had but a few more chances to hold her, even like this, he didn't want to miss them. He had never believed himself to be a masochist before, but he gladly tortured himself now when it came to this woman.

TABITHA WANTED TO BURY HER FACE AGAINST FITZ'S throat, but she resisted. Barely. There were witnesses to this moment, after all, and she couldn't let anyone know how she felt about Fitz—especially not Hannah and Julia. Instead, she tried to think about what she was going to tell her friends once they were alone. They were going to question her, and she needed to figure out what she was going to tell them.

Hannah rushed ahead of them up the stairs to open

the bedchamber door while Julia stayed by Fitz's side, her hand on Tabitha's shoulder in silent support.

Hannah pulled back the coverlet on the bed. "You may put her here, Your Grace."

Fitz set her down, and for a brief instant when his back was to Hannah, Tabitha saw only Fitz's face. He was so close to her, and those eyes, so full of storms, made her heart race madly. He nuzzled her cheek as he bent to fluff the pillows behind her back. She leaned in that extra half inch, her lips now touching his . . .

Oh no . . . She shouldn't have done it. That bittersweet pang in her chest became unbearable. Why did she crave this man the way she did? Why did he affect her this way? They couldn't be more different, more *ill-suited* to each other, and yet the sweet agony of her longing to be left alone with him made her ache so deeply that it carved lines upon her soul. Before her friends could see this forbidden moment, he pulled away from her.

"I shall send the doctor once he arrives. Please send for me if there's anything else I can do, Miss Sherborne." Fitz stepped into the corridor and closed the door behind him. Julia and Hannah whirled on her the instant he was gone.

"What happened to you?" Julia asked.

"Why is Helston wearing someone else's clothes?

Why are *you* wearing someone else's clothes?" Hannah asked. "What happened to his head?"

"Did you really sprain your ankle?"

"Does anything else hurt? Why did you leave the house alone?"

Tabitha groaned. The throbbing behind her eyes grew worse amid the onslaught of questions. "Please, just let me breathe. It's been a difficult morning."

Both of her friends fell uncharacteristically silent and waited patiently for her to speak.

When she was ready, Tabitha explained what had happened during the walk, the accident, and being taken in by the tenant farmers.

Hannah and Julia exchanged worried glances.

"You're truly all right? Helston wasn't cruel to you, was he?" Hannah asked.

"No, he was quite the opposite. To be fair, he was a little concussed, but he seemed quite deeply concerned for my welfare."

"Oh . . ." Hannah cleared her throat. "Well, as he should be."

The bedchamber door opened, and Liza slipped inside.

"Oh, thank heavens you're here, Liza. We must get Tabby out of these clothes and put her to bed."

The three women quickly stripped Tabitha out of

her borrowed clothes and dressed her in a warm night-gown. Then she was tucked back in and bed warmers were placed under the sheets by her feet. It felt so wonderful to be cared for like this. It reminded her of how cozy she'd felt in the Cresses' little cottage.

I shouldn't grow used to this, she thought. Someday the gem stealing would be over and she would be facing the next step of her life, whatever that may be, and it was that uncertainty of the future that left her feeling weary and anxious. When she'd lived as a pickpocket, she'd had only her concerns of the moment, finding food, shelter, and safety. But now that she'd managed to obtain those, her mind was always focused on thinking forward to the "What then?" questions about her future. She couldn't pretend that she would always have a life like this where she was tucked into bed and cossetted by servants and cared for by a man like Fitz or even her friends like Hannah and Julia.

"Liza, could you please have those clothes I was wearing washed and pressed? They belong to a farmer's wife nearby. I want to make sure they are returned to her."

"Of course, Miss Sherborne."

"Thank you, Liza. You're wonderful." Tabitha yawned, and the maid chuckled her thanks.

It was against every instinct for Tabitha to let her

guard down and fall asleep, but she reminded herself she was safe.

"One of the two of us should go after the diamond tonight," Julia murmured to Hannah. "It is the perfect opportunity. Helston will likely be resting. No one will expect it."

Their words forced Tabitha to fight sleep, and she sat up enough to speak.

"No, let me do it," she insisted. "It must be *me*." Then she burrowed into her pillow and closed her eyes. She had to be the one to take the diamond. If she didn't do it, she might risk telling him the truth about who she really was and why she was here. Stealing from him, as terrible as it was, would keep her heart guarded against him just enough to keep her safe.

It must be me.

EVAN JOINED FITZ IN THE BILLIARD ROOM THAT evening after dinner. "I heard you had quite the day," he mused.

"I suppose I have." Fitz resisted the urge to touch the cut on his brow. A doctor had been summoned, and the man had assured him that the cut would heal quickly and that no major harm seemed to have been done to his head. Ever since he and Tabitha had returned to the house, he'd been battling a headache, which he suspected had been in part caused by the curiosity of his guests about the accident. For a duke and an unmarried woman to have been together in an accident and return to the house wearing clothing that wasn't theirs was quite the fodder for gossip. It was only his sterling reputation with unmarried ladies that kept Fitz from being compelled to offer Tabitha marriage. Every man in this room tonight knew he would never take advantage of a woman like that. Stealing that kiss from her in the drawing room and again in the hothouse . . . that had been so completely out of character for him that no one here would ever have suspected him capable of it. The gentlemen guests had been teasing him mercilessly about Tabitha and being lucky enough to be injured by such a beautiful young woman.

"Beck thought perhaps you got carried away with passion," Evan said.

"You think I would bed a woman in the middle of a rainstorm in some field?" Fitz snorted. "I like to seduce women in far more comfortable places than that, and I certainly wouldn't have injured myself."

At this, Evan grinned wickedly. "If you're not

making love in a way that sometimes risks injury, you might be going about it all wrong, old boy."

Beck, who stood opposite them as he bent to line up a shot on the baize-covered billiard table, smirked.

"Evan's not wrong, Fitz," Beck chuckled. "The best nights I've had with women have been on the wilder side."

Fitz ignored their teasing. "She didn't come down to dinner. What if she's taken ill?" he asked them. "She was cold and wet long enough to give anyone a chill."

The doctor had said Tabitha's ankle was a little swollen, but it didn't seem to pain her much. She was clearly a strong creature, but that didn't mean she couldn't catch a chill from being in wet clothes too long.

"Whatever you do, old boy, do not, *I repeat*, do not go and check on her. That is a perfectly laid parson's mousetrap," Evan warned.

"Stay here and play with us." Beck offered him a cue. "It's been more than a year since we all played billiards together, hasn't it?"

Fitz accepted the cue and curled his fingers around the wooden pole. It had been too long since he'd enjoyed an evening with his friends like this.

"Which of us is on duty tonight?" Evan whispered as Beck came around the table to join them.

"Me again," Fitz said. "You both need to focus your efforts on watching our gentlemen guests."

"Are you sure? Shouldn't you rest after knocking that hard head of yours?" Evan asked.

"If I feel I need to switch with someone, I'll have a servant wake one of you."

"Very well, but be careful, Fitz," Beck said. "If the thief is here, they have only another day or two to make their attempt."

"If they do," Fitz said as he bent and aimed at the cue ball in front of him, "we'll be ready." He snapped his cue stick forward, striking the cue ball, which cracked against a cluster of balls that burst across the table in perfect, chaotic beauty.

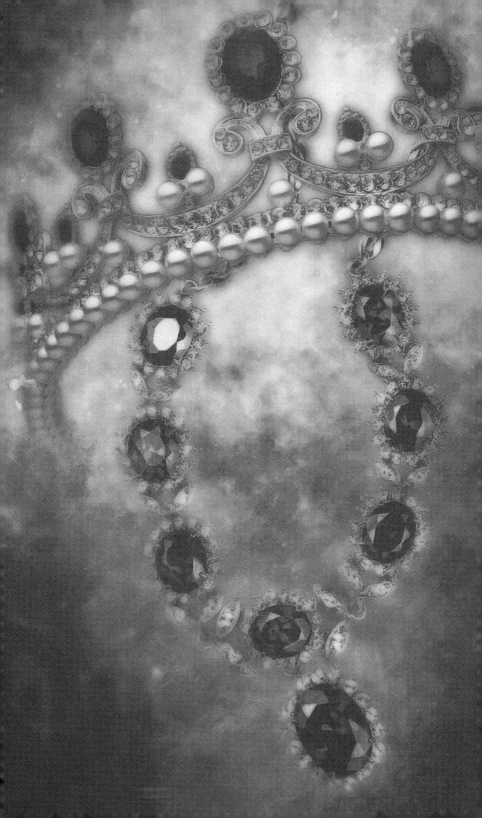

Chapter Nine

Dressed once more in her black thief's garb, Tabitha crept down the corridor to the servants' stairs. With each step her ankle twinged, but living on the streets had made her a tough creature, and she pushed past the pain.

The oil lamps in the halls gave only a dim light, and she was able to stay close to the shadows along the walls as she moved. No servants were moving about. She cleared the servants' stairs and headed straight for the rear door. As she passed by the portraits of ancient Helston ancestors, she felt their silent gazes upon her, judging her for the crime she was about to commit.

This diamond will do much more good in our hands than being worn upon someone's head, she reminded herself. She tried to bury her increasing guilt. She couldn't let it stop her this time. She had to get the diamond. Tonight.

Tabitha turned the latch of the door and stepped outside into the night, breathing a sigh of relief. So far, everything was going according to plan.

The cold night air filled her lungs and cleared her head. Above her, stars winked and glittered like diamonds on black velvet, too far out of her reach to steal. She took the same path she had used the night before to reach the study window.

She raised her head slightly, peering into the darkened room. She saw no one inside. The room was half in shadow, but the desk and part of the room was lit with moonlight, enough that she felt confident she could search the room without lighting a candle. The darkness in the deepest corners of the room gave her momentary pause, but she knew nothing was there. The guards were outside the door, not within.

Feeling more confident, she reached up and tested the window. The large glass pane swung open slowly, making no sound. She'd tucked a small grease rag into the pocket of her trousers that had oil which could be rubbed on creaky hinges, but thankfully she wouldn't need it tonight.

Pressing the window open wider, she hoisted herself up on the stone ledge and slipped her legs over the sill and inside the room. Her soft-soled black slippers made no sound as she landed with catlike grace upon the floor.

Tabitha surveyed the room, noting the large cherry-wood desk covered in letters and business ledgers, with newspapers at its center. She bent behind the desk and examined the back where Fitz would sit when he was working. There were seven drawers in the desk, three on each side and one directly in the middle. She carefully pulled each one open, her eyes taking in every bit of bright moonlight to examine the contents. A lit candle might be spotted by any servant outside in the gardens, and she couldn't risk being spotted.

She checked each drawer for a false bottom before moving to the cabinets along one wall. The desk had revealed nothing of consequence besides the usual things one would expect. Letter openers, wax seals, a few cigars and bottles of unused ink.

The rest of the room contained walls of bookshelves and one tall cabinet. Leaving the bookshelves for last, she tested the cabinet's door. It was locked, but it was of a make she had picked before. She removed a small set of hairpins, one straight and one with a bent end, and tucked them into the lock. She worked them deftly until she felt something catch against one and then twisted sharply. Then she found the next tumbler and did the same, and finally, a third. A satisfying click at the end told her the lock had turned. She tucked the pins back into her sleeve cuff and opened the cabinet door.

She grinned in triumph as she at last located a large velvet box, the perfect size to store the Helston tiara in. She opened the box and set it on the desk. Diamonds studded the surface of the impressive tiara. The stones sparkled and glinted at her. The piece was more beautiful than anything she'd ever seen in her life. Her hands trembled a little as she took in the visual poetry of these diamonds in the moonlight.

The large diamond at its center was the only thing she would be taking with her tonight. The gemstone was affixed to a silver setting that was tucked into the rest of the tiara. She neatly plucked the diamond from the setting and slipped it into her trouser pocket. She had just returned the tiara to the velvet box when she heard the sound of a pistol cocking behind her. Her stomach plummeted to her feet.

"Make one move and you're dead," a cold voice rumbled from behind her. A chill swept through her body. *It was Fitz. He was here in this room. But where?*

"Here's how we shall do this. You will put the jewel down, lift your arms, and face me."

Tabitha's breath stilled in her lungs, and her body froze. Everything she and her friends had worked for had been for nothing . . . because the man she'd grown to care about, the man she was quite certain she might be in love with, had a pistol aimed at her back.

"I said put it down and turn around," Fitz ordered.

She didn't dare speak, not when she knew her voice would betray her identity, just as his had. Protecting her identity was vital so that she could keep Hannah and Julia safe from prosecution for the thefts.

She could feel the weight of the diamond in her pocket. It was secure. If she could just reach the window, she still had a chance of escaping. The real trick would be getting into the house again safely without being seen, as Fitz would likely raise the alarm the moment she escaped. As they'd planned the previous night and would do again tonight: Julia's assignment was to keep an eye on Tabitha's chambers to give her the all-clear to return. She would no doubt be waiting with a nightgown and a robe to help Tabitha once she returned. Hannah's task was to monitor for servants and say she was in need of a glass of milk before bed if anyone spotted her in the corridors while she patrolled. It would also give Hannah the opportunity to claim she'd seen a figure running in the opposite direction of Tabitha's planned escape route if someone were to come in search of her.

It had all been so *carefully* planned between the three of them. Except for Fitz. She hadn't planned on him at all. How could someone plan for a man with burnished gold hair, stormy eyes and a voice that dripped like honey as he seduced her with the language of flowers? How could she have known that she would fall in love with her target? And how could she have been so bloody foolish to have ended up in that man's trap, as *his* prey?

"I *will* shoot you," Fitz warned in a hard voice.

She didn't doubt it. Tabitha took her chance and lunged for the window just as the crack of a pistol echoed across the room. Pain pierced her left arm, but she didn't stop moving until she reached the window. Suddenly, his arms were around her body as he tackled her to the floor. His hands tightened around her, and she had to swallow down her desire to scream. Instead, she fought, kicking hard at his shins and ramming an elbow into his stomach as she climbed to her feet.

Fitz tried to hold her, but she went limp in his arms, forcing him to drop her with a curse. She then leaned back and kicked him hard in the stomach with both her feet, sending him toppling over the back of his desk with a grunt of pain.

She almost ran to him, fearing she'd harmed him, but the need to survive kept her blood pumping and left her jumpy and panicked. She did what she had to do . . . and fled for her life.

Get out! Don't look back! her instincts screamed as she climbed out the window and ran across the garden path toward the back door closest to the servants' stairs.

By the time she slipped inside, she could already hear the faint echo of men shouting, *"Thief!"* throughout the house. She darted from shadowy alcove to shadowy alcove as she tried to reach the safety of her room. Tabitha clutched her injured arm, keeping the blood flow stanched as she stumbled the last few steps into her bedchamber.

"Oh my God!" Julia was at her side in an instant. "Tabby, what happened?"

Tabitha pulled off her black mask and drew in a deep lungful of air before she lifted her arm. Blood oozed from a deep gash along the side of her arm. The bullet had only grazed her, or so she hoped. They couldn't have a doctor look at her wound. If they did, she would be done for.

"He shot me," she gasped, still in shock.

"Come, sit by the fire. I'll find some bandages." Julia wet several cloths in a basin of clean water, then returned to her. Tabitha collapsed into the chair by the fire and winced as Julia pushed the sleeve of her blouse up to examine the wound. "Do you know who? Did they see you?"

"Fitz shot me." Tabitha closed her eyes, not wanting

to see the blood as Julia cleaned the wound. "And no, I had my mask on the whole time."

Julia nodded as she applied pressure. "I think it's only a graze, but it will take time to heal. I'll put some salve on and then bandage it. We will have to leave immediately before breakfast. We will tell everyone that you are ill after the accident on the hill and that you need to see your doctor in London at once." Julia lifted her head as she seemed to finally process what Tabitha had said. "Wait a moment . . . you said *Lord Helston* shot you? Not the footman guarding the door?"

"No, Fitz was waiting inside his study. There was a dark spot in the room, pitch black. I couldn't see him while he stood in that corner. It was a trap. He was expecting us." She reached into her pocket and pulled out the diamond, holding it up in the light. "But I still got it."

"Good God, Tabby. No diamond is worth your life! You should have left it and ran!"

"I already had it when he announced himself. And I assure you, I *did* run . . ." Tabitha sighed. "Think of all the good we shall do with it." She'd been thinking of the wounded and mentally sick veterans of the war and wanted to use Helston's diamond to care for those men. Men who'd served just as Fitz's father had. Fitz would never know the fate of his diamond, but at least it would benefit a cause she suspected would matter greatly to him. She curled her fingers around the diamond while Julia wrapped a bandage around her arm.

"We'd better get you out of these clothes and into your nightgown," Julia said.

Once Tabitha stripped out of the garments, they tossed the items onto the canopy over the top of the bed, where no one would look when searching the room. They tossed the diamond up there as well.

"We should burn the bloody cloth," Tabitha said as she handed the bloody shirt to Julia. Her friend cast the blouse into the fire, and for a moment both women watched the flames consume the fabric. It came not a moment too soon because someone knocked frantically at the door.

"Let me get it. Put your robe on and lie down on the bed," Julia urged Tabitha. "You're supposed to be feeling ill," she reminded her.

"I've been shot," Tabitha muttered. "It won't be hard to feign feeling unwell."

Julia opened the door to the bedchamber, and Hannah's face appeared.

"Helston just raised the alarm. Servants and gentlemen are searching the house for a thief. Did . . . did it happen?" she asked. Julia nodded and pulled her into the room and closed the door.

"We have a problem, Hannah." Julia nodded at Tabitha. "That beautiful bastard shot our Tabby."

"What?" Hannah gasped.

"I'm all right," Tabitha insisted. "It's only a light graze . . . I think. Hannah, we have the diamond, but we will have to leave first thing in the morning."

"Yes," Hannah said, a bit calmer now. "Yes, of course. Where's the diamond?"

Tabitha pointed a finger at the canopy of brocade fabric hanging over her head.

"Good. Leave it there until we are ready to go. Then someone will tuck it in their hair and pin it in place before we depart. No one will dare search our hair."

Tabitha sank back into the bed. "You should both return to your rooms. We should not be seen together until tomorrow morning."

"She's right," Julia said. "But, Tabby, if your arm gets worse, you must get one of us immediately."

"I will," she promised.

After her friends departed, she lay back in the bed and let out a deep sigh. She had done it. She'd taken Fitz's diamond, and he'd shot her like some common thief . . . which she was. She could have been killed, but that didn't erase the guilt she felt at having kicked him so hard or having stolen the gem. Whatever had been slowly growing between them, that delicate flower blooming in the hothouse of their hearts . . . had withered away from an unexpected frost. And that loss hurt her more than the bullet that had struck her arm.

Remember all the people it will help. It isn't as though you could have the duke and his diamond. This is no child's fairy tale.

Fitz held the candle up to shed light on the windowsill of his study. Crimson drops dotted the bottom of the sill, and a faint smear of blood shimmered in the light where the thief had brushed his arm on the window frame as he'd climbed out of the study.

Evan peered at the blood. "What did the fellow look like? Big chap or small?"

"Smaller than me," Fitz said. "But that won't help much. Most men are."

Aside from himself and his two friends, a few of the male guests had volunteered to help search the house for the thief. He'd carefully checked them over for signs of injury, of course, just to make sure the thief hadn't been clever enough to come back and pretend to offer assistance. But the guests who'd come down to help him had all been cleared of suspicion.

"You certainly winged the fellow," Beck said as he

joined them. "I don't think he will die, but he will be showing an injury. That gives us something to work with."

"I was only trying to slow him down. I tried to aim for the man's leg. It would have been a better target, but I lost my balance during the struggle and my aim was off. Have Tracy fetch our brightest lanterns. I want to follow the blood trail through the garden, see where it leads."

At Fitz's direction, everyone began a careful sweep of the estate grounds, but the blood trail halted only a dozen feet away from the study window. The man must have covered the wound to stop the bleeding, and it had effectively terminated any easy trail to follow.

Fitz glowered into the darkness of the gardens.

"Search the house. Every room, servants and guests," Fitz ordered.

"Well, not *every* room, surely," Evan laughed. "We ought to let the ladies sleep."

"No, even their chambers. It's entirely possible the thief has hidden himself in a room while a lady lies sleeping."

Fitz and the servants he trusted divided up to cover the entire house. He slipped his pistol into a holster that he secured at his hip and began knocking upon doors. Each time he woke one of his guests, he explained the situation and made a quick search of their room. Thankfully, only a handful had heard the gunshot. The house was large enough, and given the chill, most windows were shut. Good stonework and English oak muffled most sounds in the house.

When Fitz reached Julia and Hannah's rooms, they waited imperiously for him to finish his search, silently chiding him for disturbing their sleep. Then he moved on to Tabitha's chamber. She didn't come to the door when he knocked at first. He tried the handle next, and it opened beneath his touch.

She was fast asleep in bed, the fire in the hearth burning low, but an oil lamp was still lit by her bed. Fitz hated to wake her. She was so beautiful as she slept. Her hair was a rich tumble of dark waves across her pillow. In the dim light, her face looked as smooth as alabaster, with a hint of rose in her cheeks.

Finally, he summoned his nerve to disturb her peace and placed a gentle palm on her shoulder as he whispered her name.

"Tabitha?"

She stirred and her dark lashes fluttered as she yawned. "What is it, Liza? Oh!" She tensed when she realized it was *him* and not her maid who had woken her. "Fitz? What's the matter? Why are you here?" She sat up in bed and pulled the coverlet up around her chest.

"I'm afraid I must search your room," he said.

"My room? Why?" She brushed her hair back from her face so that it fell in tumbling waves over her shoulders.

Lord, he wanted to touch her hair, to brush his fingers through the silken strands. But he couldn't. To touch her was to always want more. He'd never get enough of touching her. And right now, he had to focus.

"We have a thief in the house. They've stolen my grandmother's diamond from her tiara, and we're searching the house."

"And you think it was me?" Tabitha asked quietly, her face hardening a little.

He almost laughed, but she looked so serious that he didn't. "No, of course not. The thief was injured when I struggled with him, and he escaped. We have searched the grounds and found no one outside. It's our belief that the man snuck back into the house, so we are searching every room."

The tension bracketing her eyes and mouth eased. "Oh . . ."

"You may stay in bed while I search." He cleared his throat and turned away from her to check her suite of rooms, the tall armoire, and even under her bed.

"Good gracious. You don't really think he's under there with all those balls of dust?" Tabitha asked.

He was on his knees, peering under the bed frame, and he glanced up at her question. She was hovering on the edge of her bed, looking down at him, a bemused look upon her face. She was beautiful. Yes, he had seen prettier women—prettier to a sculptor or painter. But what made Tabitha irresistible was the animation of her face and body, the way her soul shone so brightly from her eyes that it made her infinitely more lovely than any other woman of his acquaintance. There would never be a moment where he would not want to watch her.

"Fitz?" She spoke his name as he let the bed skirt drop back down. He halted in his motions as he noticed a drop of red on the sleeve of her nightgown.

"Tabitha, are you hurt?" He got to his feet, certain it was blood that he was seeing on her nightgown.

"What? No—" She tried to draw her blankets up over her body, but Fitz caught them in his iron grip and prevented her from moving them.

A faint ringing started in his ears as he reached for her arm with his other hand.

"No, Fitz, don't!" She tried to scramble back from him, but he leaned forward, catching her by the collar of her high-necked nightgown. He released the bedcovers and grasped the elbow of her left arm, gentle but firm, as he stared at the darkening red spot. He slowly lifted his gaze to her face, his body cold as he spoke.

"Open your nightgown. I want to see your arm."

Tabitha shook her head in defiance, and he slid his hand up her elbow. When she flinched, he let go. The spot of blood grew slightly on the sleeve of her nightgown.

"It was you . . . ," he said, still not wanting to believe what his eyes were telling him. This was not a truth he wanted. "I . . . shot you . . ."

He stumbled a little on the words, horrified by his actions. He'd shot a woman. He reached for Tabitha, his instincts demanding that he hold her safe in his arms and be sure that she wasn't gravely injured because of his foolish actions. But a moment later the heavy truth of her betrayal struck him like a blow.

She met his gaze with fire and pain.

"*You* took the diamond . . ." He could barely breathe, his chest was too tight. "*Why?*" None of this made any sense. How could Tabitha be the thief?

For a long moment he feared she wouldn't say anything. But at last, she spoke.

"I'm *sorry*." Her words startled him.

"Did you need money?" he asked, his tone quiet. But his mind was shouting with rage at her betrayal. He had opened his soul to this . . . *thief*. She had just tried to steal his diamond and in the process had betrayed his trust.

She cradled her arm and pulled away from him a little. "It's more complicated than that."

"Madam, you would be surprised at how very *un*complicated matters of a financial nature can be. You either needed the money or you did not." He braced one hand on the bedpost at the foot of the bed and kept his back to her. He was furious with her. So much so that he couldn't bear to look at her.

"I can't believe you are the Merry Robin thief." He stared unseeing at the flames in the hearth.

"If I admit to it, will you send for the investigators at Scotland Yard?" Tabitha's voice held a hard edge that infuriated him. *He* was the only one with any right to be angry, not her. He spun to face her, ready to tell her that he would contact the Yard at once. But the second their eyes met, he saw her fear. She thought he would hurt her. And that realization knifed through him. He wouldn't . . . *couldn't* hurt her.

He drew in a deep breath, his hands shaking as he tried to calm the rushing chaos of his thoughts.

"I should . . . but I won't. Lord knows why, but I can't do that to you. I could never hurt you."

She relaxed a little at his words, and he didn't miss the relieved exhale of her breath. He would keep his promise. He wouldn't do anything to cause her pain, but he had to understand *why* she'd done what she'd done . . . and why she'd done it to *him*. After everything they'd shared, the betrayal he felt was so profound, an ever-deepening black pool that threatened to drown him.

"But I *will* have answers from you." He was not going to let her get away from his questions. "Where's the diamond?"

She pointed above her head to the canopy.

"Tell me you're joking."

She shook her head. With a low curse, Fitz climbed up on the bed and punched the fabric from beneath with his fist, and something bright glittered as it fell to the floor by the bed. They both stared at it for a long moment. Then he got down onto the floor and retrieved it. Fitz curled his fingers around the stone. It was fake, but she didn't seem to know that yet. He almost gave it back to her. It would serve her right to try to fence a bit of glass.

"You should have asked me for the money you needed," he said as he closed his eyes. "I would have given it to you without a moment's thought." The chasm widening in his chest made it damned hard to breathe.

"You still don't understand," she replied.

Fitz opened his eyes. "Then *make* me understand. Tell me, what would drive a lady to steal?"

"That's just it, Fitz. As I told you before, I'm no lady. I'm a pickpocket. My father died and I had no one. A gang of female thieves took me in and taught me how to survive."

He snorted harshly. "Those other Merry Robins, I presume?"

"No!" she snapped. "I work alone. I only left those notes to suggest there was more than one of me to confuse the authorities."

"And how did you meet Hannah and Julia? I already knew you weren't actually cousins with Hannah."

"We aren't related," she admitted. "I tried to steal Hannah's necklace. That's how we met. She felt pity for me and let me come home with her. I think she sees me as some sort of charity project. She introduced me to Julia as a friend in need. Neither of them knows about any of this." Her pleading look dug into his heart, and he assured her with a stiff nod.

"So you steal to afford your life as Hannah's companion?" He had known many gentle-born ladies to become companions as an occupation when met with financial difficulties.

"No. I use the money from selling those jewels to

help those who need it. Orphans, widows, wounded war veterans, the elderly. The money goes to charities."

Had anyone else fed him such a story, he would have called for a constable at once, but he actually believed her. From the moment he had met Tabitha, she'd spoken of the needs of others. She couldn't have known then that he would catch her stealing his diamond, so she wouldn't have thought to lie that early on when they'd first met. He stared down at the glass diamond in his hand and then tossed it into the fire.

"Oh no!" she cried out softly from behind him in surprise. When he turned to face her, he saw that more of her sleeve was dark red now. More blood was seeping through whatever bandage she had made.

"It wasn't real," he said, nodding his head at the paste jewel. "The real diamond is somewhere safe." He approached the bed, and she shrank back from him. He halted as, a fresh flash of pain in his chest making him wince. She still didn't trust him.

"I would *never* hurt you," he whispered. "You must know that."

"Do I?" she countered.

"Tabitha . . . From the moment we met, I've been my truest self with you." He held out a hand. "Please, let me look at your arm. The bleeding is growing worse."

He couldn't deny the small but very strong sense of

216

relief he felt when she crawled to the edge of the bed and let her legs drop off the side.

"You'll have to unbutton your nightgown to let me see," he said gently.

With trembling hands, she undid the row of buttons down to the tops of her breasts and peeled the nightgown off her shoulder before carefully sliding her arm from her sleeve. He saw the makeshift bandage and cursed. It was soaked through. She must have reopened the wound when he'd woken her up.

She apparently seemed to notice what he had. "It wasn't so bad before. I think the wound has reopened."

"Christ . . . I can't believe this has happened. How bad is the wound?"

"I think it's only a graze. I didn't have time to make the bandage tight enough."

This was his fault. He had hurt her, though he hadn't known it was her. He never would have fired if he'd known it was a woman. He'd thought he was aiming at a man.

"Let me take a look." He reached for the wrapping around her arm. "But if I don't like the look of it, I am sending for the doctor."

"Please, Fitz, you can't—"

"That is for me to decide. I will not have you die of an infected wound that I've caused in my house." He unwound the wrapping until he got a better look. He breathed a sigh of relief. The bullet had only sliced the edge of her arm, not even reaching the muscle. However, the blood was thick, and although it was clotting, it still was bleeding in places. He fixed Tabitha with a glare.

"Do not move. I must retrieve some supplies and I will be back. Lock the door behind me. Men are still searching the house for the thief, and I cannot let them know you've been found."

He exited the bedchamber, his mind racing as he headed for his butler's office belowstairs. Mr. Tracy kept a medical bag behind his desk to handle minor cuts and scrapes that the staff might acquire during the course of their duties. Fitz prayed that his tending to the wound would be enough. The sight of her blood had not only turned his stomach—it had fractured his heart.

His Tabitha was the most infamous thief in London . . . and he'd nearly killed her.

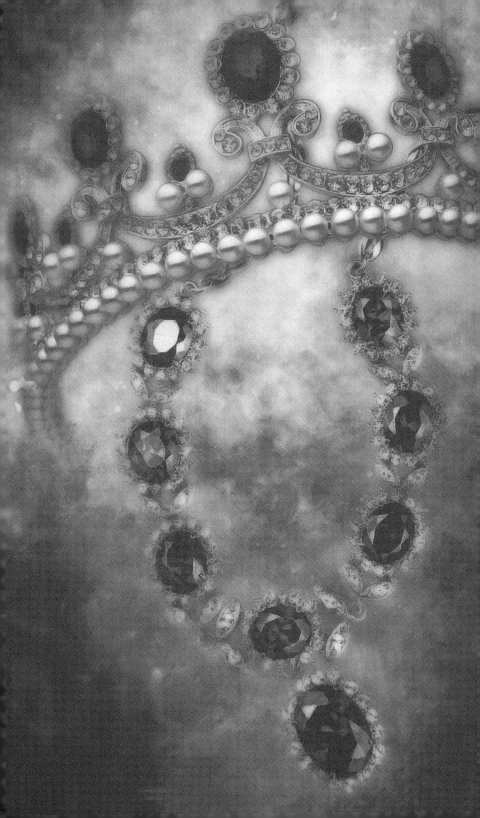

Chapter Ten

Tabitha paced the room and tried not to think about what would happen when he stepped back through the door. He'd said he wouldn't turn her over to the authorities, but she doubted he would just let her resume her thieving, no matter how noble the cause might be. What if he forced her to reveal Hannah and Julia's involvement or tried to extract something from her in return for his silence? What if he spread word to his friends to keep her from being invited to any other engagements that she, Hannah, and Julia would need access in order to steal more jewels? The house of cards they'd built was on the verge of collapse—all Fitz had to do was breathe a word against her.

She truly didn't know what Fitz was capable of, and yet, as she ran through each possibility of what he might do, she just couldn't believe he would blackmail her into anything, nor did she think he would intentionally do anything to hurt Julia or Hannah. He was far too much of a gentleman to treat true ladies like criminals. But whatever he did do could have unintended consequences that could send the cards toppling all around them. Hannah and Julia could be tainted by association and would be forced to choose her or their own social lives, and she knew which they would pick, which meant she would need to leave them to save them.

Tabitha would be back on the streets again and with a scandal hanging over her head employment at a shop would likely be impossible. Shopkeepers would not want women working for them who would drive customers away. Fitz could act with the best of intentions and still doom them all . . .

But all these worries paled against the twist she felt in her belly each time she recalled the moment Fitz realized *she* was the thief. That would leave a shadow in her heart for the rest of her life. She'd wrecked something beautiful between them, something she'd never dreamed of having. And it was gone forever because she'd taken that bloody diamond.

Too weary to pace any further, she settled herself down in a chair to await her doom. She ignored the throb of pain in her arm from the graze of Fitz's bullet as she watched the flames attempt to burn the diamond. The *fake* diamond. She had risked her life for a bit of glass. She'd destroyed the golden memories she had made with Fitz, destroyed her future, for nothing. She'd ruined everything except Hannah and Julia's lives, and even they were not yet safe.

Their involvement was a secret for now, but someone could put the pieces together if they examined Tabitha's whereabouts during each theft. Tabitha had to make certain that Fitz would not only let her go but would also agree that he would never tell anyone what she had done, not even his friends. And in order to do that, she knew he would likely exact a promise from her that she would never set foot in polite society again so that she might not be tempted to steal from those around her. If only he knew she had no compulsion to steal, no desire to take anything from anyone else, but did it only because it was necessary. But such an argument would likely fall on deaf ears. So she would have to agree to whatever terms he set forth to keep his silence. It would be the only way she could be certain she could protect her friends.

Someone knocked on the door. She padded across the carpets to open it up. Fitz's face, still shadowed by quiet anger, appeared in the space between the door and the frame.

"You may let me in. The corridor is empty."

She stepped back, and he quickly entered before he closed and locked the door behind him. He held a small black leather satchel under one arm.

"I have called off the search in the house. Everyone is returning to their beds." He set the bag down at the foot of the bed and opened the silver clasps at the top before digging around in the contents.

"Fitz," she said, breathing his name.

He stilled at that. "Helston or Your Grace, if you please. Only my *friends* may call me Fitz."

The words, though softly spoken, were delivered so formally that it felt like a slap across her face.

"Come here," he commanded and pointed to the bed.

Tabitha obeyed and eased onto the edge of the bed beside the satchel. She freed her arm from her nightgown and allowed him to use a bottle of clear alcohol to wipe the blood away from the gash in her flesh. He then dabbed the cotton cloth over the wound itself. It burned viciously, but the only sound she allowed herself to make was a soft hiss.

Fitz's lowered brows and silent glare softened slightly, but he said nothing as he continued to clean her wound.

"I don't keep the jewels," she whispered softly. Her words seemed to startle him, and he glanced at her.

"I don't," she insisted. "It's as I told you before. They are sold, and nearly all of the proceeds are then given to charities that we are acquainted with."

"*Nearly* all? What, pray tell, do you do with the rest of the proceeds? Is that where your lavish gowns come from?" His words were sharp, but she deserved the sting of them and didn't shy away.

"No, the gowns are from Hannah. You know what sort of person she is. She is all heart. She insists that I have fine gowns, but I always try to stop her. I wanted to wear nothing but dull colors and fade into the background, but she refused to let me."

"I doubt you could ever fade into the background," he murmured.

She blinked and glanced away from him for a brief moment. "Oh, but I do, quite easily. It's possible you've passed me upon the street. I would have worn old clothes, my hair up in a knot and covered by a boy's cap to guard against the cold. I would have been covered in dust from the carriages, my palms calloused and dirty. I would have begged a man like you for a bit of coin to fill my belly." She let out a breath. "And you, like every other man, would have kept on walking, your head high, your cane ready to strike if I drew too close to your perfect world."

His fingers curled around her elbow, the hold firm, but he didn't hurt her. He gazed at her a long moment.

"I would have seen you," he promised. "I would have, I know it."

Their gazes held, and she felt her heart shattering and reforming and shattering all over again.

"But would you have seen my sisters of the streets? Or the children starving as they sell you fading blooms? Would you see the men who've lost limbs in war as they gaze unseeing at the stone walls of the alleyways? Those men who served alongside your father, those men who saw friends and brothers die . . . Why haven't you lifted a hand to help them? They gave up their lives, their homes, their families . . . their very futures for this country, and you treat them as though they do not exist."

She'd gone too far, but she only wanted him to see what she'd seen, to understand that her mission was beyond the selfish need to care for her own person.

Fitz was quiet as he finished cleaning her wound.

"You give the money to these charities—how does that work? How can you be sure the funds are put to good use?"

"Because I've seen the results for myself. Your friend, Lord Brightstone, I stole the diamond earbobs off his cousin . . . and when I resold them, the money paid for more than twenty children to have new clothes—not simply new clothes, but two sets of clothing, one for winter and one for summer. Some of the children at the orphanage had never owned a pair of shoes in their lives. Do you know what that means? When the snow and ice cover the roads, these children can walk without fear of frostbite and losing toes. It changes their lives . . . and the woman I took those earrings from has only suffered a pang of pricked pride."

"Did you ever walk in the snow without shoes?" he asked quietly.

"Once, my second winter being alone. One of the girls, one of my friends, she stole a fine bracelet and sold it, bought me shoes she took all of us girls buy sweet cakes. I was so grateful to her that I gave her my cake . . ."

"Christ, that's one of the girls you mentioned who perished from the adulterated food, isn't it?"

She nodded mutely, the old memories still too raw to get too close to.

"And my diamond? What could you do with it?" he asked.

"A great many things . . . I planned to use it to help a woman who owns a boarding house. She takes in wounded veterans and gives them food and shelter. I wanted to help her. She has so many mouths to feed and so little to live on since many of the men can't find work. Not everyone could go home to a dukedom like your father."

"Yes, he was a lucky one, yet he still shot himself when the nightmares and memories became too much for him." Fitz's words were gruff with emotion, and she ached to put her arms around his neck and hold him so that he didn't have to mourn his father alone. But she didn't dare touch him. She had no right to any intimacy with this man, not after breaking his trust.

Fitz dipped the tip of his finger in a pot of salve that smelled faintly of eucalyptus and rubbed it along the injury. After that, he carefully patted the wound with a cloth and wrapped it snug with some bandages.

"Is that too tight? There should be some pressure to restrict the wound from bleeding, but I don't wish to cut the flow of blood off to the rest of your arm." His voice was gruff, but there was no ignoring the tenderness she heard in each word as he focused on caring for her. It tugged at her heart to see his hands tremble as he tended to her wound.

"It feels fine," she replied. For a moment, their gazes connected. His eyes, usually so stormy, were dark and fathomless now, still as a windless sea. She could read nothing in their glass-like depths. He had shuttered the windows to his soul, blocking her view. It was a fresh stab to her heart to lose that ability she once had to read him and see his feelings. He hadn't acted that way with anyone else. She'd been the only one he'd let his guard down with, and she'd repaid him with betrayal.

"I'm finished. You may . . . er . . . dress." His gaze flicked along the skin of her arm and shoulder that had been exposed these last few minutes. For a moment, she saw that heat and desire that so called to her own. A low heat pulled in her belly, and that inescapable desire for this man flared to life again. Even after all that had happened, she still wanted him with a hopeless, ardent longing.

As she reached up to adjust her arm and slip it back into her nightgown, he blinked and turned his back to her.

He put his tools away and tossed the bloody rags into the fire. Then he closed the medical bag and started for the door. A chill grew between them once more, so frosty that she expected snow to start falling from the ceiling above them. There was a finality to his manner that filled her with a panic that she'd never known before.

"Helston." Her voice was pitched higher with desperation at the thought of truly losing him. He halted. He didn't turn, but his tall, powerful frame went rigid, as though he'd stopped breathing.

She summoned her courage. "You said you were your truest self with me. Despite what you learned of me tonight, I swear on my word—whatever it may be worth—that I was my truest self with you as well."

The tightness in his shoulders and neck seemed to make his body vibrate.

She waited a heartbeat before continuing. "I learned early in my life to hide myself. I had to. Only by hiding could I protect myself. But you . . ." She struggled for the right words. "You made me forget to hide. You made me feel like the woman I should have been . . . had I not lost so much so early in my life." It pained her to speak these words, but this was a moment where the truth mattered more than life itself.

Still he didn't move, didn't even so much as twitch or shift his weight. He was as still as stone. But she held out hope, because he hadn't left.

"I'm not mad . . . am I? To believe that there was something between us . . . something wonderful?" She shook her head, smiling bitterly. "Whatever it was . . . I know I have ruined it forever. I would give anything to go back and never steal the diamond and just stay the night in your arms in the hothouse and speak in the language of flowers until dawn. I wish I had that memory of *being* with you to take with me when I leave."

She held her breath, knowing how foolish it was to open herself up to him like this. But among all the other regrets she would carry away this day, speaking these words would not be among them.

"I would have given everything to you in that moment . . . Fitz. Everything that I am would have been yours." Her mind, her body, her heart . . . even her soul would have forever belonged to him, had he only continued to kiss her with the flowers blooming around them in that endless night.

Fitz let the medical bag fall to the floor, and he slowly turned, his hands at his sides fisting as though he wasn't sure what to do with them. His handsome face was a stream of emotions, ranging from anger to sorrow. It was a long moment before he spoke.

"I wish I had that too . . . because I can't wipe the memory of your lips from my mind, no matter how hard I try. You were a light in the darkness that I never expected to see. You have carved yourself into my bones, and I *cannot* get you out." His voice, so gruff with pain, made her eyes burn with tears. "And I do not know if I want to."

She knew then . . . this change in her heart, this feeling of breaking apart so completely that she'd never feel whole again unless she was in his arms. She stifled a sob, and he looked heavenward, his face so beautiful, so haunted, so pained. It was as if he was standing upon a cliff of his own control, teetering at its edge.

"I'm damned to want you so fiercely now—even knowing what you are."

What you are . . . How harsh, how utterly wounding those words were. Yet he was right. She was a thief. A liar. But she also cared about him.

She rubbed her forearms, trying to warm herself from the sudden chill inside her chest. That burning intensity that filled his eyes hadn't faded, and it was the singular flash of hope she needed. She had one last chance to know him, to feel like the future she'd secretly craved with him was possible, even if for just one night.

"One night," she whispered. "Give me one night of you . . . of your touch, your kiss. *Please.* I'd sell my soul if the devil would take it, just to know what it means to be loved by you." In her life, she had begged for food, for shelter, for safety. This was the first time she had ever begged for love, and she was certain that if he rejected her, she wouldn't survive.

He stared at her a long moment, unmoving. Then the tension bled out of him as he took a single step toward her. The move was so decisive that she caught her breath in her throat. She slid off the bed, coming toward him. They met in the center of the room, and his hands rose, one coming to rest on her hip and the other cupping her face. The hold was possessive yet so completely tender that Tabitha trembled in his arms. She leaned into his touch and briefly closed her eyes.

"One night," he agreed. "Just one."

She nodded, relief washing over her. It was not the end between them, not yet.

"Lift your arms," he ordered.

She hastened to obey, raising her arms in the tight space between their bodies. His hands left her hips to clutch the folds of her nightgown. It came off over her head with little resistance, and he let it drop to the floor at her feet. She lifted her gaze to his, the heat there sealing their bittersweet bargain in the darkness. His eyes swept over her, and she wondered what he saw. Her skin told the story of a life lived hard—faint scars from her past and fresh bruises from tonight's struggle.

"I'm sorry. I didn't know . . . I thought you were—" He swallowed hard, his Adam's apple bobbing as he bit his bottom lip.

"You thought I was a man," she said, finishing his thought. "It's all right, Fitz, please don't think of it. Not tonight." She'd said his given name without thinking, but he didn't correct her. For this night only, he would be Fitz.

He trailed the backs of his fingers over her throat, her collarbone, and down to her breasts, teasing one of her nipples into a taut peak. His touch felt exquisite. Wanting to give him the same glorious pleasure and sense of connection, she touched him in return, tracing the line of his jaw, feeling the prickle of his beard growing in, the delicate shells of his ears. He turned his face, allowing her to explore him as he explored her. There was something so wonderful, so intimate about being allowed to touch him like this. To be close and to know that she could kiss him, and glide her hands over his form.

She'd seen so little of Joseph's body when they'd come together long ago. Now she wanted to see Fitz with an almost violent desperation. She tugged at the buttons of his waistcoat and then peeled it away from him before pulling his shirt free of his trousers. He stopped touching her body only long enough to remove his shirt and boots. Then he pulled her against him. Her breasts rubbed against his chest, teasing her so much that she moaned. A faint smattering of dark-gold hair on his upper pectoral muscles was soft beneath her fingers as she placed her hand on his chest to feel his heartbeat. She leaned in and kissed his skin, which made him shudder and tighten his hold on her.

"Why does everything feel a thousand times more intense with you?" he asked, his voice full of wonder.

She had no answers to give. All she knew was that if she did not claim his body tonight and let him claim hers, something they both needed would be lost to them. This was her only moment to be with Fitz, and she would not lose this memory for as long as she lived.

He dug his hands into her hair, his fingers finding the last few stray pins she had missed, and he spread her hair out in a waterfall.

His hand dove inside that hair, and he tilted her head up to seal his mouth over hers. She abandoned herself to the sweetness of his mouth, the coaxing, the gentleness, as it turned deeper, harder, more desperate. He flicked his tongue between her lips, and she groaned as his free hand gripped her bottom in an almost punishing hold. That hint of pain only heightened the intensity between them.

"Dawn will be here in a few hours," he whispered before kissing her again. "I *need* you."

She felt his unspoken warning. He would leave the mark of his passion upon her soul so that any man who dared to come after would never own her, would never fully possess her. There would always be some part of her that was forever his.

"Yes," she begged, her eyes blurring with tears. She

wanted that too, to know that he would carry a part of her with him, even though they would never come together like this again. At least tonight they would have parts of each other deep within the wells of their hearts.

He brushed away her tears with his thumbs, his gaze softening as he kissed the shining tracks of tears upon her cheeks. His mouth covered hers again as he lifted her up onto the bed and laid her flat beneath him. He kissed a path from her mouth down to her breasts, sucking hungrily on each tip, making her cry out at the exquisite feeling. She dug her hands into his hair, urging him not to stop.

The connection between them grew as he lavished kisses upon her skin. She whimpered as he released the tip of her breast, and then, to her delight and relief, he took the other nipple between his lips next. Her body arched upward, trying to rub against him, seeking that need that was too powerful to name. The need to join her body and soul with this man was overwhelming. This throbbing, pulsing, pounding need to surrender to her own desires and his.

He slid lower, his mouth kissing her hips, then the thatch of dark curls between her thighs, and finally he was grasping her knees and widening them. Part of her wanted to hide herself, but she was driven by a need so ancient that modern modesty lost its battle.

"Keep your legs open," he growled as he settled at the foot of the bed and pressed his lips to her inner thighs. "Trust me, Tabitha." She trembled as he breathed warm air upon her exposed feminine core. "Trust me to never hurt you."

Then his lips and tongue danced in wild, lazy patterns in the most sensitive part of her flesh.

It was almost too much to bear, both frightening and wonderful in equal measure. She felt as though she could reach the sky and stir up new galaxies with her fingertips as she collected stars like precious gems. A burst of brilliant light behind her closed eyes overwhelmed her, and she surrendered to the explosion of pleasure that followed between her thighs as he explored her with his mouth. Every muscle, once tense with fear and anxiety, was now so relaxed that she didn't want to move ever again.

She opened her eyes as the bed shifted slightly. She felt the heat of his body as he moved over her. He had tossed his trousers away. She hadn't seen him remove them, but she'd also been blissfully unaware of anything but pleasure for the last few minutes.

Tabitha tried to sit up and look at him but collapsed back upon the bed.

"Be careful with your arm," Fitz murmured with compassion as he settled between her thighs.

"It's all right. It doesn't hurt just now." He'd given her so much pleasure in the last few minutes that she doubted she'd ever feel pain again.

He was so much larger than she was, so packed with muscle, and yet she cradled him with her body. She felt an ancient feminine strength flare within her. She was made to hold this man, to touch him and love him, just as he was made to touch and love her. Her heart stuttered as she sensed that in another life, this man could have been her husband, her other half. Yet in *this* life, it could never be. Tonight was all they would have. A stolen moment, one gone too soon.

His eyes searched her face as if he seemed to sense her sorrowful realization. Tabitha cupped his cheek with one hand while her other curled around the back of his neck. She pulled his head down to hers.

"In all my life," he began, his words drifting over her lips between kisses, "there has never been anyone like you . . ." A hint of terrible longing and desperation laced the meeting of their mouths. Like a fire burning late in the dark autumn months, defying the coming snow.

She lifted her hips, seeking him, and he moved above her, guiding himself into her. Then he filled her, creating a connection that stretched into an infinite amount of space, beyond rational thoughts and words.

She dug her fingers into him, pulling him deeper,

urging him to move and let them both feel alive. There would be no moment beyond this. No diamonds, no guilt, no struggle. Only that unimaginable peace that came with discovering something *perfect*. She was a butterfly slowly crawling out of its chrysalis. Her wings were wet and new and oh so bright. Now she lay upon the ground of her soul and breathed for the first time, waiting for the moment when she could fly.

Fitz murmured soft, wonderful things, his lips teasing her ear and making her laugh breathlessly in the dark as he made love to her. The joy of their joining was stronger knowing they would soon part.

Their fingers laced together as he pinned her hands to the bed on either side of her head. Their gazes held as he drove into her urgently, the soft sounds of their bodies meeting and the panting breaths surrounding them in an exquisite sphere of their own making. Sweat dewed upon their bodies and Fitz's skin shimmered as he moved above her, moved in her. He truly was the most handsome man she'd ever seen as he opened himself to her, letting her see his soul in his eyes once more.

"Tell me no other man shall own your soul," he demanded, his breath hard in the dark. He drove into her, the exquisite pleasure of him sinking deep making her cry his name.

"*Tell me,*" he said again.

"No one," she gasped. "No one but you."

Her reply seemed to set him on fire as he claimed her, his roughness the only hint that his passion and possession of her had given him what he needed. She exploded with pleasure beneath him, her body straining as she reached that bursting star horizon.

"You're mine, Tabitha," he said as he slammed his hips against hers one last time. He braced himself above her, but his large shoulders trembled as he released their laced hands. She moved to embrace him. Her palms slid over his burning skin and her knees hugged his lean, muscled hips, locking them together so he could not withdraw from her body.

Fitz pressed soft, lingering kisses to her cheeks, her closed eyelids, her forehead, and then her lips. They struggled for breath as they drifted down from their lovemaking like downy feathers weaving through a lazy sunbeam.

They listened to the fire popping and cracking in the hearth. Bit by bit, an awareness of the rest of the world around them came back to her. She knew that she needed to hear the words spoken before she lost her chance.

"Tell me you're *mine*, Fitz."

He lifted his head to stare down at her. For a

moment she feared he would deny her claim on him, but his eyes softened as they always seemed to do whenever he looked at her, and the world spun wildly around her as he spoke the words she would replay over and over for the rest of her life.

"There shall never be another for me but you," he said. "*Never.*"

Never was such a permanent word, but she saw the truth in his eyes. If he married someday and produced an heir with another woman, it wouldn't matter. He would love no other but her. And she would love no other but him.

They lay in silence, neither wanting to speak. Words would only bring the end closer now. She could not bear the dawn, not anymore.

FITZ COULD TELL THE MOMENT SHE FELL SLEEP. And now, feeling her surrender to exhaustion and knowing their lovemaking was over . . . a slow, bitter ache grew inside him. He was losing her now, moment by moment, because he would have to leave this bed and leave her and return to his life . . . without her.

His chest tightened as he struggled to resist the need to wake her, and make love to her again, and deny the night its right to end. He burrowed beneath the bedsheets and pulled her into his arms, kissing the crown of her hair. No one would ever know about this. About a duke falling in love with a common thief.

No, she was not common—she was *exceptional*. She'd stolen a diamond under cover of darkness and fought him as valiantly as any man to evade capture. If he hadn't come to check on her tonight, he never would have known she was the thief. He also never would have known what her real life had been like before they'd met. The vague stories she'd told him were filtered enough for him to have remained ignorant of the truth if he'd chosen to. But now he knew what she'd endured, what strength she needed to overcome her circumstances and still have a heart open enough to fight for others who needed help.

In another life, she might have been a saint, such was the goodness that came from her actions. And he, the man with all the means in the world to change things for others, hadn't. But he could change. He could give her the diamond and let her do what she could to help others. It would give him a small measure of peace to let the gem go under such circumstances. It eased the shame he'd felt over knowing he'd failed to see what he could have done all these years to help others.

He stroked his fingers over Tabitha's cheekbones

and nose, then played with the tendrils of her hair that curled into dark wisps near her ears. There were so many delightful little things about Tabitha that enchanted him. It broke his heart to think that he would never have the chance to learn everything about her, to have the intimacy that a lover, a husband, might as they grew old. Too much had passed between them, too much pain and heartache that he could not see any other path but one that led away from her.

He checked the bandage on her arm, wanting to make sure the bleeding hadn't started up again.

A wiser, saner man would not have taken a woman while she was so injured. But when Tabitha was near, he was anything but wise, and this had been their one and only opportunity. She'd said she wanted him, and he couldn't deny them what they both needed.

As the pale-pink hue of the coming morning filtered through the curtains, he knew he had made his decision about their future. With great reluctance, he slipped out of bed and dressed. Then he tucked the sheets up around Tabitha.

He'd come to the decision that he didn't want his grandmother's diamond anymore, so while Tabitha was sleeping, he went to his study to remove it from its hiding spot. When he returned to Tabitha's room, he stared at the diamond in his palm, weighing it and thinking about what Tabitha had said, how this gem could help men who'd fought alongside his father. Men who hadn't had dukedoms and money to come home to. Men who'd given up their futures so that he and Tabitha and all the rest would never know what it would mean to see war upon English shores. These were men with honor, yet they'd been denied even a humble life. Their lives were taken from them and they lived as ghosts upon the streets.

Tabitha had been right. He hadn't seen them, those dust-covered faces and pleading hands held out, needing a bit of love, a bit of care from their fellow humans. He had walked past, determined to make his appointments, and he'd had no care for the souls who needed him.

He couldn't keep the diamond because whenever he looked at it, it would remind him of tonight, of Tabitha's betrayal and the night they'd shared that he could never experience again.

The diamond had become a manifestation of Tabitha's presence in his soul. This jewel didn't belong to him, not any longer. He knew his grandmother wouldn't miss it. She'd insisted time and again that he take ownership of it, but he knew once he had the diamond in his possession, she would expect a wedding announcement to follow shortly afterward. Since he'd had no desire to marry yet, he'd refused taking the diamond into his care and insisted she keep it in her tiara.

But after what he'd shared with Tabitha, he understood what his grandmother had wanted him to see all along. Giving that diamond to the woman he loved would feel special. *Special* was not a strong enough word for what he felt knowing he was giving the diamond to the woman he loved. It belonged to her and he wanted her to take it, to do whatever she needed or desired to do with it. It was the only thing he could give her now. He could not take her as a bride, could not give her his name, but only the diamond...and his heart.

He placed the diamond on the table beside the bed and retrieved paper and ink from the writing desk in the corner to leave her a message. Before he wrote the words upon the page, however, he studied her sleeping face.

He would envy the man who would someday have this view each morning, and he would curse himself for not knowing what he could do to keep her. He couldn't trust himself, and he couldn't trust her. He had to do what he did best, run away from the pain. Bury it. Hide himself from the world and all the things that could harm him.

I'm a bloody coward . . .

Too afraid to love, too afraid to risk losing another

person or trusting someone with his heart. Too afraid to do anything but run and hide.

Fitz placed the folded note under the diamond and let himself out of the room, closing the door, and his heart, forever.

There would never be another for him. It was the only thing that gave him any peace in that instant, however small it might be. His heart would not break a second time.

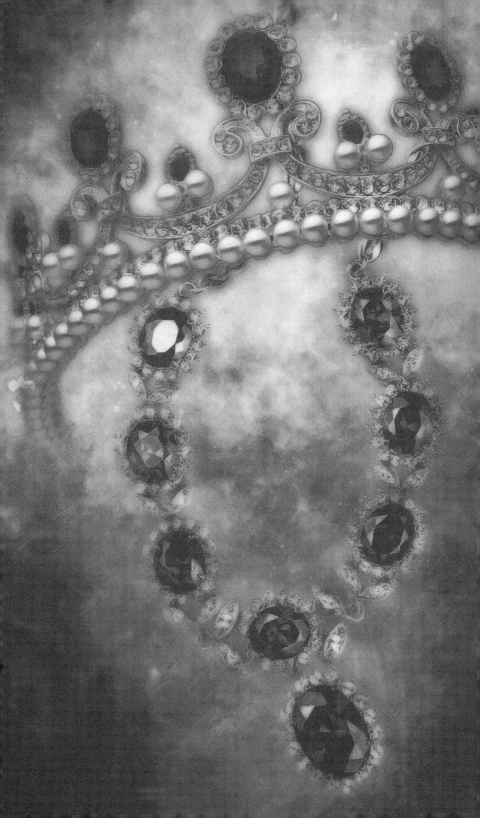

Chapter Eleven

Tabitha woke with tears in her eyes as a dream faded from her mind. What had she been dreaming of? She tried in vain to resurrect the sparse flashes of what had made her weep. She remembered joy, but also sorrow, as though she had known in the midst of her happiness that it would all end. When she wiped her eyes, the room came into focus. The fire in the hearth had gone out and morning light cast soft beams through the gaps in the draperies surrounding the window.

Fitz had been here. With her. Her body still felt languid and relaxed, though her arm ached from its wound. She stared at the rumpled sheets and the empty bed for a long moment and hugged herself. It was only then, as her gaze moved around the room, that she noticed the large diamond softly sparkling on the side table. She reached for the gem, her fingers closing around it. She turned to the ashes in the fireplace, where she saw the partially burned paste jewel still there.

Surely this can't be ... but if it is ...

The note beneath it bore a solid, confident script of handwriting that she guessed belonged to Fitz. It took her a moment to bury the flash of pain she felt knowing that whatever she was about to read would also be a message of goodbye.

This diamond is yours. Do something good in the world, and I shall sleep without missing it. Know that I will be true to you in my heart. Always.

Fresh tears escaped her, and she buried her face in her hands. The diamond and Fitz's letter toppled to her lap, and her body quaked as she sobbed. It was a long while before her tears finally ceased and she stopped quivering with grief. Numb and weary, she stared at the diamond. A beam of light had landed on the stone, and a prism of colors burst from the other side, painting the walls in a rainbow of light.

So much good could come from the gem if she sold it. But to do so, it would have to be broken up into a dozen smaller diamonds. *This* diamond would be gone forever, and she selfishly wanted this gift from Fitz to remain unchanged. It was a symbol of what lay between them, the pure, ancient perfection of something that shouldn't be destroyed. She clutched it to her chest and drew in a deep breath. She couldn't keep it, but she could make sure it would always be safe.

Tabitha hid the jewel in the vase of flowers that Fitz had give her, then tucked the letter from him in her travel case. She'd just finished washing her face in the basin on the washstand when Liza entered with a breakfast tray.

"Morning, Miss Tabitha," she greeted brightly as she set the tray down on a table. As she came closer, she lowered her voice. "Everything go well last night? Did you get it?"

"Yes. It is safely hidden away," Tabitha reassured her.

"Good. All the servants are buzzing like a hive of bees. The downstairs is dripping with gossip about what happened last night."

"Oh? What are they saying?" Alarm pitched her voice slightly higher.

"Well, that the diamond was stolen, of course, that everyone's rooms were searched, and the men were up half the night looking for the thief. They found no diamond and no thief, of course." The lady's maid winked at her. "Then, this morning, Lord Helston called off any further searches of the grounds and the house. The strange part is that he left for London and told his valet that they would be traveling to London and then Edinburgh tomorrow with no plans of returning!"

Tabitha's stomach plummeted to her feet. "He left his own house party?"

"Yes, as did his two friends, Lord Brightstone and Mr. Beckley. They were quite stunned by the entire business. The three of them were heard arguing in his study before His Grace got into his coach and left for London."

Tabitha collapsed into a chair, her breakfast ignored.

"I thought you'd be happy with the news that you got away with it." Liza lifted an exquisite pale-pink-striped satin walking dress out of the wardrobe and laid it out on the bed for Tabitha.

"I should be," she agreed, though her mood only fell deeper.

Fitz had run away from her. It was the wisest thing to do. If he had stayed . . . they would have made a terrible mess of everything. The truth might even come out. It was far better, far safer, to make a clean break of things and start over. Apart. Forever.

She touched her stomach. They hadn't taken any precautions last night. Neither of them had been thinking clearly. What if the flutter of life now blossomed within her? She would do *anything* to have a piece of him, just one part of him for her to hold.

Liza helped her change into the walking dress and arranged her hair as a thousand thoughts raced through her mind: what to do if she was with child, what to do with the Helston Diamond, what to do about her feelings for Fitz, which were never going to go away. But the pain of knowing she would never see him again was so great, it left her adrift rather than being able to devise any plan of action she could draw comfort from.

But she had to do *something*. She could not keep the diamond, and she could not bear to have it broken up into smaller pieces, which left only one option.

By the time she was presentable, Tabitha had made her decision. She told Liza to inform Hannah and Julia that she would be ready to leave soon. When the lady's maid was gone, Tabitha retrieved the diamond from its hiding place and tucked it into the pocket of her skirts. She then went in search of Mr. Tracy to ask for a private audience with Lady Helston on a very important matter.

She waited a short while in the corridor before she was shown into a private salon. The dowager duchess sat at her desk, perusing letters. Her fine satin gown of a rich hunter green was trimmed with Belgian lace and decorated at the hem and sleeves with gold tassels. She wore a delicate necklace of emeralds, and her silvery-gray hair was set in a classic style that made her seem rather ageless. Tabitha had never seen any mature woman look so splendid in her life.

The dowager turned at Tabitha's approach and gestured at a nearby chair.

"Please sit, Miss Sherborne." The dowager smiled warmly at her, but that only twisted the blade in Tabitha's heart deeper.

"Your Grace, I am here to return something to you." She knew better than to try to explain away her actions with words or delay the inevitable. It was best to just get it over with.

Lady Helston's eyebrows arched a little in curiosity. "Oh?"

Tabitha removed the diamond from her pocket and cupped it in her palm, then placed the glittering gem in the older woman's hand.

"This is yours."

"Goodness, how on earth did you . . . ?" Lady Helston suddenly lifted her gaze to Tabitha's face, a look of comprehension dawning in her eyes.

"I'm sorry, Your Grace," Tabitha whispered, her voice breaking a little.

"For what, my dear?" The duchess's eyes softened, and Tabitha saw a resemblance to Fitz so clearly in the older woman's face. Tabitha's shoulders trembled as she tried not to cry. She had expected Fitz's grandmother to be furious, possibly even to call for her butler to restrain her so she could not escape. She had not expected to see such compassion from the woman she'd stolen the diamond from.

"I was wrong to take it."

"Were you?" Lady Helston mused. "It was my understanding that the clever Merry Robins only target those who deserve it. My grandson was admittedly in need of a comeuppance as to his behavior."

Tabitha's lips parted in shock. "The diamond is yours, not his. I never should have—"

"My dear," Lady Helston gently interrupted, "gems belong to the earth. They do not belong to *people*, certainly not the men who plunder them. I believe women are the proper guardians of them, but even *we* could never own such things. We simply care for them for a while." She lifted the diamond up into the light. "Do you know the story of this particular stone?"

Tabitha shook her head. The walls around them were bathed in colored light as the dowager moved the jewel, twisting it slowly in the light from the windows.

"This diamond was discovered in 1698 in the great Indian mines of Golconda. Its cut is brilliant, and it is nearly flawless. It is four hundred and twenty-six carats and took two years of painstaking cutting. It was bought by Philippe II, the Duke of Orléans, regent of France. Louis XV, Louis XVI, and Marie Antoinette have all worn this diamond at some point in their lives. Napoleon even displayed it upon his sword hilt. It was once centered on Empress Eugénie's diadem. It has seen blood, tears, joy, greed, and love. It has reflected sunlight for nearly two centuries. You see how it has a yellow hue, faint but still visible?"

Tabitha peered at the diamond and nodded.

"All diamonds from Golconda have this color, while diamonds from other places appear more white. Some believe that to be a flaw of this particular jewel, but I do not see flaws in any diamond, nor anything that comes from the earth. Even raw and uncut, diamonds are in their own way *perfect*." She turned the diamond again, then tossed it in the air and caught it as it fell back down, surprising Tabitha.

"But this is only a stone. Its value is not monetary, even though men always seek to put a price upon nature. Its true value is in its natural beauty and what it reminds us about ourselves. That beneath our rough surface lies a brilliant jewel that has traveled up from the depths of the earth toward the surface. So much about diamonds is still a mystery, but that can also be said of ourselves, don't you think?" She set the diamond down on the desk and met Tabitha's gaze.

"I assume my grandson knows that you have this?"

"He used a paste jewel in place of the real one last night. It was the paste jewel that I stole, but after he discovered I was a thief, he gave me the real diamond. He left it by my bed—" She halted as she realized what she had just implied.

The dowager merely smiled. "Do not be embarrassed, my dear. I was once young. You must have made quite an impression upon Fitz for him to gift you this." She picked the diamond back up and held it out to Tabitha.

She leaned away from the dowager's offering hand. "No, I can't take it."

"It's only a stone," the dowager said. "I have been following your career with great interest, and if I am correct, you do not keep the items you take for yourself. I assume you do something useful with them instead, don't you?"

"I do. I sell the stones, and the money is provided to charities that are often overlooked by the upper echelons of society. But I can't take this one. It was a mistake to ever consider it." She wished she could explain to Lady Helston what the diamond meant to her. That it was precious because it was a gift from Fitz. His way of proving he cared for her, even though they could only ever have one night together. She didn't want it to be broken apart and sold or even hidden away. She wanted it to remain with Lady Helston,and Fitz, so that he understood that she loved him. That was her gift to him, the only gift she had to give.

"You love my grandson," Lady Helston said.

A painful lump formed in Tabitha's throat. "It wouldn't be right to admit to something I cannot act upon."

"But you do." The dowager put the diamond on the desk again. "Is it because you have no family? No connections? You believe yourself inferior to him?"

"Yes, but it is more than that. We are so different. We are ill-suited, and he can be so—" She halted once she realized she'd been about to complain about Fitz to his own grandmother.

"Oh, he can be terribly stubborn and focused on the wrong things, can't he? But I rather believe that this shortcoming is my fault. I did not push him as I should have. When he lost his parents, we clung to each other in our grief. His way of moving forward was to focus on the rules of his world and make them immutable. But that world, unlike this diamond, is terribly flawed. And so he has built rationalizations around those flaws. It has, I'm afraid, led to some limiting life choices. Now here you are, tearing down his walls and breaking all his rules. No wonder he fled the house this morning." A hint of a smile played upon the dowager's lips. "And yet, I believe that's exactly what he needs."

Tabitha stared at Lady Helston in confusion. "He does?"

"Oh yes, he *needs* you, Miss Sherborne, just as I suspect you need him." She tapped her chin thoughtfully. "Leave the diamond with me. As far as I'm concerned, it was never stolen, and last night's fracas was a simple misunderstanding. Let me think on the matter, my dear. In the meantime, I believe you should return to London. Don't you?"

Tabitha was more confused than ever, but she knew she'd been politely dismissed.

Hannah and Julia were waiting for her in the front entryway, while Liza was outside by their coach, seeing that their travel cases were properly packed.

"Where have you been, Tabby? We've been so worried," Julia said in a whisper as the three of them hurried down the steps. A footman opened the door and assisted each of them inside the coach.

But Tabitha shook her head and didn't speak until they were alone and the coach was moving down the road. She had to be certain no one would overhear their conversation.

"I had an audience with Lady Helston this morning."

"Did she suspect you?" Hannah gasped.

Tabitha closed her eyes, dreading this confession. "No, she didn't, but she didn't have to suspect me of anything because I . . . gave it back."

"You gave the diamond *back*?" Julia gasped. "Why? What if she reports us to Scotland Yard?"

"She doesn't know about you or Hannah being involved. As far as she knows, I'm the only one behind the thefts. And she doesn't intend to report me. She . . ." Tabitha couldn't bring herself to mention how that conversation had ended. Not yet.

Julia's face tightened with tension. "We're in this together, Tabitha. We will not let you take the fall alone. But *why* did you do it? We needed that diamond."

"I know." Tabitha tried to ignore the creeping misery inside her.

"Then why give it back?" Julia's voice rose a little.

Hannah put a gentle hand on Julia's arm to calm her down. "It's about Helston, isn't it?" she said softly to Tabitha. "You gave it back because of him."

"Why would she—?" Julia's eyes widened. "Oh no, Tabby. You . . . tell me you didn't fall in love with *him*." The way she said *him* with such horror, it sounded like Julia felt betrayed.

It was all too much. Tabitha wiped at her stinging eyes.

"Oh dear," Hannah said and gave Tabitha a hand-kerchief. "You'd better tell us what happened."

The next hour of their coach ride was spent reliving the past. Tabitha shared her meeting with Fitz that first night in London, how that moment during the musicale had connected them at once and how it had deepened during her time at the house party. She told them of the moments in the hothouse when she'd seen the softer side of Fitz and how he'd kissed her. She kept some details to herself, but she wanted her friends to understand that she'd never felt like this about anyone.

"And he found out you stole the diamond?" Julia asked.

"Yes. After you left my room, he came to see that I was all right. He thought the thief might have snuck in while I was sleeping. When he saw blood on the sleeve of my nightgown, he realized I was the thief he'd injured. Oh, he was so angry, *so hurt*. And I had done that to him."

Julia's eyes softened. "I always thought Helston had a heart of stone after what he did to our Anne . . ."

"He saw the error in doing what he did to break up your friend's engagement," Tabitha said. "Even though he thought he had done it with good intentions, he realized it cost him his friendship with Louis Atherton."

Hannah went back to the more pressing matter. "So he used a paste jewel as bait . . . then gave the real diamond to you anyway?"

"He left it beside my bed this morning," she whispered. She put her hand to her stomach, a gesture Hannah didn't miss.

"Oh, Tabby, what if you're with child?"

Tabitha wiped away more tears. "I know I can't ask for you to let me stay with you. It would be too scandalous to have an unwed mother under your roof. I thought perhaps I would try to find employment, if I could have you as a reference."

"Nonsense, you can't leave," Hannah protested. "Baby or no baby, you're family to me, Tabitha. We can handle a child if one comes; in fact, it might be rather wonderful to have a child about the house. We've set aside a small bit of the proceeds from each of our adventures for your future. We could use that toward the child if we need to."

Julia touched Tabitha's knee. "Hannah is right. We're all family. You won't leave us, will you, Tabby?"

Tabitha sniffled and smiled. "I'll stay with you as long as you wish me to."

"Now now, there's no need to cry," Julia replied.

"It's all settled. You're staying with Hannah, and everything will be all right." She said this with such confidence that Tabitha almost laughed. But after a moment, Hannah seemed to grow concerned again.

"You don't believe Helston will tell anyone about us?"

"He doesn't know about you. He told me to do something good with the diamond, but I couldn't keep it. It would have to be cut up to hide its origins."

Her friends didn't argue with her decision, but that didn't stop her worries about the future of the Merry Robins. There was still so much to be done to help those in need. They would have to find someone else deserving of their unique attentions.

Tabitha stared out at the landscape that was now turning colors with the approaching winter. She felt a chill, a wintry *emptiness* settle inside her. She hoped that wherever Fitz was, he didn't feel the same way. She wouldn't wish this feeling upon anyone.

She closed her eyes, relishing the night she'd spent in his arms. The way he had felt, the taste of his lips, and his scent that reminded her of rain and winter. The way his gaze seemed to melt when he looked at her in the candlelight. The beat of his heart in time with her own. How did a person live with only half of their heart?

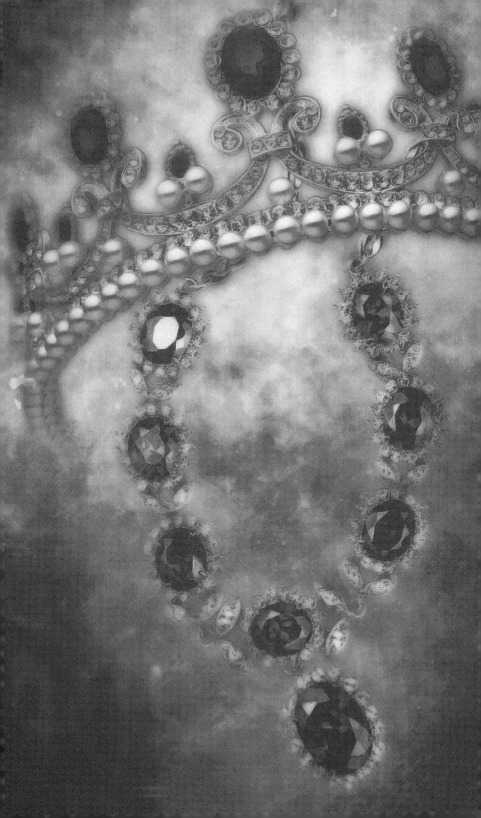

Chapter Twelve

Two weeks later

Running away to Edinburgh hadn't worked as Fitz had intended. Two weeks later, he returned to his London townhouse no less haunted by his night with Tabitha. Those memories of her in his arms clung to him like a faint perfume, or perhaps a faded dream. He had tried to bury himself in work with tasks meant to make the days spend themselves quicker.

But no matter what he did, he dreamed of Tabitha late into the night and woke with her name upon his lips. The knowledge that he could not turn to her and pull her into his arms in his bed was killing him day by day, hour by hour. He could not get her out of his mind or, it seemed, his heart.

Fitz stared at the fire that burned in the fireplace of his study. He braced a hand on the mantel and swirled his brandy, his thoughts a thousand miles away.

Where was she now? Was she dancing in another man's arms, with him believing she fancied him even as she deftly removed his gold pocket watch? The image almost made him smile, although the feeling was bittersweet.

His Merry *Robin Hood*. Lord, he *missed* her. What mischief would she be up to now?

After he'd returned to London this morning, Evan and Beck had showed up at his door and were all too eager to tell him that he had been wrong to leave the house party the way he had. Not to mention, he had let the thief go.

He told his friends that he'd confronted the thief and came to understand the person's true motivations behind stealing. When pressed about this, he would only say that he did not believe a prison sentence would be appropriate. Evan had demanded that Scotland Yard be notified, but Beck had been more reserved. He only wanted to know the identity of the thief, which Fitz had refused to give.

Now that he had returned from Edinburgh, their insistence on answers had only grown stronger. He told Beck and Evan that he'd allowed the real diamond to be stolen. He informed them that he given the thief the real one by choice. When his friends had stared at him, still confused, he then told them the one thing that he believed mattered about this situation. He believed the thief's cause was just, and they deserved to have the diamond more than him. That was the end of the matter.

His friends had reluctantly left him to brood alone for the rest of the day, and so he had. His desk was still littered with newspapers full of articles about the robberies when he'd first been keen to catch the Merry Robins, but as he'd read the articles and examined the newspapers, he'd found mentions of mysterious gifts to various charities by unknown benefactors. Knowing what he knew now about Tabitha and what she did with the jewels she stole, he saw clearly where the money was going.

Tabitha had told him the truth. She had been doing her best to help those who needed it. Now that he saw the truth so clearly he felt a strange sort of peace, despite the hollowness of not having her in his life. The Helston Diamond was his legacy, but it was one he'd never deserved. Now the jewel would be put to good use.

Turning away from the fire, he finished the last of his brandy before he sat at his desk and wrote several checks to the charities mentioned in the articles, as well as a letter to his estate steward to see that those same charities received two hundred and fifty pounds each to start. He had plans to make more frequent donations throughout the year.

With that done, he knew what he needed to do next. This was going to be the hardest part. He retrieved his hat and coat from a footman waiting by the front door.

"I shall be back later this evening. Please have Stewart pack my luggage for a month's journey and tell him to be ready to leave with me tomorrow morning."

The young man nodded. "Yes, Your Grace."

Fitz left his home and walked down the lamplit streets alone, his thoughts turning to the uncomfortable task ahead. When he reached his destination only a few streets away, he hesitated a moment on the bottom step before finally going up and rapping on the door knocker. A butler answered a moment later.

"Good evening, Your Grace. How may I help you?" the butler inquired, his face passive though he knew Fitz very well.

"I would like to speak to Atherton."

"Please step inside, Your Grace. I shall see if my master is available."

Fitz removed his hat and stepped inside. Normally, no such formality would be required in visiting his friend. But things had changed, and he had a terrible feeling as to why. It left him feeling even more as though he was walking upon broken glass.

As Fitz stood in the entryway, the butler walked down the short corridor to Louis's study and stepped inside. The door was left slightly ajar, and given the quietness of the night, the butler's voice traveled enough for Fitz to hear.

"Sir, Lord Helston is here to see you. Shall I show him in?"

"Helston?" There was a painful beat of silence before Louis spoke again. "No. No, tell him I am not able to see visitors this evening."

"Yes, sir."

Fitz stood still, his hat in his hands, his chest tightening. He had hoped that he'd only imagined the slight in the cardroom the other night, but it seemed he hadn't. Louis had given him the cut direct.

The butler returned and with an apologetic look said, "The master is not at home for visitors this evening. He is indisposed."

"Thank you." Fitz cleared his throat. "Would you mind terribly giving him a message from me?"

The butler nodded solemnly.

"Tell him . . . tell him I've been a damned fool and I'm traveling to New York tomorrow to make things right."

The butler's eyes widened. "I . . . I will relay that message, Your Grace," the servant promised.

"Thank you." Fitz put his hat back on and let the man show him out. As he stood on the sidewalk and looked up at the distant blanket of stars, he drew in a slow, steady breath.

Tabitha was right. He had been wrong to separate Louis from his beloved Anne, and they had both suffered terribly because of it. All he could do now was try to fix it. He only prayed he could.

Fitz's voyage to America had taken more than two weeks, and yet he still didn't feel prepared for the reason he'd traveled all this way. He stood inside the ballroom of the current queen of New York society, Caroline Astor. As he searched the crowd, he was amazed at the number of men and women who'd braved the wintry weather just to be seen by the rest of New York society at the grand Fifth Avenue home.

As he entered the house a few moments ago, he'd passed through a domed vestibule lined with the busts of Mrs. Astor's ancestors. Past the vestibule, there was a great marble hall and a large cantilevered staircase. He followed the other guests into an Adam style reception room with curved domed ceilings and intricate plaster-work. Beyond the reception room, he came to the entrance to the ballroom, which was flanked by two large vases and gold satin curtains. He felt like he was stepping through the curtains on a stage and was about to become an actor in a play.

The Astor house could easily rival many of the homes back in London, and Fitz admitted he was impressed by it. He had always thought of Americans as a bit desperate in how they showed off their wealth.

As he stood half a head taller than most of the men near him, Fitz felt the curious gazes of people settling on him. He'd only been in the city a few days, just long enough to book a room at the Fifth Avenue Hotel and let the evening newspapers print his arrival, when Mrs. Astor's calling card and invitation to her upcoming ball had arrived. He was grateful for his title and the opportunities his dukedom presented to him.

And that was how it came to be that he now stood at the edge of Mrs. Astor's ballroom.

A dark-haired woman in her forties came toward him, her eyes bright with mischief. He supposed that some would call her plain upon a passing examination, but there was something about her presence that made her captivating and powerful.

"Good evening, Your Grace," she greeted as she reached him.

He bowed over her hand and pressed a kiss to her gloved fingertips.

"My goodness, the reports from London simply do *not* do you justice," the woman exclaimed, a blush heightening the color on her cheeks. "I expected a handsome man, but you are something far beyond that."

"I am pleased that I live up to your expectations, Mrs. Astor," he said with his most charming smile.

She flirted back with an amused chuckle. "I believe you do, Your Grace. Now, you mentioned in your response to tonight's invitation that I could assist you in some way. I would be more than happy to do whatever I can for the Duke of Helston."

He proffered his arm, and Mrs. Astor slipped her arm through his as they moved around the edge of the ballroom, keeping away from eavesdroppers. Dancers swirled to the music, their colorful gowns painted in a thousand different hues. It made the women appear like beautiful exotic birds taking flight as their bustled skirts swirled around their legs. The wealth on display was staggering. It seemed as though all of the ladies' gowns were designed to rival one another in decoration and detail, just as the houses on Fifth Avenue had been built to rival the castles of Europe.

English society liked to display their wealth as well, but never to such a fierce degree of competition as this. Fitz wondered what Tabitha would say if she were here tonight. He'd passed a breadline in Greenwich Village, seeing the poor men and women waiting for scraps. It deepened his resolve that much stronger to do the right thing. If Tabitha saw such wealth, he knew she'd be wishing that the men and women here tonight would spend more on helping others than gilding their own cages with luxury.

"Well, Your Grace? What may I help you with?" Mrs. Astor pressed in a conspiratorial whisper. "Are you bride hunting? I know quite a few young ladies here who would be more than fit to be your duchess."

"Alas, I am not bride hunting. Well, I suppose that's not entirely true. But she would be a bride for a friend, not me. She was engaged to him, you see, and . . ."

He paused, swallowing his pride. Mrs. Astor needed to know the truth, at least enough to get her to assist him.

"I foolishly interfered and the match broke up. The young woman was forced to pursue a match here instead."

"Did she perhaps come here to also escape the rumors as to her *suitability* as a bride?" Mrs. Astor guessed astutely. "You are speaking of the Girard girl, aren't you?"

He shouldn't have been surprised that Mrs. Astor would know who he meant, but he was. She chuckled and patted his arm when she saw his face.

"This is my city, Your Grace. There is not one person in high society that I'm unfamiliar with when they arrive. The Girard girl was a special charity case. I do not typically allow the nouveau riche into my realm, but she met a friend of mine on her journey from London and impressed her with her genuine sweetness and charm. I chose to overlook the rumors that followed in her wake and have taken her under my wing."

"Very magnanimous of you," Fitz murmured.

"So what is it you've come to do, exactly?" Mrs. Astor asked.

"I've come to beg the young lady's forgiveness." He paused, considering his next words. "And if that doesn't result in her demanding that I leave or being slapped, I will ask her to return to London with me so that I might restore the union between my friend and Miss Girard."

Mrs. Astor was quiet a long moment. Her gaze swept over the dancers with the eyes of a woman who ruled over her people as a social monarch.

"I admit, this is most intriguing. A woman *must* wonder what could bring about such a change in a man like you. From what I've read in the papers, you are not the sort of man to make apologies."

"I harmed an innocent woman and lost my friend because of my pride and vanity," he replied. "I intend to fight to win him back, and that means I must first win his lady back. I trust that you will handle my presence with discretion?"

Mrs. Astor chuckled. "My dear duke, I shall not breathe a word, but people here are aware of your opinion of Miss Girard. Your sudden appearance might raise questions, and a few assumptions."

"That is unavoidable," Fitz admitted, "but my desire to mend this situation outweighs all concerns as to my own reputation."

"Very well then, Your Grace. I believe I see Miss Girard sitting among the wallflowers over there. I could call her to you for a private meeting, if you desire."

"No, thank you. I believe what is required of me is a very *public* action. I shall ask her to dance."

"A dance would send quite the message, wouldn't it? To have been chosen by the Duke of Helston? It would help recover some of what she's lost."

Fitz hoped it would do far more than that, but he would worry about that soon enough.

"If you require my assistance, you have it," Mrs.

Astor assured him as they moved together through the row of ladies wilting sadly against the wall.

"Thank you. I shall owe you a favor, Mrs. Astor," he promised.

The woman smiled. "And I shall be glad to collect on that favor someday. Good luck to you, Your Grace." She moved away to speak to some guests nearby, leaving him to enact his plan. Fitz squared his shoulders and walked toward the lovely young woman in a merlot bustle gown.

Anne Girard was a blonde beauty with a faint smattering of freckles upon her nose and hazel eyes that once held light and warmth. She sat in the middle of the row of wallflowers, her face downcast. As he drew closer, Fitz saw a quiet brokenness in her expression, and despair seemed to drag her shoulders down in a slump.

I've done to this to her.

He had played his powerful hand and driven his friend away from a good and decent woman whose only crime was her family's humble beginnings. Damn his pride and vanity. All this because he had clung to the idea of social status as a life preserver, to the point where he could not bear the idea that even his friends might put their social lives at risk.

Tabitha had been right. Loving someone was worth the risk, worth the struggle.

Anne was no different than Tabitha. Fitz had fallen in love with Tabitha in just a few days and then lost her. He couldn't begin to imagine how Louis must have felt to lose his love only a few days before they were to be married.

As Fitz journeyed across the Atlantic, he had stood on the deck of the steamer ship at night countless times and stared into the dark, churning waters of the sea. He let himself imagine that he and Tabitha were to be wed, only to have Evan come to him in the final hour before their ceremony and tell them that he must break it off.

The very thought turned his stomach, and he found it difficult to breathe. He had done that to Louis . . . *he* had caused that great and wrenching wound to someone he cared about and to this young woman.

I will not be a coward now. I will own up to my follies, no matter the price.

He stepped in front of Anne and cleared his throat. She raised her head in mild surprise, then recognized him. Horror and shock replaced her surprise.

"A dance, Miss Girard?"

She stared at him, her lips parted, her eyes wide as she realized her dilemma. Everyone knew she had no dances taken on her dance card, and it would be rude to refuse him.

"*Please*, Miss Girard." He softened his voice a little.

"There are things I wish to say, and I believe you would like to hear them. I would not have crossed an ocean if I did not believe you would wish to hear what I have to say."

She slowly stood up, and when she met his gaze, he saw her courage as she chose to accept his offer and hear him out. Fitz had the strangest feeling that he'd been blind to a great many things until he'd met Tabitha. Now he was truly *seeing* the world around him.

She placed her hand in his and led her to the floor as a waltz began. She placed a hand on his shoulder and her other hand in his. He kept a careful eye upon the crowd and steered her away from anyone who came close enough to overhear them as they spoke.

"What are you doing here, Your Grace?"

"I am here to apologize," he said, and her dark-gold brows arched in surprise.

"You want to apologize to me?" She inhaled sharply, and he pulled her a little closer and kept his voice down as they danced.

"I shall be brief and to the point, Miss Girard. I *never* should have said anything to Louis about his engagement to you. I was a damned fool, and I've hurt you both beyond words. For that, I am truly sorry. I swear it on my honor, what little I still possess."

Anne looked away, her eyes overbright with unshed

tears. She swallowed hard and cleared her throat before speaking.

"What . . . what did I do that was so abhorrent to you that you would tell Louis I would destroy his life? What could I have done that would have made you convince all of London to believe the worst of me? I've asked myself that every day since Louis broke off our . . ." Her voice hitched. "Louis said you were the *best* man he'd ever known, and if you thought me unsuitable for him, I must have done *something* for you to think so."

Her assumption stunned him. Louis had thought so highly of him that he'd believed Fitz could do no wrong. How wrong that belief had been.

A lump formed in Fitz's throat. "It was nothing you did. The fault was entirely mine. My assumptions, my foolish beliefs. I thought I was helping my friend, but in truth it was my own insecurities that cause me to act the way I did." He saw now the power his words had, and it was a power he never wished to wield again.

"Louis listens to you because he loves you like a brother," Anne said, her tone gentle as she spoke of him. Somehow that only made the pain in Fitz's chest worse to know that he'd hurt a woman who would love his friend so well.

"He still loves you, Anne," Fitz said, daring to use

her given name when he knew he had no right to take such a liberty.

"How could he? If he loved me, he would never have broken our engagement."

"He didn't want to—he believed he had to. I painted a picture of financial ruin that would destroy you both, and I had built that image out of nothing but my own fears. I convinced Louis. It wasn't until much later that he saw my words for what they were. Now I am being punished for it, and rightly so. I am his trusted friend no longer. He has cut me from his life in retribution for losing you, and I cannot blame him," Fitz confessed. "Please come back to England with me. Let me right this wrong I've done to you and Louis."

The waltz ended, and Anne stepped back, studying him carefully.

"What's changed, Your Grace?" she asked softly. "The man I knew wouldn't have crossed an ocean for this. He wouldn't have cared what became of me."

The barbed comment stung, but it was well deserved.

"I met someone not unlike yourself in many ways. She is brave, beautiful, her heart is full with a level of compassion that I can never match. It has filled me with wonder to simply be near her. And I realized . . . I *wasn't* worthy of her. Not even close."

Comprehension lit Anne's face. "You did something terrible to lose her, didn't you?"

He swallowed hard. "I'm afraid it's worse than that. I let her go. We've lived such different lives. She tested me and found me wanting. It made me realize she was right, I am not the worthy one. I played God amongst my friends, and it cost me Louis. She showed me that truth."

He couldn't have told anyone else this, only Anne, the woman who would understand his pain the most yet had the least cause to show any sympathy.

Anne reached out and touched Fitz's forearm. "I will come back to England with you, if you think I still stand a chance to win back Louis's heart."

Fitz shook his head. "He is the one who must win you back. A lady's heart is the gift, not the man's. I may have led him astray, but it is still he who must earn your trust and love again. But I shall do all that is in my power to remind him of that."

"Then I must pack everything as quickly as possible," Anne said.

"I must warn you. There will certainly be talk when we return, scandalous gossip and rumors," Fitz warned. "I will do what I can to quell them, but it won't stop everyone speculating about your return. Especially if it is with me."

"If Louis and I marry, I will have no care as to what people say about me," she replied without hesitation, and he believed her.

After briefly thanking Mrs. Astor for her assistance once again, Fitz escorted Anne from the ballroom and helped her inside his coach. Once she was safely at her house packing her things, he returned to his hotel and sent his valet to purchase their fares for the journey home on the first ship available. It turned out the next ship bound for Southampton was leaving the day after tomorrow.

As Fitz undressed that night, he couldn't help but think of the woman who had sparked this change in him. He closed his eyes, touching his fingers to his lips as he replayed their last kiss as they lay in bed together.

He wished he could go back to that moment, to bury himself forever in that brief stretch of time. But that was the thing about life—those perfect moments were so exquisite because they could never be repeated, only *remembered*. Tabitha was in his heart, no matter how the years would stretch and grow between them. And for that, he was grateful.

He knew his last conscious thought upon this earth would be of her, and when he faded into deepest night, she would still be a part of him and whatever he became beyond death.

So many things could be lost in the passing of time, except one. Love, true love, never surrendered to time. It endured in spite of it, and for once the pain of love and loss he felt was something Fitz welcomed . . . because it was all for *her*.

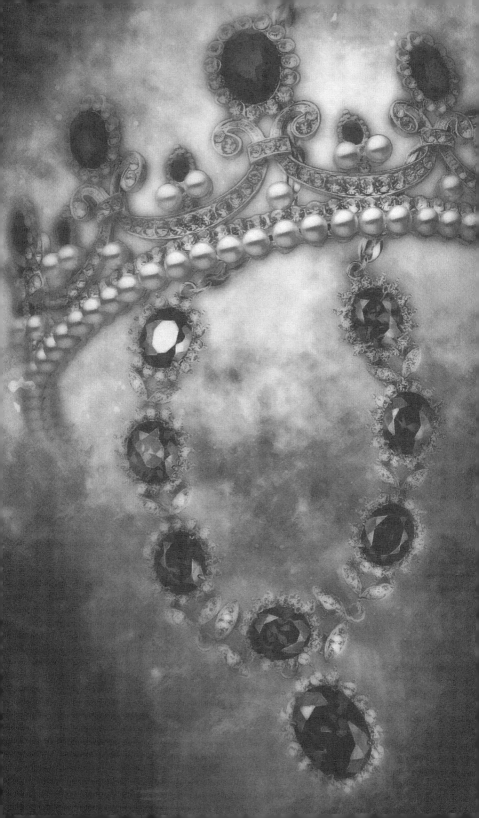

Chapter Thirteen

"**A**re you certain that he will still want me?" Anne Girard asked. Beneath the small lamplight inside his private vehicle, Fitz saw the young woman twisting her kid gloves between her trembling fingers in apprehension.

"He would be a fool not to," Fitz promised her. He felt a twist in his gut knowing that he'd reduced this once vibrant, confident young woman to someone who doubted herself. Fitz couldn't help but think of Tabitha and how restoring a couple who were meant to be together, wasn't just for Tabitha, but for himself. It was a new beginning for him, but it didn't ease the breaking of his own heart any less.

The coach came to a stop outside the townhouse belonging to Louis Atherton. One of Fitz's footmen opened the coach door. Fitz stepped down first before he turned to offer Anne his hand. She accepted it and descended from the carriage. As he led her up the steps to Louis's residence, he was painfully aware she'd once planned to call this townhouse her home.

He rapped the knocker and waited for Louis's butler to answer the door. When he did, the man's eyes bulged at the unexpected sight of Fitz and Anne standing there.

Fitz met the butler's stare coolly, but secretly he prayed the man wouldn't turn him away a second time.

"Please ask Atherton if he is available to see me. And tell him I have a gift that he would be mad to refuse."

The butler waved them inside. Anne reached for Fitz's arm, clinging to him nervously. In the last month at sea, he'd spent quite a bit of his time with Anne and had regained her trust. In a moment like this, it felt good to realize that she knew now that he would support her. Fitz patted her hand in silent reassurance. The last time Louis and Anne had spoken, it ended in tears. This time, things would be different. He would see to it.

The butler left them for only a moment and then returned. "The master is in his study and will see you, but I must caution you he's deep in his cups. I do not think he is suitable for a visit from a lady," the butler warned with a glance of regret toward Anne.

Fitz turned to Anne. "Let me speak to him alone for a moment. I shall call for you to come inside when I believe he's ready." Fitz gave her fingers a gentle squeeze before letting them go.

She nodded and followed him to the door of the study but remained outside as instructed. Fitz straightened his coat and entered Louis's sanctuary, closing the door behind him.

His friend was slumped in a chair by the fire. A glass of brandy sat abandoned on the drink cart in favor of a full bottle of Scotch that currently rested in his friend's hand. Louis's ascot was missing. His hair was rumpled as though he'd dragged his hands through it repeatedly, and his shirt was partially undone as if presenting his heart to the world, begging for someone to drive a dagger into it. There was a stuffiness to the room that made Fitz feel as though Louis had not left this place in a long time.

"So, you've come back?" Louis's voice wasn't slurred, which gave Fitz some relief. However, the bite in his friend's words was a clear warning.

"Yes, I've returned from New York," Fitz said. "Aren't you curious as to the gift I brought you from that illustrious city?"

"I've had enough of your *gifts*, Fitz. Your precious *advice!*" Louis suddenly lunged to his feet and slammed the bottle of Scotch down on a nearby table. "I let you in so I could say these words to your face. We're finished. You're *not* my friend," Louis growled.

Fitz scowled back at Louis. "Hold your tongue and listen to me." He knew if he didn't get a word in now, his friend would never listen to what he had to say.

Louis's brown eyes darkened with rage. "Hold *my* tongue? That's rich, coming from you. Listening to you destroyed my life!" Louis swung a fist, and the unexpected blow caught Fitz on the chin.

Fitz stumbled back, his fists raised in defense, but no other blows came. Louis rubbed at his knuckles, eyes bright with pain.

"You turned me into a coward, Fitz. You, the man I called brother, you made me despise myself. I was a fool to let you convince me to break it off with Anne. She was my *world*. But you can't understand that, can you? You have no heart, *none* at all."

Louis's words burned inside Fitz, hurting him far more than any blow. "If only that were true," he muttered to himself. If he had no heart, then he would not have suffered the pain of his own heart breaking the way he had. His own heartbreak would feel infinitely less if he had no heart.

"What?" Louis heard him, but not clearly enough.

He cleared his throat. This wasn't quite going

according to plan. "Perhaps you should see what I've brought you?"

"I *said* I want nothing of yours," Louis said and spun away. "Get out!"

The door opened behind Fitz, and Anne stepped into the room. She looked as poised as any princess, but Fitz didn't miss the slight tremble in her shoulders.

"Louis," Fitz said softly.

"No." Louis spun around, but the fire in his eyes died the instant he saw Fitz was not alone. He staggered forward a step as all the fight drained out of him, and he seemed a mere instant away from collapse.

"Anne?" He uttered her name with such anguish that Fitz felt his own pain at losing Tabitha burn fresh all over again. He knew this pain, this agony. The knowledge that he'd hurt his friend like this, that he'd been the one to cause such wretchedness to two souls . . . Fitz felt like a man doomed to hang for his crimes against the heart, including his own.

"Louis." Anne spoke her lover's name with tenderness. "His Grace brought me back from New York. For you."

Louis's confused gaze moved between the two of them. "He what?"

"He said that you still love me. That you might still . . . take me as your wife." Such words required great courage to say, and Anne had plenty of it. Fitz could not imagine saying such things himself. She was far braver than he could ever be.

Louis stared at him blankly, as if trying to decide this was a dream he was having due to the amount of Scotch he'd drunk or if it was real.

"You are right, Louis. About *everything*. I never should've stopped you from marrying Anne. Marry her because you love her, because she is *yours*. Never let a friend, or a former friend, convince you to ignore your heart ever again."

Fitz made a polite bow to Anne and exited the room before either of them could speak. Louis and his love had much to say that was private, and he had no desire to burden them with his presence any longer.

He put his hat back on and let the butler show him to the door. He was halfway down the steps when someone called his name. Fitz turned to look back at the doorway of the townhouse. Louis stood there, one hand braced on the doorjamb, his chest rising and falling as though he'd run to the door to catch up with Fitz.

"You went all the way to New York to speak to her? Why?"

"Though my words harmed you both, she suffered far more and I owed it to the lady to apologize to her in person. Even though I have no heart, I would do anything for you. Because you're my friend."

Louis's face grew ruddy. "I didn't mean what I said, Fitz. Truly I didn't. I was angry and . . ."

"Ah, but you did mean them, and I deserved to hear them. I will ensure that the polite society of London welcomes Miss Girard into its circle. She will have only friends from now on, not enemies. I vow that I will see it done."

Louis took a step closer to Fitz until he stood at the top of the steps, looking down.

"What happened to you?" Louis asked. "The Fitz I knew wouldn't have done this."

Fitz didn't answer right away as he considered his response. There was so much he regretted now, so much shame he felt for the way he'd been acting toward not just strangers but his friends. Tabitha had given him a glimpse of another life, a better one he could have if he only dared to admit his follies and vowed to change. He let out a soft sigh and looked back at Louis.

"The Fitz you knew was a blind and ignorant man. That Fitz is gone. I see myself in a new light now, and I mean to change."

Louis was quiet a long moment. "You know, I believe this is the Fitz I always thought I had as my friend since the day we first met. I'm glad to finally see him again." Louis paused again. "You don't have to leave. You could stay for a drink with us."

Fitz smiled, trying to keep the melancholy he felt out of his face. "I thank you, but I must go. You and Anne need time alone to discuss things. But if you do wish to see me again, you always know where to find me."

Louis nodded his understanding, and Fitz returned to his coach.

As he sat down in the darkness, he let out a heavy sigh. He had done all he could to bring Anne and Louis back together, and he was confident he had succeeded. Time would tell if Louis wished to renew their friendship, however. All Fitz could do was hope for forgiveness. Anything beyond that would be a blessing.

When he returned to his townhouse, he was more than ever aware of its silence. He wanted this house full again as it had been when Beck and his family had stayed here. For the first time in his life, he was willing to admit he wanted a family of his own. His eyes sought the landing on the staircase where he'd first seen Tabitha. He removed his hat and gloves, staring at the spot, remembering the moment that she'd turned to look at him. Even then, he had known something wondrous had come into his life. If only he could go back in time and fix the mistakes he'd made so he could have her back.

He would have pulled her close and whispered that she didn't need to steal a diamond, not when she could have him instead. He would have given her anything she desired, money for her charities, and he would have draped her in jewels and dressed her in the finest gowns. Of course, he knew better now. She wanted no fine gowns or jewels. She wanted love. She wanted time with him, like those hours spent in the darkness and warmth of a shared bed, or the gentle teasing of their conversation in the hothouse. That was what she wanted. Time and love. But he'd let too much come between them, and he didn't know if she could ever trust him not to be a cold bastard who cared little for others. Could he prove to her that a man could change? Would it be enough? For a man used to having answers about everything, it upset him greatly that to these burning questions he had none.

"You're finally home, my dear boy?" His grandmother's voice pulled him out of his thoughts. He hadn't seen her since he'd left the house party almost two months ago.

"Yes." He turned to face her as she approached. She was dressed for a night at home in one of her more comfortable dark-blue gowns, and her silvery hair was braided over one shoulder.

"How was New York?" She folded her arms over her chest, her frown deepening. "I assume your mission was successful?"

"Yes, very successful. Although I do owe Mrs. Astor a favor." He smiled, but his grandmother's face remained solemn. "I'm sorry, I should have informed you of my plans to travel."

"Yes, you should have. I don't think those steamships are seaworthy. Something could have happened to you. Did you even think of that?"

He came over and kissed her forehead. "But nothing did. I'm all right, Grandmother. The ship was quite safe, I assure you. You should consider a voyage yourself sometime."

"Not bloody likely." She scowled at him and then reached into the pocket of her dress. "I never had a chance to see you before you left for New York. I wanted to give you this." She held out her closed fist.

He opened his hand and she dropped something cold and heavy into it. When he realized what it was, his heart stilled.

The Helston Diamond. The real one. The one he'd left beside Tabitha while she'd slept.

"How did you . . . ?" His voice trailed off as his mind

flashed with that final image of Tabitha in bed, her hair spilling across the pillows in the dawn light. Everything he'd felt in that moment came rushing back to him.

"A very remarkable young woman returned it to me."

Tabitha had given it back? A sudden violent pain in his chest made it hard to breathe.

"She didn't want to keep it," he said, half to himself.

"Oh, but she *did*," the dowager said. "I rather think that was the problem. She wanted to keep it because it was all she had of you. But if she kept it, she would have no choice but to use it for what she had originally intended. The diamond would be broken up and sold. She gave it back so that it might stay just as it is. To preserve the memories she has of you."

Fitz curled his fingers around the diamond, holding it tight. "What did she tell you about those memories?"

"Not much, but I have lived and loved a long time, and I see love more clearly in my old age than young people do. That woman is hopelessly in love with you. The question is, what will you do about it?"

"There's nothing I can do." Fitz felt betrayed by his own words.

"I rather thought the people of your generation married for love and damn the rest?"

He chuckled at her words. "Oh, we do, do we?"

"You're a *duke*, Fitzwilliam. If you cannot marry for any reason that you please, then what sense does this world make?"

"Grandmother, you don't understand. She has lived on the streets. She has no family, no connections. She is a pickpocket. A thief. She's one of those Merry Robins you so admire, wanted by the police. Are you telling me you would allow such a woman to be the next Duchess of Helston?"

"Why yes, she is rather the perfect kind, don't you think?" his grandmother replied without hesitation. "Family connections can be such a pain. Once she is your wife, she will be *our* family. She will be my grand-daughter. She will have every connection she requires. That is one of the many benefits of marriage, aside from being with the one person you love. What point is there to life other than to embrace the act of loving others and receiving love from them? Love is the only thing a person can take with them when they die." She patted his hand that held the diamond. "The rest is merely window dressing. Besides, the question was never whether *I* cared about the wife you would choose. What matters is whether *you* care about her. Is this girl a fleeting diversion, or is she your world, Fitz? To that question, only you know the answer. And if she's your world . . . what are you still doing here talking to me?"

Your world. Louis had said Anne was his world. A wellspring of hope suddenly blossomed in him.

In the nearly two months since he had parted from Tabitha, it had become clear that she *was* his everything. Even knowing that he could not be with her, he had risen each day and gone to bed each night with his heart aching for her.

He'd once thought poets were fools to speak of love as all-consuming, but now he understood their words. His grandmother was right. Love was the only thing that mattered. Romantic love, familial love, love for one's friends, even love for strangers who perhaps need it most. Tabitha had known that truth all along and had tried to show him. His beautiful, brave, brilliant thief with a heart of gold.

"I am told she is at Lady Crawford's ball this evening," his grandmother said. "You received an invitation, so you may attend if you choose."

"How do you know where she is?" he asked his grandmother.

"I'm a grandmother first, darling, and a duchess second. It's my job to know where the woman my grandson loves is at any given moment. Now go and change. You mustn't be late."

She gave his hand another squeeze. Then he was rushing up the stairs, taking the steps two at a time.

Every fear and worry he'd had about a future with Tabitha had become pale and inconsequential when weighed against the thought of a life without her. He didn't care at all what might happen if the truth of her past came out. The only thing that mattered was not spending one more moment of his life without her.

He shouted for his valet. "Stewart! I have a ball to attend!"

He wasn't here.

That was all Tabitha could think each time she'd attended a ball in the last month. The Duke of Helston was in New York, not here in London. Yet it didn't stop her foolish heart from leaping every time a gentleman entered the ballroom.

Everyone knew Fitz had left London. The rumors had been flying as to *why* ever since his arrival in New York had been telegraphed back to England. She'd heard that he had attended one of Mrs. Astor's balls. Not knowing who Mrs. Astor was, she'd asked Hannah about the woman. This prompted a discussion as to *why* Tabitha had asked her, which led to a second discussion about the fact that Tabitha's feelings toward Fitz hadn't lessened since their parting.

None of that had been pleasant. She didn't want to talk about Fitz, let alone think about him. It simply hurt *too* much. Yet she did think about him every single day.

Why had he gone to New York? Gossip had ranged from business to bride hunting, but none of the sources were reliable. Reports had mentioned that he'd stayed only a few days before boarding a boat back to England, which had caused even more wild speculation.

He should be back any day now, but she had given up hope of ever seeing him again. He would no doubt avoid her and refuse to attend any events where she might be, and she could not blame him.

Julia suddenly joined her in the row of chairs where women were resting between dances. "Tabby, you won't believe it!" Her friend arranged the skirts of her pale-green and berry-red pleated gown as she sat down beside Tabitha.

"What is it?"

"He's back."

"What?" Tabitha asked, though she had no doubt from Julia's tone who she meant.

"Lord Helston apparently arrived in London late this afternoon and was spotted escorting a woman off the ship and into his private coach."

A woman? That didn't make any sense . . . unless

the bride hunting rumors were true. But he'd been in New York only a few days and—

"And you will not believe who it was he was seen with departing the ship!" Julia announced, interrupting Tabitha's panicked inner thoughts.

"Who?"

Julia gave her a knowing look, a slight smile on her face. There was only one name she could think of that might cause that reaction. Julia would know that any other young woman being seen with Fitz would have broken Tabitha's heart.

"Anne Girard?" Tabitha said softly.

"The same." Julia's face was flushed with excitement. "She's back! It's simply wonderful! You will adore her, Tabby, I promise you will!"

Tabitha still didn't understand. "Why would she be traveling with Lord Helston? You don't suppose they were married?"

"Anne married to Lord Helston? Goodness no, what on earth would give you that idea?"

Tabitha had no answer, only confusion and irrational fears.

"Don't you see, Tabby? He went to New York to bring her back. For Louis. He's trying to make amends. Oh, this is marvelous. Wait until I tell Hannah! She won't believe it! And to think I called him a bastard . . .

Well, I suppose he was at the time, but even a bastard can change!" A few women nearby gasped at Julia's use of the word *bastard*, but Julia never seemed to care what anyone thought of her.

She abandoned Tabitha as she spotted Hannah at the refreshment table and rushed over to whisper the news in her ear. Hannah's eyes widened, and they shared excited looks before they glanced in Tabitha's direction.

Tabitha looked away and toyed with the dance card wrapped around her wrist, staring at the couples dancing in front of her. Fitz was home. Had he really brought the young lady home for his friend? She wanted to think so, but she wasn't sure. Had he truly changed his mind about her? If he had, the grand gesture of traveling all the way to America to bring the woman back was impressive, to say the least.

The dancers on the floor parted, some of them stopping in their steps as a man strode through them with purpose. Beneath the lamplight, his hair shone a deep gold and his blue eyes were fixed on her, filled with the same storms she'd grown to love. Her heart pounded wildly and her mind reeled as she tried to arrange her thoughts, but all she could think was his name over and over.

Fitz.

She couldn't think past that single realization. He was here.

Fitz stopped in front of her, bowed, and held out a hand to her. She rose as if in a dream and placed her gloved hand in his. He curled his fingers around hers tightly, and her skin broke out into goosebumps as that electric connection shot to life between them once again. He pulled her into his arms, and taking their cue, the musicians dove into a new waltz.

She gazed up at him as they danced together beneath the crystal chandeliers in the shining light, neither one speaking. This was where she belonged. In this man's arms and nowhere else. Her heart fluttered in her chest now, like a songbird stretching its wings and readying to sing on a clear winter morning. This man was her *home*.

They gazed into each other's eyes as their feet moved in time to the music. His large hand on her waist was warm, his hold firm. His other hand clasped hers tight, as if he feared she might vanish when the last note of the waltz ended.

She finally spoke, breaking the spell between them. "Is it true that you went to New York?"

"Yes. I had an apology to give," he said, his voice soft. "One long overdue."

"And did you?"

"I did." That look of peace, that sense of knowing he'd done the right thing, had changed his once imperious face to one far more welcoming, which only enhanced his already sinful good looks. "I asked Miss Girard to return home with me. She and Louis are getting reacquainted. The future is up to them now. I've done what I can to make things right."

Tabitha stared at him, unable to form words.

"It is only the beginning," he confessed. "I still have much to fix in my life."

"You do?"

He smiled sadly. "I certainly do."

She had a sudden flash of understanding. All the charities she and her friends had been supporting had recently received checks in the last few weeks from a new anonymous donor. It must have been him, but she didn't want to force him to admit it.

"I spent so much of my life building walls to protect myself after I lost my parents. I was terrified of getting hurt, but those very walls kept me from living. I thought I didn't need to live, that being safe was better . . . but you changed everything for me," he said. "I never expected you to get past my walls, Tabitha. You slipped in like the thief you are and stole me away from myself and showed me that living . . . that *loving* was worth the pain. You didn't just take the Helston Diamond—you took my heart."

She held her breath, but when he remained silent, she finally dared to speak. "Are you asking for it back?"

"The only way I would want my heart back is if you came with it," he replied, his eyes softening. "I know I've made a mess of things. I left you and I shouldn't have. I should've stood with you against world, slaying dragons in your name . . . but instead, I fled."

She stopped dancing abruptly, and he grasped her tighter, as though he feared she would flee. "Fitz . . . I never asked you to slay dragons or protect me from the world. All I want, all I ever wanted, is to be loved by you."

He was silent a long moment, unaware of the growing crowd that had stopped to watch them talk.

"Fitz, everyone is watching us," she warned in a whisper.

"Then let them. I am done letting my fear rule over me. I choose to be ruled by love instead."

He clasped her hands in his, and in front of the crowd of people he got down on one knee and reached into his waistcoat pocket. He pulled out something large and glittering in his palm.

"I believe this belongs to you. I offer it, my name, and my life as your husband."

"You wish to marry me?"

"Yes, if you will have me." He held her hands steady and placed the great diamond into one of her palms. "*You* are the only jewel I desire."

His eyes were now clear of storms, and in that instant, Tabitha glimpsed the future they would have together, the years slowly spinning past, leaving a tapestry of two lives that were always meant to be entwined. Someday those threads would end, but those of their children and grandchildren would continue on, carrying that tapestry of their love into the future.

This sense of *knowing* her destiny and the rightness of it left her stunned. Those years of grief that had threatened to consume her soul and Fitz's as they suffered loss after loss had now given them a chance to grow, to stretch beyond that grief and expand their hearts so that love could burst forth once more.

One word held the power to unlock the hidden gate that led to the garden their hearts shared. She was so full of joy, so full of disbelief at her own good fortune, that it took her two tries before she could speak it.

"Yes."

Fitz surged to his feet, pulling her into his arms as he kissed her hard, desperately, the way a man does when he fears he will lose something precious if he ever lets it go.

Tabitha clung to him, kissing him back, reassuring him without words that he never needed to doubt the vow of that single word.

When their lips broke apart, the room had grown as quiet as a church, and she smiled up at him through happy tears.

"Yes," she said again, stronger this time.

Fitz glanced around at the guests, spotted Hannah and Julia, and nodded solemnly at them before he scooped Tabitha up in his arms.

"Fitz! What are you doing?" Tabitha gasped. The guests around them covered their mouths with gloved hands in shock.

"I'm taking you home, *wife*."

"But we're not married yet," she protested with a laugh.

"My heart married yours that night we met. The rest is merely ceremony."

She had no response to this except to cling to him a bit tighter.

"Where are we going?"

"Home, because I cannot stand another moment of not kissing you."

Fitz carried her from the ballroom and out to the street, where his coach waited for them.

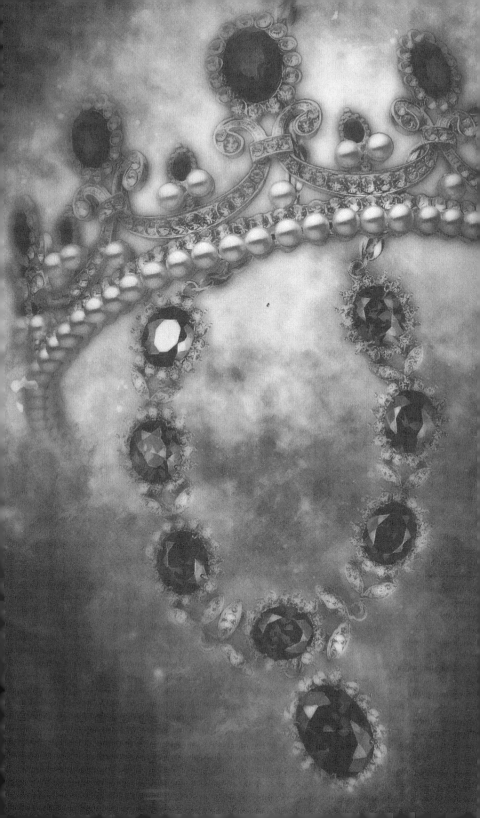

Chapter Fourteen

The coach stopped in front of Fitz's townhouse, and Tabitha gazed up at the beautiful home through the small window. She was cradled on Fitz's lap and had no desire to move off him at that moment. In the coach ride over they'd had a chance to talk for the first time they'd parted the night they'd made love. She'd confessed everything to him then, even telling him about Hannah and Julia. She truly trusted him to keep her secrets and keep her friends safe and he'd assured he would. He in turn had told her more of how he'd gone all the way to New York and everything about that night in Mrs. Astor's ballroom when he'd groveled for forgiveness from Anne and brought her back. He'd even shared his meeting with Louis and his fearful hope that his friend would forgive him now that he'd done all he could to make things right.

For the first time in her life, Tabitha felt...whole. She was with the person that her heart belonged to and she had no more doubts...except one.

"My grandmother is home this evening . . . I wanted you to meet her...as my future wife."

"Your grandmother!" she gasped. "Oh heavens, Fitz. We can't . . . she can't possibly approve of me as a wife for you—"

"Actually, she is the one who knocked some sense into my head," he chuckled. "I assure you, she *does* approve."

"But she can't. She knows that I stole her diamond and what I am..." That was the only thing that Tabitha feared. She didn't want Fitz and his grandmother arguing over her. She would not be the reason for a break between them.

He stroked a fingertip down her nose. "She doesn't give a fig about your past. In fact, she is a great admirer of the Merry Robins. She's already claimed you as family."

Tabitha couldn't make sense of his words. It simply wasn't possible that a duchess would approve of her, let alone like her.

"I promise you she will be happy to see you." He

leaned in to nuzzle her cheek, and she closed her eyes, wishing they could stay here in this carriage a little longer, cocooned in the warm darkness, and not have to face the world outside.

"Come now, darling," he said. "You've met her already, and she was quite impressed with you."

"But not like this, not being carried in your arms like some Viking's prize."

Fitz laughed. "Viking, eh? Well, I am told we Helstons have Vikings in our blood. So you'll have to forgive me when I carry you off in my arms to ravage you."

Despite her fears, she laughed at that. This playful Fitz reminded her of the man from the hothouse, the man she'd gotten to know when he'd let his guard down.

"Very well, O Viking. Carry me off." She waved an airy hand like a Saxon princess.

"With pleasure." Fitz called for his footman to open the coach door. And the moment she was out of the carriage, Fitz had her scooped up in his arms again. Fitz's butler was waiting for them inside when they arrived, a look of shock upon his face at the sight of them both or rather with his master carrying a woman in his arms.

"Tracy, is my grandmother still awake?"

"Yes, s-she's in the library," the man stuttered as he blinked at Tabitha.

"Oh yes, Tracy, you've met Miss Tabitha Sherborne. I'm happy to announce she will soon be my duchess."

The butler quickly recovered from his shock and bowed to Tabitha.

"Welcome, Miss Sherborne."

"Thank you." Tabitha clung to Fitz's neck while he carried her upstairs to the library. He thankfully set her down the moment they stopped just outside the open library doors.

The dowager duchess was seated by the fire, she read a book spread out in her lap. She glanced up at their entrance.

"Grandmother," Fitz said solemnly as he led Tabitha to her.

The dowager set her book aside and stood, offering Tabitha a warm smile.

"So, you brought back the thief who stole your heart," Lady Helston said, her eyes roving gently over Tabitha, inspecting her from head to toe.

Tabitha waited patiently for the older woman to pass judgment. Though they had met before, Tabitha sensed this moment was the one that mattered most.

"Yes . . . you will do quite well, my dear. Quite well indeed." She reached up to cup Tabitha's cheek the way a grandmother would. "Welcome to our family."

Tabitha's lips parted in shock. She hadn't expected that, despite Fitz's reassurances.

"You don't mind that we are to be married?" She wanted no arguments or resentment to come between them later and had to be certain of where the dowager stood.

"Mind? I rather insist on it, my child. I knew there was something about you that first night we met at my musicale. You were genuine, and now I know why. You have lived, suffered and *fought* for every moment in your life. The Helstons are a strong family. We support each other and share our strength. You and Fitz will be an even match in all the ways that will guarantee a successful and happy life together." She turned to her grandson. "Now, I shall start wedding preparations tomorrow morning with you both, but for now I shall retire." She smiled at them. "Do not *talk* too late into the evening." She emphasized the word *talk* as she drifted out of the library with a natural grace that Tabitha envied.

Fitz waited until they were alone to pull Tabitha back into his arms, and she melted against him. It was impossible not to burn with desire when this man held her as he did now.

He kissed the shell of her ear, and she shivered with anticipation.

"Shall we continue this in my chambers?" he asked, his voice deep and inviting.

She reached for the buttons of his waistcoat. "Your chambers are too far away." She actually wanted him here, now, and didn't care if there was a bed or not.

"Here?" His voice turned rough as he dug his hands into her skirts, starting to jerk them up.

"Here. Anywhere. Just *now*." She needed to be joined with him, needed that intimacy they once shared restored, and she couldn't wait another moment. A knock at the library door halted her fingers halfway down the buttons of his waistcoat.

Fitz cursed under his breath and released her skirts. She dropped her forehead against his chest and blew out a frustrated breath at the unexpected interruption.

The butler cleared his throat from the doorway. "I'm sorry to interrupt, Your Grace, but you have visitors that I believe you'll wish to see this evening."

"Oh?" Fitz turned his body slightly to shield Tabitha a little from Mr. Tracy's view, though she was completely clothed. "I don't suppose they could wait an hour?" he teased the butler, which shocked the poor man so thoroughly that he blushed. "I'm jesting. How many guests are there?"

"Er, yes. Several guests, in fact, are here. They are all *quite* insistent upon speaking to you and Miss Sherborne."

Fitz glanced down, silently questioning her, but she had no idea who could be at the door.

"We should see who they are, then," he said and clasped her hand in his. Even a simple hand-holding such as this made her feel warm all over and connected to him.

When they reached the top of the stairs, the place where they had first met, Fitz stole a slow, lingering kiss from her that made Tabitha's head fuzzy in the best way.

"I think you quite scandalized Mr. Tracy, the poor dear, his face was so red. I don't believe he's used to you teasing him," she admitted with a soft smile. "But I like this *you.* I like this side of you, Fitz."

"The human side?" he asked.

"The *true* side." She smoothed her hands up his waistcoat to his collar, curling her fingers in the cloth as she breathed in the wintry scent of him. "This is the man you've always been inside, and this is the man I love. Never let the world change you again. *Stay this way with me.*"

He tipped her chin up with his fingertips and nuzzled her face with his.

"Always, my heart," he promised and wrapped her in his arms, the heat of his body pouring into hers and making her feel safe and cherished in a way that she'd never thought possible.

The sound of arguing downstairs disrupted the sweet moment.

"What the devil?" Fitz muttered as he stared down toward the entryway. Four people were clustered together there, speaking in raised voices.

Hannah and Julia were squared off against Lord Brightstone and Mr. Beckley. It didn't escape Tabitha's notice that this argument lay between her closest friends and Fitz's.

"I want my cousin's earbobs back," Brightstone demanded.

"Well, you can't have them. They're gone," Julia answered triumphantly.

"Gone where?"

"I'm afraid they've been sold, my lord," Hannah said with a hint more politeness than Julia.

"*Sold?*" Brightstone hissed. "You bloody thieves. I can't believe either of you would stoop to such low actions." Despite Brightstone's harsh words, Tabitha could swear she heard a hint of something...playful? No, that wasn't quite the right word, intrigue perhaps?

Whatever it was, she didn't think Brightstone was as angry as he was feigning to be.

"I rather think *your cousin* is the one who needs to have her conduct addressed," Hannah replied. "You should be comforted by the fact that the sale of those earrings went to fund a lovely charity that supports the elderly who can no longer support themselves."

Brightstone blustered at that. "That's all fine and good, but damnation, did you have to *steal* them? I would have donated money to you. You need only have asked."

Tabitha didn't miss how Brightstone's tone had softened considerably.

"That would be missing the point of why we stole them in the first place," Hannah said.

Beck seemed to be the only one not participating in this argument and therefore was the first to notice Tabitha and Fitz upon the stairs.

"Fitz, Miss Sherborne," Beck greeted them with a nod, his tone neutral, as if all that was happening around them was normal. The argument abruptly ceased as Hannah and Julia rushed toward Tabitha.

Julia shot a suspicious look at Fitz, then one of concern to Tabitha. "Tabby, are you all right? When he carried you off like some barbarian, we feared what he planned to do next."

317

"It's all right. I'm quite fine, and it was rather silly of you to worry," Tabitha assured her. "You and everyone else saw him propose to me."

"I assumed that was some kind of strange delusion," Julia said. "Either mine or his. You have to admit he's not exactly the romantic type."

Sometimes her friends were far too overprotective of her. A man she adored carrying her off into the night in his arms—well, that was something to be celebrated not to be concerned about.

"Oh, but he is, Julia. If you'd only give him a chance, you'd see that," Tabitha defended him, and Julia cast her eyes down as though a little embarrassed. Tabitha understood her friends were still suspicious of him after all the harm he'd done to Anne Girard and Louis, but he'd changed, and done the right thing.

"Your Grace, could we have a moment alone with Tabitha?" Hannah asked.

"Of course. My study is just up the stairs and on the left." He pointed toward the staircase.

"Thank you."

Before Tabitha could say another word, she was bustled upstairs and into Fitz's study and the door firmly closed behind her. Her two friends faced her.

"Tabitha, have you considered what it would mean to be married to a duke? To have the scrutiny of all of high society upon you? We want you to be happy, but we also want you to be prepared," Hannah said gently.

"I have. I am ready to face whatever comes, but Fitz and his grandmother seem quite determined to defend me against the world. That to me makes any struggles I face worth it. They see me as family. I never thought such a thing would be possible," Tabitha confessed. Hannah's eyes softened and welled with tears.

"This is what you truly want, Tabby?" Hannah asked. "I know you say you love him, but are you certain? Do you need more time to think about this? No one would judge you if you wished for a longer courtship."

"How long did your husband court you before you married him?" Tabitha asked Hannah.

Her friend blushed and smiled. "Officially...only a month. It was quite scandalous to be married so soon, but to be fair, we'd known each other for years." She cleared her throat. "Very well, your point is made. We just want you to be happy and safe. Everyone deserves that."

I am," Tabitha assured her. "I have always felt incredibly safe with him. He treats me like I matter more than anything in the world to him." She let out a soft breath. "I wish you both could understand. He's simply wonderful to me."

Her friends exchanged a look, and she continued on, hoping to show them how wonderful the real Fitz was.

"He went to New York to bring back your friend. How many men do you know who would cross an ocean to apologize to someone they've wronged? And he brought her back with him so that she and Louis Atherton might be reunited. He did all of that because he wanted to change. He wanted to be better for me, *because* of me. I still can't believe it."

"Neither can I," Julia muttered.

"I suppose I can," Hannah said slowly. "True love can change anyone. I just never expected a man like Helston to find it. But you must understand that we want to make sure that *you* want this, that you want *him*."

"I do. I want him more than anything," Tabitha confessed. "He's my every dream. I never thought I would have a life like this, a life filled with love."

"Very well, then. We will let him have you, but you are still the sister of our hearts. Never forget that."

Hannah and Julia hugged her for a long moment, and she felt that bond of sisterhood between the three of them.

"Now tell me, what are Lord Brightstone and Mr. Beckley doing here?" Tabitha asked.

Julia's face reddened. "It seems they were just as

concerned for Helston's well-being when he carried you off. It is quite unlike him, you must know, to act so . . . gallantly romantic in a public place. We ran into Lord Brightstone and Mr. Beckley on the steps outside. It seems that Mr. Beckley figured out that we were the Merry Robins because Fitz was acting so strange about you and you were the only guest Fitz wouldn't have reported to Scotland Yard because he was in love with you. Then Mr. Beckley deduced you had help and he guessed we were the other robins. Naturally, Lord Brightstone was furious since we stole from that dreadful cousin of his."

"Heavens, what a night," Julia sighed dramatically. "Our secrets have been exposed, and Tabitha's been proposed to by a duke."

"Not exposed," said Hannah. "Discovered."

That splitting of hairs concerned Tabitha as to what would happen next. "Oh dear. Do you think they will report us?"

"Mr. Beckley won't, he seemed quite amused by the entire thing once he'd pieced it together and he stated he had no intention of going to Scotland Yard. He said the people we stole from quite deserved it. As for Brightstone, I shall make sure he keeps our secret," Hannah said.

"How?"

"Lord Brightstone had an affection for me when I first debuted. He would have tried to court me had I not accepted Jeremy's proposal first. I believe he will agree to be silent if I ask him to."

Julia seemed unconvinced, but she let the matter go for now. "What do you suppose will happen next? Perhaps the queen will invite us to Balmoral for Christmas."

Hannah chuckled. "Tabitha, do you wish to come home with me tonight?"

"Actually, I would like to stay here, if you don't mind." Tabitha was relieved when her friends said they would let her remain with Fitz tonight. She didn't care about propriety. She only cared about being with him after missing him so deeply for so long.

"I suppose we should go now, Julia. There will be much to do tomorrow."

"And we had better make sure that Brightstone and Mr. Beckley aren't bothering Helston," Julia added. "It won't be good if Brightstone manages to convince Helston to be on their side."

"Fitz won't say anything," Tabitha assured them.

"Don't be too sure," warned Julia.

Hannah came to Tabitha's defense. "No, she's quite right. A duchess cannot be the subject of an investigation, so he will protect her."

Julia tapped her chin. "I suppose. But we still need to get Lord Brightstone off our backs, then."

"Don't worry. I will handle him," Hannah said.

But right now, Tabitha couldn't help but wonder how Fitz was handling his friends.

"You knew, didn't you?" Evan demanded of Fitz the moment the ladies retreated to Fitz's study.

"Knew what?" Fitz feigned ignorance.

"That the three of . . . of *them* were the thieves."

"I knew about Tabitha. I only found out about the others' involvement tonight." He had been surprised to learn on the coach ride back from Lady Crawford's ball that Hannah and Julia had in fact been her accomplices.

"When were you planning to tell us?" Beck asked.

"Once we were married and Tabitha was protected. The authorities would have a more difficult time investigating a duchess than a single young woman from the streets."

"So you are to be married, then?" Beck asked. "I wasn't quite sure I could believe what I saw at Lady Crawford's ball. You must admit, it's rather out of character for you."

"A display like that is out of character for anyone," Evan added.

"Yes, I suppose it was a bit daring," said Fitz. "But the truth is . . . I like the kind of man I am with her. I've been pretending to be someone I'm not for a very long time, and when I'm with her, I am free to be the man I want to be. The man I *should* be."

His friends stared at him, but the concern quietly vanished from their faces.

"I admit, I rather like this version of you," Beck said.

Evan finally smiled. "Agreed, but damnation, man, you've got to warn us before you go and do something like propose to a woman in front of everyone."

"Or like running away to New York without telling us," Beck added. "We're your friends, Fitz. We want to help you."

Fitz found himself grinning sheepishly. "I'm glad, because I wish to wed Tabitha as soon as possible. I see no point in a lengthy courtship when I know exactly who I want to be with for the rest of my life."

Beck smirked. "So let me understand this. She steals your diamond, *then* steals you as a husband? She must be quite the thief."

"Indeed she is," Fitz chuckled.

"Yes, well, that doesn't get me back my cousin's earbobs."

"Evan, you have been quite insistent about those jewels. Did they have some value to you?" Beck inquired.

"What? No, but my damned cousin won't shut up about them. I am weary of hearing her moan and whine about them."

"Ah," Beck chuckled. "Now we got to the heart of the matter. Why not buy her another pair to keep her quiet? You could always hire a paste jeweler to make her a replacement pair. I doubt she'd know the difference."

"Absolutely not. She's not even on the list of my favorite cousins, and I have dozens," Evan snorted.

"Then we can all agree to let the matter rest?" Fitz asked his friends. "I should like to start off my marriage without any trouble from Scotland Yard."

"You'll have no trouble from me," Beck promised.

"She's still a thief and broke the law." Evan let out a defeated sigh. "But for your sake, I'm happy to overlook it, assuming their thieving days are over."

"Good. Now, will you both stand up with me at my wedding?"

Evan and Beck nodded. "And what of Louis?" Beck asked.

"I will ask, but I don't know what he will say," Fitz admitted. "I will hold him no ill will if he refuses."

"Did you really bring back Miss Girard from New

York for him? The ballroom was buzzing with the news." Evan looked at him expectantly.

"I did."

"Good. It was quite the romantic gesture to bring Miss Girard back for Louis and then propose to Miss Sherborne like that. You're setting high expectations for the rest of us gents."

"Perhaps that's a good thing." Fitz chuckled and turned at the sound of the ladies exiting his study, Hannah in the forefront.

"Well, my lord," she said, "we're leaving Tabby in your tender care tonight, but we will be back tomorrow for her. There is much to plan for the wedding, and we wish to help your grandmother if she will let us."

"You are most welcome in my home anytime, ladies," he informed them. "And I assure you, my grandmother will welcome your assistance."

"I suppose we'd best be off as well then, eh, Beck?" Evan nudged Beck in the ribs. But Beck's attention was focused on Julia as though he was examining a very intricate puzzle and was clearly fascinated. Fitz noticed it, but Julia seemed to be oblivious.

Beck finally shook himself out of it. "Yes. The love-birds want to be alone. We can't fault them for that."

Fitz chuckled as the two women escorted his friends

out to their waiting coaches. Once they were gone, he pulled Tabitha into his arms.

"Thank God, I thought they'd never leave."

"Nor I." Tabitha giggled and buried her face against his chest.

He clutched her tighter, delighted to hear her laugh. The girlish sound made his heart swell. He wanted her to be filled with joy, to have some of her girlhood happiness restored. She had been forced to grow up far too fast.

"Now . . . where were we?" he asked her as he leaned in for a kiss that lingered. Long moments later, he kissed the tip of her nose and brushed a loose lock of her hair back behind one ear. "Shall we go upstairs?"

"Yes," she replied with a soft smile that turned his heart over.

Fitz led her to his bedchamber upstairs and marveled at how calm he felt. It was as though everything in the world was right, and it wasn't until this moment that he realized how wrong things had been before he had found this gift from the universe.

"It all feels rather like a dream," she confessed.

"It does, doesn't it?" He had never believed that he could come to love another person so quickly. To him, love was something that grew slowly over years, like the trees in the ancient forests in the north. But now he realized that love could be born in an instant.

"When I was a boy, my father took me to Brighton. Have you been there?"

She shook her head. Fitz pulled her close. "I shall take you there for our honeymoon."

"All right," she replied as she waited for him to continue.

"When I was visiting there, there was a terrible storm one night and lightning struck the sand on the beach. The next morning, Father took me on a quest for something he called a fulgurite."

"What is a fulgurite?"

"Well, when lightning strikes wet sand, it turns the sand into glass and forms a pattern of tubes that matches the path the lightning took."

He brushed the backs of his knuckles over her cheek. "It happens in less than a blink of one's eyes. Fulgurites are like veins of glass within the living earth. That was how I felt the night we met. I was the sand, you were the lightning. The veins of our love were created in that first instant."

He paused a moment to reflect. "The rational man in me wants to think this through, to take my time in proposing marriage, but the part of me that isn't rational is humming like a tuning fork, and the notes I hear are pure in their message. *Marry her now, love her forever, never look back, never question it.* Does that make sense, or do I sound mad?"

Tabitha sniffled and shook her head. "Mad? Far from it. You sound quite *wonderful.*"

"And yet you're crying." He brushed away a tear with his thumb.

"I suppose you should be warned that women often cry from being happy. I am no exception."

He grinned. "I consider myself duly warned, then."

"We have so much to discuss, so much still to plan that my head is spinning a little," she said.

"Then allow me to distract you." He tilted her chin up and lowered his head. Their mouths fused in a kiss. No longer a bittersweet goodbye, but rather a welcoming to one's home. How simple life had become, Fitz realized. All he had to do was choose to be open to love. There was every chance he could lose this woman or she could lose him, but the thought of living without her now, that was a fate he could no longer bear to think of.

Tabitha's lips parted beneath his and he devoured her, flicking his tongue against hers while his hands unbuttoned her gown at the back. The strains of a half-forgotten waltz echoed in his head as he surrendered himself to his love for this woman. He gave her everything he had of himself and reveled in her gift of herself to him in return.

When he ran out of buttons on her dress, he broke the kiss and gently had her turn away so he could help her out of her gown and all those silly layers of under-garments. He tugged the laces of her blue-and-gold corset until she was free and tossed her chemise away.

"My God, you're breathtaking," he said as he watched her seat herself at the end of his bed. He nearly tripped attempting to shed his own clothing, such was his eagerness to join her. She covered her mouth to hide a laugh as he finally lunged for the bed and they toppled back together. He fit her to his body, cradling her against him as he once more captured her mouth.

Her hands moved boldly over his skin, claiming ownership over him. She hesitated when her hands fluttered at his hip.

"Yes, touch me, darling, anywhere you wish," he encouraged in a low growl as her fingertips teased his shaft and then closed around it. She stroked him lightly, and it felt like heaven.

Her thumb brushed over the crown of his shaft. He nipped her bottom lip as he was possessed of an almost feral need to make love to her. Her exploring touch was going to be the death of him, but what a glorious death it would be.

"Not yet," he breathed against her lips as she stroked him again, urging him to enter her.

"Oh, Fitz, please . . . I *want* you . . ."

He sensed she had reached the same desperate need he felt and wished to wait no longer.

"How do you want it, darling?" He'd done his best not to think of all the ways he'd wanted to make love to her while they'd been separated, but he had, and now he felt like a child given access to a table full of desserts with no one to tell him he couldn't try each one.

"You mean there's more than one way to . . . ?" She waved shyly between their bodies.

"We are limited only by our imaginations," Fitz said with a grin.

"I've only ever been familiar with the way we did it before . . . and I've seen a few times men on the street . . . in the alleyways with women, but I didn't seem to quite understand how they could do the act . . ." She blushed wildly and buried her face against his shoulder.

"Never hide from me," he said. "We will have the rest of our lives to explore these intimate adventures together." He lifted her face to his and kissed her softly for a long moment, simply enjoying the art of kissing her. And it was art to touch her lips to his, and far lovelier than any painting.

When their lips broke apart, Tabitha smiled up at

him, a hint of mischief in her eyes. "About those other . . . ways?"

"Oh yes, let me show you." He chuckled and gently rolled her onto her stomach and covered her body with his, careful not to hurt her with his weight.

"Like this . . ." He used one knee to spread her legs from behind and then nudged her wet heat with his cock. She groaned low as he slowly entered her. There was nothing to describe it, this *loving* of his wife-to-be, except that it felt like coming home. This was why love was everything. All life held the risk of pain, of losing such a wondrous thing as love, but to never know it, to never possess it for even a few brief moments . . . that was no life at all.

Fitz placed soft kisses upon her neck and shoulder as he moved above her and within her, drawing out the pleasure for them both by changing the pace of his thrusts.

He gave her a light love bite in the sensitive spot in the crook of her neck and she moaned, closing her eyes as her inner walls clenched around his shaft. She'd come so quickly, but he wanted her to come again. He withdrew from her and rearranged their bodies so that he leaned back against the headboard in a seated position. Then he eased her down on his lap, once more sliding into her welcoming heat.

"Wrap your arms around my neck," he murmured.

Their faces were close enough to kiss, but he resisted the temptation instead and watched her eyes. She lifted herself up and down on him experimentally, riding slowly as she learned this new position. Her full breasts rubbed against his chest, and he gritted his teeth to fight off his own release. But the moment her eyes darkened and she cried out his name in a second climax, he gripped her bottom and moved faster until he could hold his control no longer. He surged into her over and over, never wanting to leave her tight, wet heat. He tensed as he found his pleasure.

It seemed a long time later when Tabitha lay down on his chest, their bodies still connected, as she spoke the words that would change his life a second time.

"I have something else to tell you, something that I hope will be welcome to you."

He stroked her hair with his fingertips and tucked a lock behind her ear. He was so full of a fierce tenderness for this woman, *his* woman.

"You can tell me anything. We are partners. We shall share everything in our lives. I trust you and I hope you know you can trust me with anything now."

She drew in a deep breath and spoke.

"I believe I am with child, Fitz. *Our* child. I visited a

physician last week, and he believes it as well. It must have happened that night at the house party."

Fitz couldn't speak, couldn't breathe. That perfect yet heartbreaking night, when he'd thought he'd lost her forever, they'd created a little life between them. He had no words to describe the gift their child would be to him. She lifted her face to look at him, her expression turning fearful as she saw the tears dripping down his cheeks.

"Fitz?"

He smiled and wiped his eyes. "Women aren't the only ones who can cry from happiness, it seems." He pulled her head to his, kissing her deeply.

The joy that shot through him at that kiss only strengthened the veins of love within him, like sand struck by lightning a second time. Life was, quite simply, *beautiful*. His love for Tabitha and their child was like a diamond discovered deep within the earth— their love was forever.

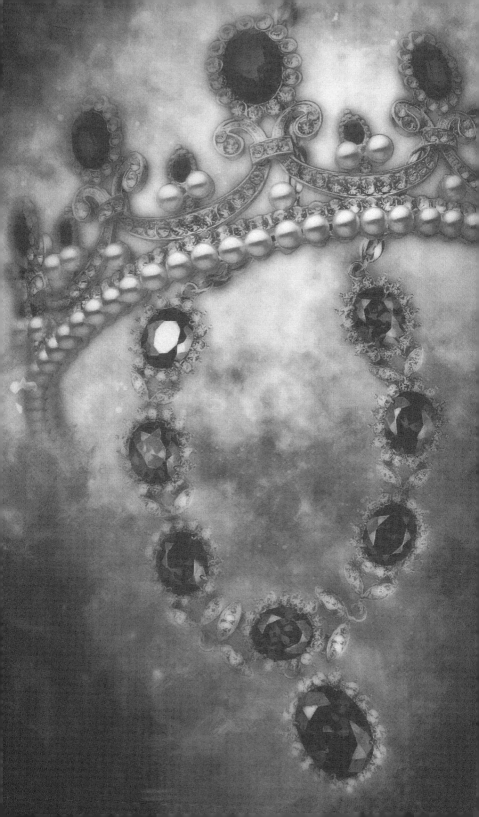

Epilogue

One year later
Tabitha played with the blue petals of a cornflower on a wooden bench as she watched the once infamously callous Duke of Helston push the pram that carried their daughter, Rose, down the paths of Hyde Park.

More than once he would stop, bend over the pram, and carefully re-tuck the blankets around the babe, then kiss the tips of his fingers and press them to the child's cheek. The look on his face, so in love with their daughter, was something Tabitha had never dreamed she would see. Yet there it was, that look of endless devotion from the man she loved. He turned back to her and waved with that charming smile that always hit her behind the knees.

She'd never imagined that life could become so utterly perfect. She was a member of a secret ring of jewel thieves who helped those in need, she had two dear friends who were as close to her as sisters, and she had a grandmother, a husband, and a daughter. Life had, after such a long period of darkness, brought forth a sunrise that shone brilliantly, and she would bask in every moment of its glow.

The dowager duchess sat beside Tabitha, both of them resting in the winter sunlight while Fitz and little Rose took their exercise. The baby seemed to be most happy when she was outdoors and in her father's care. Thankfully, the early winter was still warm, but both she and Fitz kept a close eye on their child to make sure she didn't fall ill.

Rose loved the attention she received from her parents and doting great-grandmother. Fitz would show Rose fresh flowers and tell her stories about the meanings behind each, just as his mother had, and she would squirm and giggle and make soft little grunts as she tried to reach the flowers but failed.

Their daughter's blue eyes, so like her father's, took in the world around her with an intense fascination. Though Rose was far too young to understand his words, she loved the sound of his voice, just like her mother. Fitz would even sing to Rose, which had surprised Tabitha and delighted her beyond words. She hadn't known Fitz could sing, but it explained his love of music. Tabitha briefly closed her eyes and let the winter sun sink into her skin and warm her.

"You must be careful with him," the dowager warned.

Tabitha opened her eyes and saw a gentle smile on the dowager's face. "Oh?"

"He will give Rose *anything* she wants. You had better make sure she doesn't get *too* spoiled. A little spoiling is fine, of course. But not too much." The dowager curled her hands around her cane as she watched Fitz pause once more over the pram to speak to the baby.

Tabitha chuckled. "I will do my best, but it is hard to argue with him." Her husband had filled the nursery with toys even though Rose wasn't old enough to use them, and he was already discussing buying her a fat little pony to ride in the park though Rose was years away from being able to ride anything.

"Oh heavens, it's nearly time," the dowager interrupted. "We must go or we shall be late."

Tabitha checked the pocket watch Fitz had given her as a wedding present to wear with her dresses. The dowager was right. They would indeed be late if they didn't leave now.

"Fitz, darling, we must leave for the grand opening." Even pushing the pram, he cut such a fine figure in his dark-blue three-piece suit. More than one lady passing him had blushed at the sight of such a handsome man tending to his child. It was an unusual sight, but an incredibly attractive one from any woman's perspective.

He returned with the pram and offered one elbow to her and the other to his grandmother. "Shall we, ladies?"

Where they were headed was thankfully not far from the park, but they didn't wish to be late. This was simply too important an occasion. As they reached the correct street, they saw a queue of people down the pavement waiting to be let into a townhouse up ahead. Men and women of the highest social circles greeted Tabitha, Fitz, and the dowager as they passed by them. The dowager lingered a few steps behind to speak with some of the people waiting in line and waved for Tabitha and Fitz to continue on ahead.

"So many people came. This is wonderful," Tabitha said.

"It's about time London did its part," Fitz said. "Of course, this is only a small start to what I'd like to do."

Hannah and Julia waited for them on the steps of the fine old home that Fitz had purchased and helped turn into a charity boardinghouse.

"There you are!" Hannah exclaimed and hurried

toward them. She embraced Tabitha, gave Fitz a quick hug, and bent down to tickle Rose's little cheeks.

"Welcome to the Helston Home for War Veterans," Julia announced with a grin as she joined them on the top step. "Everyone's been waiting to come inside, but we didn't want to start the tour without you."

In the last few months, Fitz had forged a far better relationship with Hannah and Julia than Tabitha had expected. She hadn't thought they would be so quick to forgive him, but when Anne and Louis had come to Fitz and Tabitha's wedding, they'd announced they'd eloped just a few days before. As a result much of the bad blood between Tabitha's friends and Fitz had vanished. It didn't hurt that Hannah and Julia had seen how happy she was with him.

Fitz followed Tabitha and her friends inside. Tabitha kept close to her husband, eager to see his reaction. He had left all the details of the boardinghouse up to the Merry Robins and was only now allowed to see what his money had achieved. He'd been a little shy at the thought of pushing his way into their world of charities, but he'd desperately wanted to support the veterans in honor of his father.

"I think you'll find this place to your satisfaction. We took all of your wishes into account." Hannah laid a hand on Fitz's arm and smiled warmly at him. She'd come to see how much this cause meant to him.

"Thank you, Mrs. Winslow. I deeply appreciate the efforts you and Miss Sterling have gone to in order to make this possible. Tabitha has told you what this means to me."

"She has," Hannah replied, her gaze softening. "Please take a look before we have the others join us."

The interior was light and airy rather than dim and gloomy. It was also well appointed with new furnishings. Fitz had requested that as one of his desires. He'd said that his father had tried to hide in the darkness in those last few months, and he believed sunlight was better for a person's health.

A woman a bit older than Hannah and Julia waited for them at the base of the stairs. Tabitha made the introductions.

"Fitz, this is Mrs. Ewing. She's in charge of the boarders. Mrs. Ewing, this is my husband, Lord Helston."

"Thank you for coming, Your Grace. Please follow me. I am honored to show you the house and introduce you to our current boarders," Mrs. Ewing said as she began a tour of the house. The rest of the guests waiting outside began to proceed in after them. Their donations, along with Fitz's, had done so much to improve the medical care, food, and lodging of the war veterans staying here.

Tabitha held her husband's arm and watched his face as he truly saw what a difference he could make in the world. She knew he wanted to be involved, but she'd also wanted this first opportunity for him to be a bit of a surprise. This house was full of veterans, most of them disabled or bearing other physical or mental scars. Some had served alongside his father, others had served in other countries, but all were tied by their service and their struggles to return to their normal lives. Now these men were healthier and happier in this warm house, all thanks to Fitz and the others now flooding inside. Tabitha knew the grand opening was going to be a success.

"We have a physician who visits every week, and each man is guaranteed to be seen by him. Some require medicine, while others simply need to talk and have someone listen," Mrs. Ewing explained.

"I imagine many of them suffer from soldier's heart," Fitz murmured. "My father had that . . . but he had no one to talk to."

Tabitha gently squeezed Fitz's arm. "Thanks to you, these men do." Tabitha had learned that soldier's heart affected *many* veterans. More than she had imagined. They would wake at night screaming or jump at any sound. Sometimes even the silence brought back the screams of horses and the roar of cannons. It drove some to madness, and sometimes they became a danger to themselves and others because they could not escape the past.

The cumbrous weight of those memories the veterans carried was vast enough to drown even the strongest of men, just as they had done to Fitz's father.

As their group entered the drawing room, one of the veterans, who was missing an arm, was playing cards with two other men. At the sight of Fitz, he stood and walked over to them.

"Yer Grace?" the man said uncertainly in a thick Scottish accent.

"Yes?"

The man cleared his throat. "My name is Patrick Dowd. I served with yer father. He was a good man. I was sad to hear he'd passed."

Tabitha noticed a tic in Fitz's jaw as he tried to fight off a wave of emotion.

"Thank you," he replied, holding out a hand for Patrick, who shook it.

"I hear ye are the one to thank for this place. Ye've done a good thing, Yer Grace. A damned good thing. Yer father would have been proud of ye."

Patrick bowed his head respectfully and returned to

his card game. Fitz was silent during the rest of the tour, and when everyone went to the dining room for some sherry and sandwiches, Fitz pulled Tabitha back into the corridor with him so they could have a moment alone.

"Are you all right?" Tabitha whispered as she brushed her fingers over his cheek. She didn't like it when he went silent like this.

"What you've done . . ." He stopped and cleared his throat. "It's wonderful. I only wish my father was alive to see this. To have met you. My parents would have adored you, Tabitha." He circled his hands around her waist and touched his forehead to hers.

"How are you feeling now that you've seen it?" Tabitha asked in a whisper. She was getting better all the time at learning to read the subtle changes in his moods, but he still kept his thoughts and emotions hidden from the world more than she would like.

"I admit I'm overwhelmed, but I daresay that is a good thing. Seeing all this, it makes me feel overjoyed . . . and yet full of sorrow. We can't help everyone, can we?" The look on his face nearly broke her heart. How could anyone have thought him cold? This man had too much heart—he simply feared showing it.

"No, we can't," she said. "But those you do help will change the world."

He pressed a soft kiss to her lips, and she felt a deep change inside her soul as her love for him flowed through it. To love him, to love herself, to love others, it all gave her life such a wonderful fullness. Even her moments of grief made the moments of happiness that followed stronger.

"When I think of my life and my future, all I see is you," he said. "If your stealing a pocket watch hadn't caught the attention of Hannah, and Julia, I might never have met you," Fitz mused.

She smiled against his lips. "Is that your way of saying you're glad I was a thief?"

Her darling husband, the once cold and brooding man who'd hidden himself away from life's joys, now smiled down at her. The sun seemed pale in comparison to Fitz's face, which glowed with his love for her.

"I suppose I am."

Though she and the others had given up their more audacious and headline-grabbing escapades, it would be wrong to say she'd retired entirely.

There were still many men and women of privilege with too much money and too little empathy who might find themselves missing a watch, wallet, earring, or even the odd necklace.

Their unintended generosity always found its way

to the right places, and the world was made just a little bit better than before.

He pulled her closer, fitting her body to his, and kissed her again. This time for far longer and far deeper, just the way she liked.

"I wonder if there's a hothouse nearby?"

"I believe Julia and Hannah can look after Rose for a bit. I'm sure we could find somewhere to go . . ." She chuckled and grasped her husband by his ascot, pulling him down for another kiss. She was a lucky woman to steal not only a diamond . . . but a duke's heart.

TWO DAYS LATER

Evan Haddon, the Earl of Brightstone, lounged in his chair at the Fox and Hound gambling hell, studying the cards in his hand. It was a winning hand, of course. They always were. He was a deuced lucky man in all ways except one. The one thing—or rather, one person—he'd give everything to have was also the only person out of his reach.

Hannah Winslow.

He tossed his hand of cards to the middle of the table, and the men around him cursed when they realized they'd all lost.

"Brightstone, you have the devil's own luck," one man muttered.

Evan grinned ruthlessly as he collected the slips of paper listing what the various men owed him. "Sorry, old boys." He had no plans to collect on any of them, but these men didn't need to know that yet. Despite his melancholy mood, he was feeling strangely charitable. He blamed it upon Hannah and her friends.

A band of bloody jewel thieves.

He dreaded to think what they would attempt if they ever got bored with pickpocketing the elite of London. There were still the occasional thefts being reported to Scotland Yard and being printed about in the papers, but it seemed more articles described donations being made to charities. That Evan had no issue with whatsoever; he'd even made a few discreet donations himself, anonymous of course, to the charities the Merry Robins supported. But the idea that a fine lady like Hannah Winslow was slipping her hand into pockets or sliding rings off fingers . . . Damned if he knew whether to curse or laugh at the thought.

"Well now," mused a nearby man in a soft Irish accent. "Will you look at that?"

Evan followed the gentleman's gaze, and his heart skipped a beat at the sight of a woman. But not just any woman—a fine lady in a deep-purple bustle gown that was fringed with silver tassels. She stood hesitantly in the entryway of the gambling hell before she entered. The pleated silk of her skirts rippled seductively as she moved and the train of her gown presented a picture of perfection that made all the cyprian ladies in attendance jealous. The neckline was rather low for this particular woman, who was far more used to being seen in high collars. It was clear she was a lady of quality, yet her exquisite beauty would soon be too tempting for even the most gentlemanly of the men in the room tonight to resist.

What in the blazes was *Hannah* doing here? Only courtesans dared to come into the Fox and Hound, and even then they stayed in the company of men who could protect them.

Her gaze drifted over the crowd of men. When she spotted him, he saw a flash of relief on her face. She headed straight toward him, ignoring the men who stopped their gambling to stare at her as she passed. A hint of a blush in her cheeks was the only outward sign that she was aware of their ungentlemanly gazes.

Evan leapt to his feet as she reached him.

"Lord Brightstone," she said in that soft, oh so sweet voice of hers, the one that always tugged at his heart.

"Evan, please," he corrected, the way he did upon their every meeting. They'd known each other for years, yet she still called him Lord Brightstone, no matter how much he insisted otherwise.

Evan had loved her since the day she debuted before the queen, and he'd never stopped loving her. But she'd never been his. She had loved another and always would, even though that man no longer drew breath.

Bloody hell, he was jealous of a damned ghost.

Her light-hazel eyes briefly left his face to dart and roam around the room of men again, then returned. "Can I speak to you privately?"

"Of course. I can find us a private room this way." He led her to the back of the den of sin and chose one of the rooms that had an unlocked door. While the primary business here was that of gambling, rooms like this provided privacy for other, more intimate activities.

A bed stood in the far corner, a small table held a bowl of fresh fruit, and a fire was lit in the hearth. It was a scene ripe for seduction—which wouldn't happen, of course. But damned if his mind didn't go to a place where he and Hannah would make thorough use of that bed. He closed the door, and she retreated to a spot by the fire to warm her hands, even though it wasn't particularly cold tonight.

"What can I do for you, little robin?" he teased.

She turned to face him, her dark hair tumbling over her shoulders in tantalizing waves that made him want to dig his hands into the strands and kiss her. Which, again, he couldn't do.

"Don't say that, not here!" she hissed, and he drew closer to her.

"Why not?" he asked.

"Because someone might think I am a thief."

"But you *are* a thief," he pointed out with a chuckle, and she rolled her eyes.

"I *was* a thief." She scowled, but the expression was adorable on her.

Evan chuckled. "Come now, Hannah, there's no one else here. You may intend to keep a lower profile for now, but I know you. And now that I know your reasoning and methods, I know you won't stop any more than I would stop making wagers or playing cards. It's not just about the good you can do anymore, is it? It's the thrill you feel punishing those who deserve it and getting away with it. You are a thief, a lovely, talented one with a heart of gold."

Hannah blushed at that. "Even if that were true, it is not something that should be said aloud."

"Your secret is quite safe here. The only thing anyone is thinking about right now is how I'm damned lucky to have you all to myself. They are certainly making assumptions, but only regarding your virtue."

"Lord Brightstone!" she gasped in indignation.

Evan shrugged, hiding the fact that he loved seeing her cheeks flush. "You came to a gambling hell, you demanded a private word with me, and here we are. Tongues will be wagging come morning—I cannot prevent that."

Hannah paled at his words, as though she hadn't considered the consequences of her actions.

"Which brings me back to my original question. What can I do for you?"

She twisted her fingers in her skirts and then blew out a breath.

"A young woman came to see me this evening. Her mother's emerald ring was taken from her. I want to help her get it back."

"How did this woman find you? Don't tell me you are now advertising your services in the papers?" He was half joking, but as he said it aloud, he realized it wasn't entirely unlikely.

"No, of course not." Hannah rolled her eyes. "Apparently, the young lady tried to speak to a few of Tabitha's old friends from her days on the streets. She was desperate to find someone to help her, and the women she spoke to gave her our names."

"You mean those street urchins know you, Tabitha, and Julia are stealing from the elite of London? That's awfully dangerous. What if one of them gets pinched by the good old men of the Yard and they drop your name to stay out of jail? Have you considered that?"

She lifted her adorable chin at him and fixed him with a look that would have frozen any man to stone . . . well, almost any man. He was thriving in this discussion with her. It was the most alive he'd seen her since . . . since she'd lost her husband.

"We have considered it. The women who know about our identities are in a small, trusted circle. They would never betray Tabitha. She's done too much for them and the people they care about who needed food and shelter. Not to mention, those sorts of bonds formed in that life, at such a young age, are almost impossible to break. These women are like Tabitha's sisters."

He understood those sorts of bonds himself—he'd do anything for Fitz, Beck, or Louis.

"Fair enough. Where do I fit in with your situation? You are the thief, not I. Can't you retrieve this young lady's ring?"

"I tried, but the men who took it from this young woman are frightening. I wasn't able to establish its whereabouts or get a lay of the building before I was made to leave, and I was rather afraid that if I pressed my luck and was caught in the act, I would end up being . . ." She couldn't finish her thought, though it was clear the kind of harm she had feared would come to her.

"Did anyone put their hands on you?" he growled. The roaring sound of blood in his ears almost deafened him. He would kill any man who dared harm her.

"No, but the threat was heavily implied. So I thought perhaps a visit from an earl might be more persuasive than a widow. Would you do it? For me?"

There wasn't a thing in the world he wouldn't do for Hannah Winslow, but he could never let her know that. If she ever learned the depth of his feelings for her, she would never speak to him again. As a widow, she'd stayed far away from other men, sending a clear message about her choice not to remarry, and he had always honored that.

"I would do it, but not without something in return," he said.

She reached for her coin purse, but he caught her hand and shook his head, almost laughing at the thought that she would try to pay him when he had plenty of money.

"If not money, then what do you want?" she asked innocently.

Before he could rethink his actions, he said the one thing he shouldn't, the one thing he wanted most.

"A night with you in my bed."

He should have expected the slap, but he honestly hadn't thought she'd strike him that *hard*.

"If you would let me finish . . . ," he said, trying to ignore the sting of her blow. "I am not talking of making love. I wouldn't touch you, nor would you touch me. My bed is quite large. We would sleep together in it with a continent between us."

Her brows arched up. "But then . . . why would you want that if not to touch me?"

The answer he wanted to give would have shocked her . . . He wanted to hear her breathe. He wanted her scent on his sheets. He wanted to see her comb her hair out before bed as she talked about her day. He craved all the small little perfect moments a husband would have with this woman that he never would because her heart would always belong to the man she'd lost. He was mad to want to pretend for one night that she was his, that they had a life together at long last . . . because deep down, Hannah Winslow had turned him into the most romantic fool ever born, and when she was near he couldn't think clearly.

Finally, he cleared his throat.

"My reasons are my own, but I assure you I will not touch you. My only request is for you to sleep beside me in my bed for *one* night." He held up a single finger, and her brows knit in confusion.

"Well . . . I suppose that wouldn't be too hard of a request . . ."

It was adorable to watch the emotions play across her face as she sought a way out of her predicament and failed.

"Very well. One night." She held out a hand to him to shake on it.

He would rather have sealed their bargain with a kiss, but a man had to earn this woman's kisses, and Evan had no idea where to begin with that task. He clasped her hand in his and shook it, giving her a confident smile.

"Excellent. Now tell me everything you know about these men and what exactly this emerald ring looks like."

THANK YOU FOR READING *DUKES AND DIAMONDS*! **Don't worry, there will be more adventures with two more stories in the series with Evan and Beck each having their adventures and romance.**

About the Author

Lauren Smith is an Oklahoma attorney by day, author by night who pens adventurous and edgy romance stories by the light of her smart phone flashlight app. She knew she was destined to be a romance writer when she attempted to re-write the entire *Titanic* movie just to save Jack from drowning. Connecting with readers by writing emotionally moving, realistic and sexy romances no matter what time period is her passion. She's won multiple awards in several romance subgenres including: New England Reader's Choice Awards, Greater Detroit BookSeller's Best Awards, and a Semi-Finalist award for the Mary Wollstonecraft Shelley Award.

To Connect with Lauren, visit her at:
www.laurensmithbooks.com
lauren@laurensmithbooks.com

facebook.com/LaurenDianaSmith
x.com/LSmithAuthor
instagram.com/Laurensmithbooks
tiktok.com/@laurenandemmabooks